What others are saying about *Coffee Rings*. . .

Coffee Rings goes straight to the heart, touching every emotion. Yvonne tackles some tough issues head-on, yet she's done it with gentle grace, creating a totally unpredictable plot filled with delightful characters whose secrets will keep you guessing until the end. It's the best Christian novel I've read in ages.

Peggy Darty,
award-winning author of 22 novels
and the *Mystery Lady* series

This is Yvonne Lehman at her best! *Coffee Rings* is a book you won't easily put down. . .if you put it down at all. Get ready for characters you can relate to and plotlines right out of this crazy thing we call "life"!

Eva Marie Everson,
author of *Shadow of Dreams*,
Summon the Shadows, and *Shadows of Light*

Yvonne Lehman is fast becoming one of my favorite authors. *Coffee Rings* is riveting. Full of interesting characters with intriguing secrets, this page-turning story grabbed hold of me and wouldn't let go. Highly recommended.

Deborah Raney,
author of *A Nest of Sparrows* and
Christy Award nominee for *Playing by Heart*

Coffee Rings

Three women.
One tragic event.
Nineteen years later,
secrets surface. . .

YVONNE LEHMAN

ISBN 1-59310-339-5

For more information about Yvonne Lehman, please access the author's Web site at the following Internet address: www.yvonnelehman.com

Acquisitions and Editorial Director: Rebecca Germany
Editorial Consultant: Becky Durost Fish
Art Director: Robyn Martins
Layout Design: Anita Cook

Published by Barbour Publishing, Inc., P.O. Box 719, Uhrichsville, OH 44683, www.barbourbooks.com

Our mission is to publish and distribute inspirational products offering exceptional value and biblical encouragement to the masses.

Printed in the United States of America.
5 4 3 2 1

Dedication

To David Lehman and Cindy Wilson for advice on discussion questions. To Lori Marett for her invaluable, unique critiquing expertise, and to Michelle Cox, who said, "Consider me *percolating* on this. . .*filtering* through every word. . .down to the final *dregs*."

Acknowledgments

So many people help with a book that it's impossible to name them all or even remember what may have triggered a scene, setting, theme, or plot. I do want to thank some who come immediately to mind. I've never asked anyone for information without their being eager and enthusiastic about answering my questions or leading me to someone else who might help.

Thanks to all who ask about my writing, which is my work and my mission. Your prayers and interest are appreciated. A special tribute goes to Rebecca Germany, my editor at Barbour, who came up with the great title *Coffee Rings,* which fits the theme of this book. Also, I appreciate her allowing discussion questions, which may be helpful to readers. Many times, my characters are asking questions about their lives that reflect some questions I may have.

A special thanks to the Blue Ridge Writers Group, listed in the dedication. They have varying abilities that work well in evaluating and discussing a work. Each one may see something no one else saw, and each comment is helpful. I thank them for prayers, editing, critiquing, reading, commenting, and/or just listening and encouraging as I talk out my concerns and wail that I'll never meet my deadline.

Thanks to Cindy at Chelsea's in Asheville for the cookbook and the lovely afternoon at their tearoom, which gave me ideas for my character's Victorian house in which she serves coffee, tea, and lunch. Thank you to Jeff Butler for the use of his name and the name of his Black Mountain restaurant, The Veranda.

Others who gave expert advice and expressed a willingness to offer information include Terry Brigman of Brigman's Funeral Home in Black Mountain; and Pat Johnston, Nurse Practitioner Susan Shinn, and Dr. David Hetzel of the Hope Cancer Center for Women.

Thanks to Jenny, a sales associate at Tanner's, who suggested the name of Lancaster's as the place where one of my characters works. I also used the names of the lovely, elegant women who work there (Sally, Judy, Melissa, Lori, Laura, Holly) in a scene with my character. They (and the clothes they sell) are special to me.

Thanks to my poet-friend Nancy Dillingham of Asheville, North Carolina, for the use of her poem "Defense." And to poets Robert Burns, Walt Whitman, and Shakespeare *(Norton Anthology of Poetry)*.

Most of all, thanks to my readers, whose responses encourage me to continue writing my stories. It is my hope and prayer that you find my stories entertaining, inspirational, encouraging, and faith strengthening. Your pleasure is my purpose.

Eunice Hogan had planned for the secret to be buried with her. But when one is given a death sentence, reality begins to take on a different look. No, that wasn't entirely the case. Somehow this had nothing to do with reality. Yet she was sitting in the doctor's office next to Henry and hearing the reality that a time limit had been placed on her life.

A numbness swept over her and apparently over Henry, too. They listened to the doctor, who said Eunice was fortunate to have been free of cancer for over a decade. He was sorry, but there'd been a recurrence of the cancer. It had metastasized and was now in the liver and pelvic area. This accounted for her digestive symptoms, her feeling bloated and having nausea. He presented options like chemotherapy, radiation, exploratory surgery.

Maybe she missed something. Maybe he or Henry said healing was possible; maybe Henry said they believed in miracles. But Eunice didn't hear anything like that. All she could hear was her mind asking, *What am I supposed to do?*

Go home and fix supper? Do the laundry? Mop a floor? She had to check herself to keep that hysterical tickle from escaping her throat. If she laughed, she'd never stop. She didn't know how to feel, how to think, what to say or do. How did one handle such a thing?

Oh, the doctor didn't set a date, a day, or an hour, but. . .six months, more or less—as if a day were a thousand years. That timelessness vanished when she and Henry left the doctor's office. The day was going all too quickly. Her life was on the highway to death. On the other side of the median strip, vehicles were going in the opposite direction toward Asheville.

She sat in the passenger seat while Henry drove. They were heading to. . .his home in Laurel Ridge. She was heading to. . .her home in eternity.

She heard him say, "We believe in miracles, you know."

"Yes."

How could she leave Henry? He couldn't pick out the right color tie to wear with his suit on Sunday morning. How could he take care of her? She'd taken care of him for half a century.

How flippantly she'd said and heard others say that we begin to die the day we're born; there's nothing certain but taxes and death; and we never know if we will draw another breath. Death could be any moment. . .except this moment. Now, her moments were numbered.

"It's a nice day," Henry said when they reached home. "Why don't you sit on the porch, and I'll make us some lunch?"

Isn't that what she normally said to him? Had the roles reversed so quickly?

She sat in a rocking chair, feeling the warmth of the sunny afternoon—a time when new life was beginning. Henry's jonquils were already popping out of the ground. Her gaze lifted to the mountains. How could she climb this one?

She took in a deep breath. She'd heard that life flashes before one's eyes at the moment of death. What did it do when you'd just been told that you have six months to live?

Would it slowly unravel like the threads in a knitted sweater you've thoroughly messed up? You pull the yarn. It zigzags across the pattern, unraveling until it lies in a pile on the floor. You knitted it for Christmas, but Christmas Eve has come, and there's not enough time to start over. You look at the mess on the floor that is indefinable, not a sweater at all.

It's just yarn. . .

signifying. . .

yarn.

The thought reminded her of a passage of Shakespeare's *Macbeth* she'd read, memorized, and taught:

Out, out, brief candle!
Life's but a walking shadow, a poor player
That struts and frets his hour upon the stage
And then is heard no more: it is a tale
Told by an idiot, full of sound and fury,
Signifying nothing.

Is that how her life would end? What was her responsibility? Her life was not going to end in some sudden automobile accident, no plane crash, no elephantine foot on her chest, no quick going.

Six months. Too little time to plan anything in the future.

Too much time to reflect on the yarn.

Just enough time to reflect on the secret hidden inside the back cover of her Bible.

Earlier that morning, unable to get back to sleep, Annette Billings rose before daybreak, fastened her auburn hair back with a scrunchy, then brushed her teeth and rinsed her face in cool water. Towel-drying her face, she gazed in the mirror into light gray-blue eyes that questioned, *Are you sure?*

She blinked the sleepiness away, applied gloss to her lips for a spot of color in her pale face, and removed the scrunchy.

Sure?

A few determined strokes with the hairbrush reminded her she could use a cut. With a defiant lift of her chin, she spoke. "Of course I'm sure."

Turning from the reflection, she shivered. There'd been a long winter. Signs of spring were right outside her door, but the mountain air turned cool at night, extending into the early morning. She felt the chill of winter still hanging on with all its might. She slipped into jeans, a sweatshirt, and tennis shoes.

She decided not to turn on the heat, since she'd be leaving soon. Later, the sun shining through the windows would warm the second floor of the big Victorian house that served as her living quarters. Before long, activity on the lower level would warm the downstairs.

While coffee dripped into the pot, Annette walked around the contemporary island that separated the kitchen from the dining area and stood beside the round, glass-topped Victorian-style table. That and two white wrought-iron chairs were the only part of the room that resembled the downstairs, known by the public as Annette's Kitchen. She knew the private and the public could be as different as night and day. Her public life was as proprietor of her business downstairs. Her private life remained within herself except what she shared with Ruby and Lara.

She stepped over to the glass doors leading out to the back deck and switched off the light. Instead of morning, she faced a barely discernable landscape beyond a closer view of her dark and shadowy reflection in the glass.

She recalled the theme of Henry Hogan's Sunday morning sermon. He used Scripture written by the apostle Paul, who described this life as being like one looking through a glass darkly. Annette knew the truth of that and God's leadership in spite of it. However, she preferred all to be crystal clear. Too many times she'd questioned the reasons things happened as they did.

The gurgle of the pot drew her attention. Clear water, passing through the grounds, turned into brown liquid. Even that reminded her of the situation she faced, changes being made. After pouring a cup of the aromatic steamy liquid, she pulled out a chair and sat in the shadowy morning. Her cold fingers curved around the cup. The liquid warmed her insides.

Morning slowly dawned. Suggestive of impressionist art, gray mist rose from the forest floor, creeping up tree trunks and along bleak, leafless limbs. Mountain peaks competed for prominence in the sky, which reminded her of a dingy towel in bleach stubbornly resisting the lightening process.

She quickly gulped down the rest of the coffee. Feeling jittery, she supposed she hadn't really needed the caffeine. She had to hurry, wanting to talk to Louis in private.

She not only had to tell her husband she planned to marry Curt, she also had to tell Curt's wife.

Annette drove her car down the winding exit bordered by pines and out to the main road. Knowing even school buses wouldn't be in evidence this early, she took the back roads and drove through neighborhoods, trying to concentrate on the bloom of spring.

The signs were there in beds, on bushes, but they looked as subdued as she felt—bleak and dull. The sky had apparently decided this was no occasion to allow the sun to show its face. She'd often felt in communion with nature, but never more than now.

No more than five minutes later, her heart beat fast as she slowed the car to make the final turn onto the long concrete drive that led to her destination. The slanted roof of the A-frame office building came into sight on top of the long, sloping hill. The light breeze teased the flags on tall poles at the back of the building. They struggled to display their grandiosity but fell in limp defeat.

She parked in front of the building. The offices would be locked. She took one of the bundles and exited the car. Keeping her mind and attention at her feet, she hastened through the breezeway and onto the concrete encircled by flagpoles. Reaching the double flight of concrete steps, she touched the cold steel handrail to steady her descent. An array of slender green stems with long leaves topped by closed, fingerlike buds extended down the inclines adjacent to the steps.

Any other time, Annette would have smiled, knowing that the lilies awaited the sunshine to make them open in splendor and reveal their orange trumpets as if ready to proclaim some kind of good news. Now, respectfully, they remained tightly shut.

By the time she reached the bottom step, the gray sky had yielded to the light. Tears washed her cheeks, making them as wet as the dew-dampened grass beneath her feet. She knew the spot by heart. Five down, ten over.

Only for an instant did she allow her glance to sweep over the veterans' cemetery at the vast display that looked like marshmallow soldiers at attention in a sea of green. Some clutched flags; others, real or artificial flowers.

She stopped in front of Louis. There was no easy way. No preliminaries necessary.

"Louis." She inhaled air that cooled her throat. "I'm going to get married again."

The breeze held its breath.

The birds began to gossip.

Annette bent to lay down the half-dozen yellow roses. Instead, she fell to her knees. Then with a cry, she lay prostrate on his grave.

"Oh, Louis. I'm not leaving you. You'll always be in my heart. I love you and always will. But there's room in my heart for Curt, too."

She cried like she hadn't since three months after Louis was buried, when she finally admitted he wasn't coming back. This was real. He was gone. In the fourteen years since he'd been killed, she'd done her best to live up to what the town expected of the young single mother, widow of the local boy who died as a hero for his country.

Sealing the finality of Louis's death, she sobbed for a long time. She knew he wasn't there, and she'd rarely visited this place. But the headstone bore his name: Cpl. Louis Andrew Billings. He'd been proud to serve his country. She'd been proud of him.

But he didn't come back. Sometimes over a decade seemed like a long, long time. Today it seemed like yesterday.

How long she lay on the ground as if it were her security blanket, she didn't know. It didn't matter until she heard a sound that brought her back to the present. She looked around and saw a man in orange coveralls on a riding lawnmower farther down the incline.

She turned and arranged the yellow roses in the funnel vase in front of the headstone, brightening the setting. Walking away, she took a good look at the cemetery, so well kept with headstones in neat rows, a miniature of Arlington. Flowers were removed upon wilting, and flags were placed at every gravesite during national holidays.

The sky had brightened, as if the sun might decide to peek through after all. Annette brushed at the grass and dampness of her sweatshirt and walked on. This time, passing beneath the flags, she looked up at the American flag. Her memory heard the twenty-one-gun salute that had honored the brave, slain soldier. Walking on through the breezeway, she heard more than that.

"What a moment, what a day," singers had sung at another funeral. "We shall rise." She'd endured the funeral of Curt's wife. She had to hurry to another cemetery and, in respect, lay flowers upon Sybil Crowder's grave.

Then no more funerals.

No more thinking about death. She'd forced such things into the back of her mind. Next fall, her son would enter college. She would not be left alone. She would begin a new life, one of safety and security with Curt.

Should she mention the past to Curt?

No. It didn't affect their relationship. That was before she even knew him.

Everything would be fine. . .fine. She looked straight ahead. No ghosts of the past fluttered around trying to get her attention. She forced herself to believe that, despite the sudden brisk breeze that blew her hair, made her catch her breath, and caused the clouds in the sky to tremble.

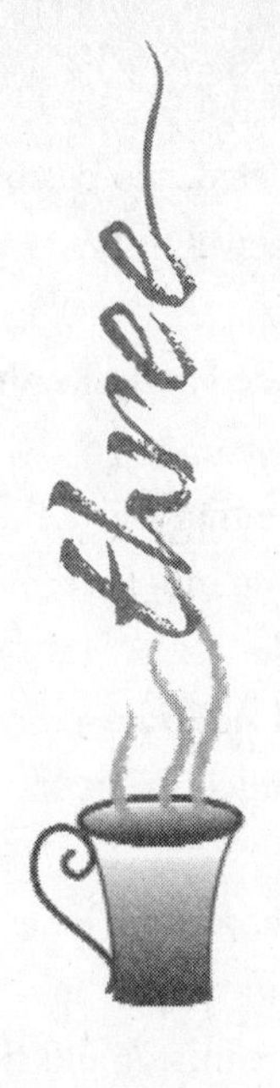

Curt Crowder left his floral shop early, leaving the responsibility of locking up to an assistant. Before Sybil died, he'd been the last one to leave, as if no one else could lock up. He'd learned the hard way that he should have taken more hours off, spent them with his wife. She was gone now, and he still had his shop. When she died, he knew he would trade all his flowers for one more minute with Sybil. That was impossible.

But he had a second chance. He and Sybil had a good marriage, but he knew with hindsight how to be a better husband. He smiled inwardly. Most parents admitted they were better as grandparents. They'd learned by their mistakes. He hoped he had learned and would be all to Annette that she deserved.

He'd taken off his wedding ring the day he was surprised by thoughts about Annette that went beyond friendship. Now the developing relationship seemed the most natural thing in the world, as if God had brought them together for the benefit of each other. Their personal losses had formed a bond between them. Annette had lost her husband years ago. He had been losing Sybil for the past four years to a rare form of dementia for which no cure had been found. Even four months ago, he would not have thought he could love another woman.

He could, and he did.

“Where’s your ring, Dad?” Shelby had asked.

He’d hedged. It was too new, too unexpected, too personal to tell his daughter. “I put it with your mother’s jewelry. That’s where it belongs.”

Shelby looked skeptical, then sort of nodded and accepted his explanation.

Now, only one thing remained to do, and that was telling his children. After that, he and Annette would openly let the world know they had fallen in love.

After showering and dressing, he turned sideways in front of the full-length mirror in his bedroom and pulled in his stomach. He grinned, remembering a quip from Shelby.

“Did you ever notice,” she’d said, “how people will look in the mirror, pull their stomachs in, straighten, and shove their chests out?” She’d laughed. “Then they turn from the mirror and slouch. Out comes the tummy.”

His wasn’t too bad, he complimented himself, shrugging into his navy sport jacket that was the color of his eyes. He patted his tie. He didn’t want to overdress but at the same time didn’t want to give the impression that this wasn’t a special occasion.

He felt more anxious than on the day he’d married Sybil. He’d been too young and foolish and eager then to be nervous. Hadn’t known what he was getting into. He was just getting the girl he loved and planning to spend his life with her.

This time he did know what he’d be getting into and eagerly embraced the thought.

He wasn’t exactly old but had to admit he wasn’t young anymore—not at forty-eight. The gray at his temples and sprinkled throughout his black hair attested to his middle age. He’d suspected Annette would think he was too old for her, but she’d made it clear that was one thing she liked about him—his. . .maturity.

This relationship sort of caught them both by surprise. It

shouldn't have. They'd been headed in that direction for a long time—just hadn't let the thoughts go beyond friendship.

He followed the aroma of Sybil's, now Shelby's, famous spaghetti sauce down the hallway. Would he walk these hallways in the future? Or would he sell this house and live in Annette's big Victorian house? They hadn't gone that far in their plans. Either way suited him. But first, there was this preliminary dinner.

He walked into the kitchen. Shelby glanced over her shoulder, then laid down the long-handled spoon and turned. "Dad!" She gave him the once-over. "Just who are you bringing to dinner?" She looked down at her jeans and T-shirt covered by an apron. "You didn't say this was a dress-up occasion."

He raised his hands. "Now, Shelby. It wouldn't be a surprise if I told you. And don't worry. You always look beautiful."

"Yeah," she scoffed. "I bet you say that to all your daughters."

He laughed. "Only two of them."

"Oh, get out of here." Shelby playfully slapped his arm. She shook her head, causing her hair, caught back in a rubber band, to wag like a puppy-dog's tail.

He was glad they could joke around again and laugh. Several months had passed before they had gotten back into that after Sybil died. Shelby had sort of taken up where Sybil left off. He'd probably let her do too much for him. But he thought they both had needed it. They'd sort of worked through their grief together. He'd even felt a little guilty at times that Shelby seemed to spend as much time at his house as in her apartment. Of course, her husband joined them on the nights Shelby cooked for him. Before long, Annette would be standing at the stove, cooking. Or he would be cooking in her house. Didn't matter. They might even eat out every night.

But Annette loved to cook. She liked a lot of people around her. She'd fit in with this family perfectly.

"What's that grin for?" Shelby asked with a tilt of her cute face. "You look like the cat that ate the canary."

"Never you mind, little girl. But I've got to get out of here. Don't want to be late."

Shelby scolded. "I told the others we'd eat at six o'clock."

"Yes, dear," Curt quipped. Nothing anyone could say would daunt his spirits today. He chuckled and headed for his car. He thought of a line of poetry his dad used to say before he died and left the floral shop to Curt. He didn't know the poet but recalled the words: *"If I stepped out of my body, I would break into blossom."*

Less than ten minutes later, Curt came to the small sign in Victorian script: ANNETTE'S KITCHEN—ENTRANCE. An arrow pointed to the right. He turned and drove up the hill, where she had a wonderful view of distant mountains and the residential area below. The sun had finally peeked through the clouds a few times, but the sky threatened to become overcast again. A profusion of yellowbuds on the right side of the road welcomed him as he drove past the house and around the back through the empty parking lot. Her business hours ended after the 3:00 p.m. tea and coffee hour. He pulled up beside her side entrance.

He got out and rang the bell. Soon he wouldn't have to put his finger on that lighted rectangle to summon her. He would have his own key. Better yet, he'd have her by his side.

The reflection of the evening sun on the glass panes prevented his seeing her until she opened the door and stepped out onto the wraparound porch.

Emotions that he'd once thought he'd never feel again made his heart race. His glance swept over her, appreciating her attractiveness and the femininity of her dress, the color of a flowering coral azalea bush in full bloom.

The color complimented her auburn hair, shiny with deep

golden highlights. In her restaurant, she wore it fastened back with a clasp. Now, it bounced lightly around her shoulders as she accepted his arm and descended the few steps to the car.

Her eyes, more blue than gray, raised to his, held warmth. The sight of her and the faster beat of his heart were welcome like a ray of sunshine after a cloudy day. Yes, she lit up his life.

After a gentle hug of his arm around her shoulders, pulling her to his side, and telling her how lovely she looked, he opened the car door for her to slip into the passenger's seat. He settled in on the driver's side. Before he could turn the key in the ignition, she placed her hand on his arm.

"Curt."

The seriousness in her voice caused dread to rise in him. Had she changed her mind? Most of the time as their relationship became more personal, he just counted his blessings. At other times, he felt he couldn't bear going back to the sense of loneliness and loss that had nagged at him for months since Sybil's death, then on unexpected occasions after that

Now that he'd opened his heart to Annette, how could he go back? He didn't see how he could take another loss like that.

He turned his face toward her. Worry troubled her eyes.

"Are you nervous?" she asked.

Yeah, he could have said. *Nervous that you'll say you made a mistake. I'm too old for you. You've been alone too long.* He forced a smile. "About what?"

She shrugged one shoulder. "Your family."

He breathed a sigh of relief. Was that all? She'd told him her son, Tom, had disapproved of her dating when he was thirteen. He was now a high school senior and approved of their relationship. Curt lifted a hand in a dismissive gesture. "My youngest is eight years older than Tom and has been married for five years." He lowered his hand and caressed hers in a gentle manner. "They love you."

Annette nodded. "As a friend." She took a deep breath. "It's different, becoming a part of the family."

He spoke with confidence. "They'll welcome you. They've been saying that I laugh more lately, getting back to my old self." He smiled. "They'll be delighted that the reason is you."

Annette returned his smile. "It has to be that way, Curt. They have to want me as part of the family."

He laughed lightly and started the car. "If that's all that bothers you, we've got it made."

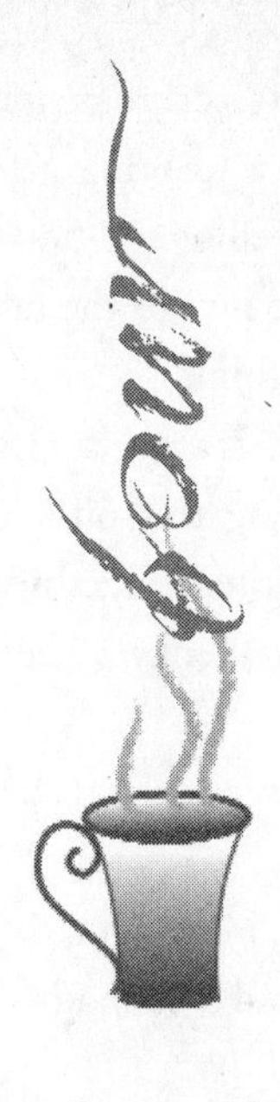

Hey, Sis, don't you have that food on the table yet?" Mike appeared in the doorway of the kitchen and headed for the stove.

Shelby reached out and grabbed his arm. "The traditional hug first, Bro."

She liked the fact they'd all begun to hug after her mom died. They had before, on occasion. Now it seemed to say they were closer than ever. They'd even started getting together for dinner once a month when it worked out for everybody. During the teen years, they'd drifted apart into their own activities and friends; then Mike had married Darla. Francine married Frank. Her brother and sister had started their families.

Darla came in. They hugged while Mike went over to inspect the pots on the stove. Darla asked the usual, "Can I help?"

Shelby nodded. "I don't know what you and Francine want your children to drink. I made iced tea for the adults. But we've got milk, juice, and water. Oh," she added, "it's warm enough for the children to eat out on the deck if you want them to. Except for the baby, of course, and the adults will eat in the dining room." She spread her hands and grinned. "Looks like Dad wants our full attention when he brings his guest and springs this surprise on us."

Darla questioned, "Who and what do you suppose this is about?"

Shelby shook her head. "No idea. He just said that since the family was getting together tonight, he'd like to bring a friend, and he has a surprise for us. He's mentioned selling the florist and traveling. Maybe he's got a buyer and wants to give us the money."

Darla grinned. "Hey, I like the way you think."

Shelby laughed, then shrugged. "I guess it's not a big deal, though, since Dad's in good spirits and doing this on a family night. Anyway, I'm using the good dishes for the adults since Dad brought home such a beautiful flower arrangement for the table. Go look at it."

Darla left the kitchen. Shelby turned to see Mike tasting the sauce. "Get out of that!"

Mike cowered in mock fear. "Just testing it for you."

"You're a pest, that's what you are. Go find somebody else to annoy."

Mike stuck out his bottom lip and slunk out of the kitchen.

Darla returned with Francine beside her, balancing little Luke on one hip.

"Great-looking table, Sis," Francine said, and Darla agreed. Shelby went over and kissed the baby on the cheek and patted his chubby little arm. He ducked into his mother's chest. Shelby hugged Francine as best she could, then stepped back.

"Not yet?" Francine said, gazing at Shelby's tummy.

Shelby heaved a sigh. "Nothing yet. But we're still trying."

Francine turned her attention to Luke. "I might just give you this one. He's a pistol. Cutting teeth, so he's fussy and slobbery. See!"

Shelby saw the wet spot on her sister's blouse and watched the precious boy trying to chew on his pacifier. She smiled, but her heart ached for a child. She and Brian had been trying for three years to have a baby. Darla with her two and Francine with her three proved they had no problem conceiving. She and Brian finally decided to be tested and were waiting for the doctor's report on how likely she was to be able to conceive.

"Where are those little sweeties, anyway?" Shelby asked.

"They ran down to see if the blueberries are ripe."

Shelby laughed. "I told them last week they wouldn't be ready for a long time."

"Well, to a kid a week is a long time," Francine informed her.

Shelby felt reprimanded, as if Francine thought she knew nothing about raising children. But Francine didn't mind calling on her to baby-sit occasionally.

"Oh, there they are," Darla said, walking to the kitchen window as voices of children and men could be heard.

Shelby walked over, too. Brian, Frank, and Mike had the three girls and boy looking at the green berries on the red and black raspberry bushes, the way Shelby's dad and mom would do if they were here. Shelby's heart ached at the sight of those precious children. She got to see them often, but they weren't hers, and that made all the difference.

Francine was only a couple years older than she. When Francine had the twins, they had talked about the joy of family and raising their children together since they lived only a few miles from each other. Now Francine had twin girls and little Luke. Shelby had none. Francine often said she had her hands full and might not have any more.

Brian and Mike turned toward the front of the house. The children began to run.

"Dad must be back," Shelby said. They all headed for the front door.

"Wonder what the surprise is this time." Francine's voice held the kind of excitement Shelby felt. Their dad had always been generous. He'd often surprised her and her siblings with some needed appliance, a gift of money, or vacations for the entire family. Mike had mentioned a boat the last time they went to the beach. Wouldn't surprise her if her dad drove up pulling a boat or leading someone else to the house with one. He'd become even more generous since their mom died.

Shelby's eyes widened.

Her dad strutted around his car and opened the passenger door. Emerging were a pair of shapely legs in high heels. Gallantly, he held out his hand, and a woman placed her hand in his.

What was going on?

Shelby felt Darla, Francine, and Luke breathing down her neck at the front door.

The children ran up. Her dad hugged them and introduced them to the smiling woman, who accepted their hugs. Brian and Mike shook her hand, then led the procession up the walkway as if some princess were coming behind them on a red carpet.

"That's Annette," Francine whispered.

Shelby's fingers trembled over the tiny pink roses on the china plate she held under the faucet. The tumbling water washed away the crumbs, but it mimicked the flood threatening her eyes. She turned off the faucet but couldn't stop the rivulets streaming down her cheeks. She grasped the silver-rimmed edge of the delicate dish. Her shoulders shook.

She could hardly believe what had transpired at the dinner table. What her dad's surprise and Annette Billings had to do with anything she couldn't have guessed. Could her dad be planning to buy Annette's restaurant? Was Annette planning to buy the florist?

Her immediate thought about Annette was how pretty she looked, less conservative than usual in a silk dress and her hair brushing against her shoulders. She looked younger than her thirty-something years. Of course, she'd seen Annette at church through the years, dressed up, but she hadn't paid much attention. She'd thought of her as Annette Billings, proprietor of Annette's Kitchen, who wore her hair fastened back with a clasp, dressed casually, sometimes wearing an apron.

As they ate and talked casually, Shelby could hardly keep her mind off what her dad's surprise might be. When Francine or Darla excused herself to check on the children or tend to one who came in with a problem, the men turned the conversation to sports.

When the women returned, so did the conversation about Annette's Kitchen, the great food served there, the enchanting Victorian house, what her son was doing.

It wasn't until after the children had finished and were turned loose to run in the backyard and dessert and coffee were served that her dad seemed ready to reveal his surprise.

He began by clinking his spoon on his coffee cup as if all eyes and ears hadn't been ready during the entire meal. He cleared his throat. Color rose to his cheeks, and his eyes looked feverish. His words, however unbelievable, were perfectly clear.

"You know," he said, "Annette has been a close friend of our family for years."

Of course, Shelby had known Annette was the proprietor of a place her mom and dad had frequented until her mom had to be put in a nursing home. She and her friends often went to the Kitchen. Her dad had gone there in memory of his wife. Shelby knew they talked because they had something in common—the loss of their spouses. Annette had joined others who brought food, sent sympathy cards, asked if she could do anything.

Shelby supposed Annette could be described as a close friend, especially if they had some kind of business deal going.

"Our friendship has become more serious," he said.

Shelby knew she couldn't have heard him right. Not even when he added, "We would like to have the blessings of the family."

His gaze rested lovingly on Annette's face, while she looked around from one to another.

Shelby was too shocked to do anything but stare at her dad.

That. . .was his surprise?

An eternal silence seemed to have settled on the room. No one spoke. The laughter and talking of children sounded from the backyard. Her dad said, "Well?"

Everyone then seemed to speak at once. At first they were

hesitant, then congratulatory. Annette and Francine conversed congenially. Shelby could think of nothing complimentary to say. When Annette glanced at her, Shelby tried to sound natural. "Dad, you should have warned me. I only cooked spaghetti." What an understatement. Her mom's prize spaghetti was not the kind of meal to serve at an occasion like this. *Occasion? Catastrophe is more like it.*

"Doesn't matter," he said.

Doesn't matter?

She'd planned the dinner, shopped for the ingredients, made the salad, bought the French bread the family liked, spent the entire afternoon making sure everything was perfect for eight adults and five children. . .but it doesn't matter?

It didn't matter!

Shelby had heard that the way to a man's heart was through his stomach. If that were so, then Annette's Kitchen was much more appealing than her mom's spaghetti.

Afraid to trust herself to speak further, Shelby began to gather the dirty dishes and take them into the kitchen—as if that mattered.

"Shelby?"

The sound of Annette's voice caused Shelby to jerk around.

She saw the dishes in Annette's hands at the same time she heard the crack of the plate against the faucet. The plate slipped from her hands. She moaned, feeling as fragile as the shattered pieces lying in the sink.

"Mom's best china," she wailed.

Annette spoke gently. "You were crying before it broke."

Not bothering to dry her hands, Shelby faced Annette. "I cannot accept this," Shelby choked out. "I know you've been a good friend to all of us while Mom was sick and since she died. But she's only been in her grave for six months. I don't mean this as anything against you, but there's no way you can come in here and. . .and. . .take her place."

Shelby hated the sadness that washed over Annette's face and sounded in her voice. "I suspected that, Shelby, by your reaction to your dad's announcement. That's why I told the others you and I would clean up together. So we could talk."

Shelby hated that self-righteous attitude of Annette's. She was trying to put a guilt trip on her. Determined not to apologize, Shelby turned toward the sink and stared at the pieces that couldn't be put together again. The pattern was one-of-a-kind, irreplaceable.

That's how she saw this situation. An important piece of her family was missing. But bringing in someone else to replace her mom would be like putting a paper plate with the china and calling it a set.

She didn't want to hurt Annette's feelings, but she had to be honest. She would try and make Annette understand she had nothing against her personally. She just couldn't be part of the family so soon after her mother's death.

She turned around.

Annette wasn't there.

"Shelby's just not thinking straight right now, Annette," Curt said on the way back to Annette's home. "I shocked her. I should have warned them."

The moment the silence had settled on them at the dinner table, he realized the others hadn't experienced their mother's regression like he had. He'd watched her turn from a dynamic, intelligent woman all the way down to having to be cared for as if she were an infant. To Shelby, her mom died six months ago. For him, Sybil's death had been a slow process for the past four years. Even then, he hadn't wanted her to die, but she had. Something in him had died along the way with Sybil. Now he wanted to live again. Was that wrong? Was it too soon?

Annette shook her head. “No, Curt. This way we got the true reaction. Shelby didn’t have a chance to cover her inner feelings.” She spoke softly. “I’m not upset with her. Or you. But I just will not do this. I told you.”

He wanted to shout, yell, hit something but felt like he was in some sort of suspended state, like a twilight zone. He’d felt that way after being told Sybil was dying. No! She was too young to die. No! Shelby couldn’t possibly have said those things to Annette. She was a grown girl—married. He might argue that Shelby was being childish.

But Annette had made herself perfectly clear before they went to the dinner. If the family gave their blessing. . .

“Don’t get out,” Annette said, when he pulled up at her door. There would be no talking it over. Not even a walking her to her door. Not even a leaning toward each other and touching their lips together like two people enjoying the warmth of each other, with the promise of a future together. Not even a hug.

He touched her hand.

“Good night, Curt,” she said softly. A sad smile touched her lovely face. She opened the car door. His hand fell to the empty seat. He watched as she unlocked her door, went inside, and without turning his way, closed the door behind her. Light permeated the inside of the house, and he watched her appear, then disappear from his sight. Would she cry? Would she be sorry?

Remembering her words, her caution, he felt she’d had the premonition something would go wrong.

He hadn’t.

The love he felt for her had happened like a bud whose petals begin to unfold and slowly grows into a beautiful flower.

One day he’d stood at the table where she was sitting. She looked up. He looked down in her face. And it happened! He saw eyes that sparked with something new, something different, something he hadn't seen before. He saw the surprise. He felt something leap inside him. Something caught in his throat. Of course he'd known Annette was an attractive woman, but he didn't expect there to ever be another woman for him. Sybil had been his life. Then suddenly, this was simply there. It existed. Like a house being built that has wires running all over but, until the switch gets flipped, remains dark. The switch flipped. The light dawned. He saw the blue-gray of her eyes, the spark in them, the life in them, the full, soft-looking pink lips, the way she laughed lightly, the way she had a habit of lifting her left hand and pushing a strand of hair behind her ear so perfectly formed. Even the lobe was alluring, not made for an earring but for a man's touch, as soft and appealing as a rose petal.

His love was like a primrose garden. You tend it. You watch it. You appreciate. Suddenly, the tightly closed bloom is a blossom. You know the potential is there, but the excitement, the breathlessness, the awe only comes at the moment of the blossom. The beauty is breathtaking. Then there's another one. Another surprise, until the garden is a paradise. Nothing exists but the garden.

One thing he'd forgotten: The evening primrose blossom falls to the ground while in full bloom. It doesn't last.

When Annette had come into the living room at his house after dinner, saying they should leave, he couldn't think of anything to say, except, "The flowers on the dining-room table are for you."

She had shaken her head, said good-bye to the air, and walked toward the front door.

Frustration rose in him. How could a sensible woman like Annette put such a stipulation on their love? If they both had small children, he could understand it better. A ray of hope entered his mind as he realized this was their first confrontation, the first time they'd disagreed on anything important. People who were close had their disagreements. They'd work this out.

He hoped it was just that clichéd lover's spat.

Doubt crowded out the hope. Maybe she didn't love him as much as he. . .

He shook his head and started the engine. Why tarry?

She doesn't need me.

For the second time that day, Eunice held her Bible. She and Henry had eaten lunch; she'd napped for a while; then they passed the afternoon as if nothing unusual had happened—except he'd taken the day off from his office at church. He said they would talk about it when she was ready.

She wasn't ready. She was still alive and went through the motions of living like any other day, except without the feeling. When Henry went to his study to work on Sunday's sermon, she reviewed the Sunday school lesson she would teach to women her own age. They'd gone through many things together. Some had survived cancer. She wouldn't. She could teach them how to live. But she didn't know how to die. Should she resign? If so, when? What would she do then?

Why was she given six months? Just to slowly waste away? How could God have a purpose in that? Would it help anyone for her to die. . .gracefully? If her life hadn't pointed anyone to the Lord, then how could her dying do so?

Around five o'clock, Henry said he would go pick up something for them to eat. She hadn't made any effort toward supper. What she ate would make no difference. Calories wouldn't have to be counted. . .now. She had kept her mind on writing cards that she needed to send to church members. She'd sent hundreds, thousands, during the years. Soon she would be receiving them.

"Do you want me to tell the congregation on Sunday?" Henry asked. "Or do you want to?"

What happened to our miracle?

"You tell them," she said.

They were both like dammed-up rivers pushing against the barrier between them. His pushed one way, hers the other, and they both pretended all was safe. She knew, he knew, something had to give. Which would be first? How long could the dam stand the pressure? When would the dam break and floodwaters spew forth and do irreparable damage?

Or were she and Henry strong enough to be like calm waters? Right now, they were both calm, too calm, like the calm before the storm. Their eyes didn't meet and hold. She didn't want to go first. Henry was stronger than she in the Lord. But he needed her. Didn't God know that?

No, don't go there. That thought caused the still water to stir.

After supper, Henry threw away the paper wrappers, poured another cup of coffee, and said he would be in the study if she needed him.

If she needed him? She'd needed him to help her live. How could he help her die? Could he? They might talk about it later, after dark, when the lights were out and they would lie in bed and hold each other and not be afraid to look toward each other, fearful of what might be in the eyes—the mirrors of the soul.

What troubled her most, other than leaving Henry, was not death. . .but a part of life she'd tried to ignore.

She held the Bible.

This was her personal Bible, her devotional Bible, which she kept on top of the nightstand. It looked so innocent there, not hidden away as if it bore a secret.

Sitting on the side of the bed, she remembered Henry standing in the pulpit, holding his Bible out toward the congregation, proclaiming, "This is truth!"

Her hand trembled over the cover, where her secret was glued. No one would suspect. She had cut the margins from around the note so that no indentation showed. Inside lay a truth—but not the whole truth.

Like white lies, there were half truths.

She'd resolved to pry up that paper and destroy the evidence.

Who was she protecting?

Someone else, out of love?

Or herself, out of selfishness?

Should this be revealed?

Or destroyed?

She looked toward the ceiling with a prayer in her heart. *Lord, I never knew the whole truth. Is it my duty to find out and meet my maker with a clear conscience, or do I pretend all is well, as I have done for nineteen years? What about the others. . .who know? What is my obligation to them? What is my obligation to You? Is this note like a broken-heart locket, where one takes half and leaves the other half with his lover until they meet again and join the pieces?*

Had enough time passed so they could now speak of it? Or should it lie. . .buried in the past?

There was a reason for everything. That's what Henry preached and she believed. God answered prayer with yes, no, wait. Was God going to reveal His answer. . .after nineteen years of waiting?

Her hand trembled with indecision on the back inside cover. Maybe she should just leave it there. No one would ever know. It didn't show.

But what should she do about the three women—Annette, Ruby, and Lara—who had the other side of the locket?

Annette stood on the stairs, holding onto the stair railing.

Yes, it was what she'd expected. The last hurdle. She just couldn't get over the last hurdle. She was like an equestrian whose horse clears all the jumps, then comes down to the last one. Just one little bump of the hoof and the pole goes down. Everybody groans.

She wasn't sure if she felt like groaning. In a way, she felt relief, like she could take a breath now. She'd been holding it, waiting for the pole to fall, so to speak.

Something deep inside had warned her she didn't deserve the kind of happiness she might find with Curt. Also, the past and the future had pressed against her like two bookends. Should she tell Curt about the past?

Now that was not an option. Shelby had made the decision for her.

She'd been alone, except for her son, Tom, for a long time. Was this too soon for Curt?

She hadn't intended to fall in love in the first place.

She'd known Curt and Sybil from church. They both had frequented her restaurant for many years. Annette bought flowers from Curt's florist. During Sybil's illness and after her death, he came to the Kitchen, sometimes with family members, sometimes alone.

Curt began to bring flowers she ordered. . .and some she didn't.

She recalled the first time he brought yellow roses. "These are the first of the season," he said. "They'll look beautiful here."

She offered to pay.

"Please," he said. "Allow me to give. I need that."

They often sat at a table, drinking coffee, talking about their loved ones who had died and those who hadn't and about the weather and food and flowers. They empathized. They became friends.

One day she sat at a corner table alone after a particularly busy coffee hour. The Kitchen was closed. Customers would frequent only the gift shop until closing time at 5:00 p.m. She was sipping a cappuccino, deep in thought about something. What happened next erased that memory and was replaced by the unforgettable one.

A male voice whispered near her ear, "And what is this lovely lady so deep in thought about?"

Recognizing his voice, she straightened, looked up into his face, so much nearer hers than she expected. Their glances met. Their gazes held. Her breath caught. She heard the swift intake of air into his mouth, through his firm, well-formed lips. She hadn't really thought about that before.

When she looked up into Curt's face, something leapt inside her. Like never before. Different than when she and Louis had been childhood sweethearts. With Louis, the love had taken many forms. He'd been her sweetheart. She liked him, then loved everything about him, had gone through the stages of being in love with love, with the idea, with one's own maturing emotions, the nearness and need for another. First love, only love, exciting love, married love, remembered perfect love—that was Louis.

She expected if she were ever to love again it would be something she wanted to happen, worked at. The desire for that had not occurred before Curt.

She did not define that incredible instant for a long time

afterward, simply basked in it for it felt good, secure, safe, new. Curt was a good man. He'd loved his wife. He'd raised a fine family. He was a respected Christian man.

She didn't know if it was his need she felt or her own latent one.

A need, a desire to love grew within her. With it grew a love for that man. Afterward she allowed her thoughts to go where they had not previously been. Without guarded warnings or the constraint one has when looking upon a married man, she began to see his physical attributes in terms of how well she related to that. She began to welcome the delicious shivers of delight at the manly look of him, the character in his face surrounded by dark hair sprinkled with gray, the gleam of hope in his deep blue eyes, his full lips turned into a smile, the growing desire for her.

He waited until she gave a sign. The eyes were the mirror of his soul. She reveled in it. She liked being special, respected, wanted. She felt young again.

Now her gaze moved from inner reflection to a corner table where she and Curt had sat—where she and her friends often sat. A lovely bouquet of fresh flowers Curt had given her graced the center of the table. The flowers had begun to wilt. They would die.

Her gaze left the corner table, swept past the entryway into the gift shop, and alighted on the white Victorian birdcage. The light delineated the pink silk flowers draped over the cage and pushed its shadow across the floor.

The church had given the birdcage to her when she opened the Kitchen. She had dared not ask who picked it out. She was the widow of the town hero. Louis had died for them, God, America, mother, and apple pie. She couldn't refuse it. But who had suggested it? Had it been an innocent gesture?

Or an accusation?

It had been an albatross around her neck.

She closed her eyes for a moment. She knew better than to go there. She hadn't meant to. No, she knew no one was vindictive enough to give such a gift in a deprecatory way. How could they? They didn't know. No one knew. Except Ruby and Lara.

A birdcage would be the last thing Ruby or Lara would have chosen. She remembered the shock on Ruby's face when she saw it and the pallor on Lara's.

Annette had accepted it, covered it with silk flowers, and focused on the flowers. Only on rare occasions did she focus on the inside of the cage. . .empty.

This was one of those rare times.

Yes, the birdcage was adorned with flowers. Like the headstones in the graveyard. Her Victorian house was adorned with flowers. She even had a plaque on the wall, given to her by a local poet, written in Victorian script:

Around the house
she built a fence
of flowers—
Nancy Dillingham, "Defense"

Nancy had shown Annette the poem and said the Victorian house was set amid such a beautiful garden and inspired her to write the poem. Patrons liked the poem and thought the title clever. So did Annette, but sometimes, like now, it felt like an accusation, like handwriting on the wall. Didn't even the title imply such?

Let the beauty conceal the stark reality.
I knew it.
I accept my punishment.
Tommy will leave. I will grow old. . .alone.

She took a deep breath and continued up the stairs.

Not completely alone.

There are three of us. The three. . . No, she wouldn't think "stooges." Ruby was the one who could say something like that, and they could laugh. Neither she nor Lara could pull it off like Ruby.

She backtracked.

There are three of us. The three. . .lifelong friends.

Curt heard the battle raging the moment he walked into the house. He strode to the kitchen. "You can stop your arguing. Annette called it off. There is no relationship."

His family members stepped aside to let him enter the kitchen. He looked at the stark faces, the silent mouths of each one. His chest rose with each labored breath he took. His gaze fell upon his youngest daughter. With difficulty, he spoke. "Congratulations, Shelby. Your surprise was bigger than mine."

With a shake of her head, she gave him a look like Francine or Darla might express when reprimanding their children. "Dad, that just goes to show you. She's pitting the two of us against each other already."

Fortunately he choked on the words that almost spewed forth. After forcing a few deep breaths, he spoke as calmly as he could. "What all did you say to Annette?"

Shelby barely lifted a shoulder while silence hung in the air like a boulder about to be dropped from a high building and everyone waited for the impact. "Dad, I'm trying to keep you from making a mistake. It's only been six months since Mom died." She had the audacity to speak calmly. "I just said that nobody could take Mom's place."

Hurt, anger, disappointment mingled with despair. He spread his hands in a helpless gesture. "No one can take anybody's place, little girl." This would be easier if she'd spoken against Annette, had some reason to dislike her. But intimating he was trying to replace Sybil. . .wasn't fair. Stifling the urge to defend himself, trying to behave like a reasonable man, he muttered, "What else did you say?"

Her defensiveness surfaced. "I. . .don't exactly remember."

Fearing he would lose control and having no idea if he'd yell, hit, cry, or run, he moved over to a chair and held onto the back of it. He moistened his dry lips with his tongue. "Okay. Let me refresh your memory. You said you couldn't accept this. Right?"

Her chin lifted. "I might've."

"Uh huh. Okay." He feared he'd break that chair back—or his knuckles. "And what did she say?"

He watched Shelby take on a thoughtful look. A few grunts and groans and sighs came from the other family members. Curt lifted his hand for their silence. His eyes challenged his daughter.

Shelby lifted her hand in a helpless gesture. "Annette said something like. . ." Her defiant glance then met his. "Something like, she thought so."

"Thought so?"

Shelby nodded. "That I couldn't. . .accept this."

He nodded, afraid of the calm that overtook him. This girl was a stranger. "Anything else?"

Shelby shook her head.

Curt tapped out the words on the back of the chair with the palm of his hand. "And from that, you come to the conclusion she's trying to put a wedge between us." He snorted. "Well, Daughter, the only one doing that is you. You!" His voice was deep and tremulous. "I'm totally ashamed of you." Disregarding the hurt that leapt into her eyes, he repeated, "Totally."

He turned toward the others. "The celebration is over. You can go home now."

"I'll round up the children," Frank said and touched Curt's arm as he walked past him.

"It'll be okay, Dad," Francine said. "Annette was just uncomfortable after what Shelby said. She won't hold that against you." She made a move toward him, but he held up his hands in abeyance. He wasn't in the mood for sympathy. He'd thought he was done with that kind of thing.

"We'll be in touch, Dad," she said.

Darla whispered something about being sorry and followed Francine out the door.

Mike laid his hand on Curt's shoulder for an instant. Brian shook his head and looked down at his shoes as he walked through the doorway.

Curt hurried out behind them. He heard children's voices. He needed to tell them good-bye, give them hugs. With his lower lip held by his teeth to still the trembling, he walked out onto the front porch.

When the hugs were done, Mike and Frank steered the children to the vehicles to buckle them up. Francine and Darla said good-bye and left.

Curt knew Shelby stood behind him. He didn't want to face her, but she walked around in front of him.

Vaguely, he heard farewell words from the vehicles.

The one he didn't want to hear said, "Dad."

"Just go."

She tried to hug him when he teared up, but he waved her away. He needed to get used to being alone. He'd lost two women he loved. One in death and the other because of Shelby's trying to run his life for him.

Shelby gave him a condescending look. Her face wore an expression like she was a mother who had just scolded a child, as if to say, "This hurts me worse than it hurts you."

"But Dad. . .the dishes."

His mouth opened, and his tongue stuck to the roof of his mouth as he tried to say the word that wouldn't come out.

Dishes?

Brian grabbed Shelby's arm. "Come on, let's go." He pulled her from the porch. His abruptness changed to sympathy. "Sorry about this, Curt."

Francine had said Annette wouldn't hold Shelby's words against him. She was right. But Annette had made it clear their relationship would not continue unless the family approved.

Oh, Shelby would come around, wouldn't she? She'd grow up? She'd realize she was wrong? By then, would Annette have realized she didn't really need him after all? She'd adjusted well through the years.

He hadn't.

He stood on the porch, feeling the brisk breeze. Winter had lain dormant, allowing a hint of spring, but would stick around for a while. No, spring hadn't come.

The sky had darkened, and gray clouds had gathered.

Was that rain?

Maybe.

Maybe not.

Could just be the condition of his eyes.

Outside. Inside. What difference did it make?

He and Sybil had done well. Their children had married nice guys. They had their mates.

He turned and fumbled for the handle on the screen door.

He had. . .

. . .the dishes.

Saturday morning dawned as an extension of the catastrophic Friday "family" dinner.

Last night, Shelby had hoped to leave her tears in the bathtub to rush down the drain and out through the pipes. However, Brian turned his back on her in bed, said they'd all spoken their minds and there was nothing more to say. Her tears had fallen like the spring rains that go on and on eliciting flood warnings.

After Brian would listen to her no longer, he got up and went into the other bedroom, saying he had to get some sleep.

Brian had even eaten a bowl of cereal before she got out of bed. Normally he'd cook golden-brown waffles for them. She loved to smear on the butter and watch it melt in the little squares before putting on blueberry or strawberry jam or sweet delicious maple syrup.

Not today! No tantalizing aroma of warm waffles cooking on the griddle. The air smelled of rejection.

She'd heard that the first big argument with your husband is devastating. She'd had that years ago, but that didn't compare with losing the support of not only your husband, but your entire family. Her sister and brother had, in high-pitched emotional voices, told her how selfish and wrong she was.

Darla and Frank didn't say so, but apparently they agreed with Mike and Francine. They had herded their families into their cars without even saying good-bye to her.

Were they so wrapped up in their own lives, their own jobs and families, that they couldn't see how wrong her dad's remarrying would be?

Maybe they and Brian would understand after thinking it over.

She hadn't been able to get through to him last night. Maybe this morning, he would be more inclined to listen.

He had made a pot of coffee. She got a cup and joined him at the kitchen table. He looked every bit of his ten years older than the teens he taught in high school. She hadn't awakened to her husband's pleasant face surrounded by rumpled reddish-blond hair. There'd been no teasing about the freckles across his nose and plump cheeks. She'd awakened to a pillow. The tired circles under his cloudy-gray eyes spoke of a restless night. The mirror had said hers were worse—puffy accompanied the tired look.

"Are you still against me this morning?" she asked.

"I'm not against you, Shelby. I think you're wrong, and I'm entitled to my opinion."

Shelby had a tendency to speak her mind without thinking. But on this subject, she had thought. All night long.

She spoke softly. She wanted no more harsh words, not from her husband, family members, or herself. "Brian, can't you see that if I approve of this, Annette will be in Mom's chair at the table, beside Dad in his bed, at functions he and Mom went to? And worse, when we have a child, he or she would be expected to call her grandmother."

Since he was four years older than she and graduated from college, she'd considered Brian wise and mature. She admired that about him. After a thoughtful moment, he spoke.

"Shelby, if your dad wants Annette in those places, it's his decision."

"Oh, Brian. He's just trying to replace Mom. When you see someone making a mistake, you tell them. That goes double when it's your own dad."

"His being your dad doesn't mean you own him."

"I'm not trying to own him."

He got up, dumped his coffee in the sink, and set his cup on the countertop. "Shelby, there's no need for further discussion. I don't know how you can have this attitude."

She stood and walked closer to him. Sarcasm welled up to join her hurt and anger. "Maybe I'm pregnant."

That got his attention. His head jerked toward her. For a long moment he looked at her with a soft expression in his eyes that had a way of melting her heart. They'd been trying to have a baby for three years. "You know how much I'd like that, Shelby. But if I had anything to say about it, I'd prefer you had morning sickness instead of. . ."

She waited. "What?"

He waved his hand in dismissal. "Never mind. This isn't going anywhere except where we've already been. It's been hashed and rehashed."

"You were going to say I have a mind sickness, right?"

He looked distressed. "I didn't plan what I was going to say, Shelby. That's why I stopped. Whatever I say will be wrong. You've taken your mom's place with your dad in so many ways. It's like an obsession." He paused and sighed. "See? Your mouth is now wide open, and your eyes are looking holes through me. I can't get through to you. You're more hardheaded than the high school students I teach. I can't say the right words. I'm. . .going."

He strode past her toward the back door.

"Going?" Had he lost his mind? "Where?"

He paused at the door. "I'm going down to the floral center to see if I can help your dad. He doesn't want you there this morning, and you're in no shape to go anyway. I can at least cut some stems off roses or just keep him company. He probably could use a friend right now."

"You're going to talk about me, aren't you?"

His head rocked from side to side. "Frankly, I think we'd both prefer to smell the roses this morning."

"You don't love me."

He didn't even deny it. Just shook his head again and walked out the door.

He hates me.

The whole family hates me. Why can't they understand? Don't they love Mom the way I do? They'll come to their senses. They will.

She went into the bedroom she and Brian planned to turn into a nursery. Normally on Saturday, if her dad didn't need her at the floral center or to clean at his house, she and Brian would go and look at baby furniture. They would even go to stores and look at those teeny-tiny little adorable baby clothes.

Not today!

And why?

Because Annette wasn't being honest with herself. She would never interfere with the Crowder family? She already had. She might have come to Shelby in private and asked her opinion instead of making a grand entrance.

Not only had she caused discord within the family Shelby was born into, it was even more personal. Now there was a rift between her and Brian. Shelby sniffed and fell onto the bed, where she'd slept alone last night. She sobbed into the pillow.

She could never even have a baby as long as her husband preferred not to sleep with her.

Where Ruby made her mistake was yelling above the children, the TV, a sixteen-year-old's idea of a music CD, and a barking dog. "Charlie, can you get that?"

He got it in the bedroom, so she hadn't a clue who called—that is, until he came into the kitchen, shrugging into his jacket, with a look on his face she didn't recognize, and she was quite familiar with all his expressions. "I have to go out for a little while. Shouldn't be long."

"What is it? Who was on the phone?"

Already halfway out the door looking like a dog about to chase a rabbit, he lifted his hand in an unreasonable facsimile of a good-bye wave. "We'll talk about it when I get back, honey."

Honey!

He never called her "honey" at home unless he wanted to reprimand her or correct her about something. *Don't be so hard on the kids, honey. How long you going to stay in that bathroom, honey? Why don't you kiss me like you mean it, honey? When's the last time this bathtub was scrubbed, honey? When are you going to make that special dessert of yours again, honey? Is that a dent in the fender, honey? What happened to all the money in the checkbook, honey?*

While the dishwater soaked out all the oil from her hands, she thought of Wednesday night after choir practice. After he dismissed the choir, Charlie had asked Maybelle to stay and practice her solo one more time. He looked at Ruby with his round, innocent-looking brown eyes. He spoke in that soft, sweet way of his. "You don't mind waiting 'til we go over the solo one more time, do you, honey?"

"I drove my own car," Ruby said, as if he didn't know he drove his because, being the responsible person he was, he wanted to be there when the choir members arrived, and she couldn't always be on time. His was a paying job, so that left her to do the free one of chauffeuring the girls to their various activities, whether church, school, or otherwise.

If she had to sit and listen to Maybelle sing one more note, she had a strong suspicion something was going to get broken, and it wouldn't be a high C that did it.

"I'll go on," she said. "All the girls are here tonight."

A dimple dented his left cheek. A man almost forty shouldn't be that cute. "I'll be home in a little while, honey."

That was Wednesday night.

Now on Saturday morning, he was saying the same thing. What did he think—that she was some kind bee who'd found a hollow tree in which to make a hive?

And, too, she wouldn't know if he returned in a little while. She had to be at Annette's by noon to help plan, of all things, a wedding. That would be easy. What the world needed was someone to help couples plan their marriages.

She sat down to eat the piece of bacon one of the girls had left on her plate and half a blueberry pancake on Charlie's. She shouldn't. But hadn't she raised her children to clean their plates? Somehow it kept children in Africa from starving. Anyway, her ire would surely burn off the calories.

By eleven thirty, she'd finished her unpaid job of washing the dishes, the table, the countertop, and the floor; making the bed; doing two loads of laundry; writing a list of things she'd need from the market; and telling the girls to fold the clothes and clean their rooms for the umpteenth time. She then put sixteen-year-old Jill in charge of the younger girls.

"Can Lonnie come over?"

"No. Your dad's not here, and I'm leaving."

"But Maa-umm. Lonnie's funny."

Ruby gave her a piercing look. "Yes, dear. But he's a rotten teenager, and who knows what lurks behind that humorous mask?"

Jill tilted her chin and raised her eyebrows. "You're funny." Lest that sound like a compliment, she added, "Sometimes."

"Exactly." Ruby grinned. "You made my point."

After Jill's groan of indignation about her disastrous plight in life, Ruby glanced at the wall clock. Ten minutes to shower and be at Annette's. Oh well, why break an "always late" habit of many years?

"Saturday is Charlie's time with the girls—after their chores. But not today." She mumbled to herself. No need to worry about the girls hearing her. They didn't hear even if she yelled.

She crunched her naturally curly hair with her fingers. Still wet, but so what? Was gray mixed with dishwater-blond any prettier dry? She thought not.

"He knows my free time is a couple hours on Saturday with Annette and Lara. That's all I do outside family and church. But he had to go out!"

"Whatever happened to your smile, Ruby? And the sparkle in your light blue eyes?" She answered herself. "They got lost in the fat. . .honey."

She put on a long skirt that was supposed to camouflage the hips. It sure did. Made her look like one big hip from the waist down to midcalf. She peered more closely into the mirror. No, she wouldn't bother with makeup. After all, she wiggled her eyebrows at herself, who would look at her face? Her skirt had a sexy split to the knee.

She laughed and grabbed a sweater from the closet.

After a quick review of the girls' responsibilities, she reminded them to lock the door; not go anywhere; call 911 in case of fire, flood, or death; and not open the door to anyone.

She grinned but refrained from saying, "Not even Charlie."

"I love you," she called.

She walked out and rang the doorbell until Carley came to lock the door. Eight-year-old Carley was the youngest, named that because it was the closest Charlie was ever going to get to a boy of his own. After three tries, she sure wasn't going to chance having another girl—no matter how often he sported that dimpled cheek. . .the one on his face!

"Love you, Mom," Carley said, and Ruby blew her a kiss.

They were good girls, active in church, and all had professed Jesus as their Savior. But they were still human girls, like she had been, full of life and energy and self-will. Only Carley curled up in her lap occasionally. Sometimes the others sat close to her, but most of the time they preferred their privacy and their friends. Thirteen-year-old Kristin was the only one who ducked down in the floorboard of the backseat when she had to ride with her and saw kids she knew. Jill was becoming such a self-sufficient young lady, she was confident in her own teenage world and not always aware her mom existed, except as one who harped at her about this and that.

But that's what a mother had to do, wasn't it? Teach them, train them, discipline them, tell them she loved them. Do her best and not be scared to death.

Ah, she thought, settling in the car. *Two hours to forget the joys of family life.* They were her life. She thanked God for her family. Without them, she had nothing—except memories. Thank God again, she was too busy for memories.

She'd escaped into family life. After the children started school, she had escaped into her job at social services, and other people's problems made most of hers seem minor in comparison. Her job had made her a likely candidate for being on the committee for their Alternate Answers for Young Women program.

She'd recently found a home and a job for a fifteen-year-old pregnant girl. At least her teenagers weren't pregnant. She knocked on the steering wheel as if it were wood.

Ruby backed up to the edge of the driveway of her modest frame house in the reasonably priced, older residential neighborhood. The living space was on ground level at the front. The front yard was small, thirty feet from the sidewalk next to the road busy with traffic when a conference was in session farther up the mountain.

Seeing a line of cars on the road, she looked through the windshield at the black lab standing at the back of the house at the chain-link fence surrounding the spacious backyard. She liked the privacy of the back. In nice weather they could walk out of the basement, spread their lounge chairs on the concrete drive or the green lawn surrounded by age-old bushes, flowering wild azalea trees, and tall lilacs. The basement served as the laundry room and a partitioned section that Charlie had turned into an all-purpose room they used to enjoy together when the children were younger. Now it belonged to the kids, the dog, and the cats.

Waiting for the cars to pass, she pondered, "Whatever happened to our family life?"

Then she remembered.

They had had children. And two of them had turned into teenagers.

She backed out onto the street. But none of that. She needed to psych herself up for helping to plan Annette's happy future of wedded bliss.

"Your weight concerns me. You're borderline bulimic," the doctor said before opening the door and leaving her alone in the examination room. "You need to put some meat on those bones."

Lara sighed. He should know.

He was the only person who had seen her naked in over fifteen years. She had the same thought each year after having her physical exam. Last year it had been fourteen years. This year. . . fifteen. . . Next year it would be. . .another year. But that's what she'd chosen. That's what she wanted.

That was yesterday.

However, the doctor's assessment had lingered in her mind. His words were quite a switch from what she normally heard.

Elegant, rich women who came into the shop where she worked complimented her. "Lara, you always look so lovely," they would say. "What a classic outfit. How perfect. I wish you hadn't bought that so I could. That is a Lancaster, isn't it?"

Sure it was. Those who worked at the exclusive women's shop called Lancaster's were required to wear their designer clothes. That was no place for a uniform or to dress down to make someone else look good. After several years of compliments, one tended to believe it.

Now, for breakfast she made herself drink a double mocha cappuccino with whole milk and whipped cream. Which had the most calories? Booze or cappuccinos?

She could smile about that. She'd tried the booze way. It hadn't made any difference. There was truth in the saying that it might make you forget for a while, but you wake up the next morning with the same problems plus a hangover.

She could have the hangover without the booze, so why

bother? Fortunately, she hadn't become an alcoholic. She'd simply been a drunk. Her co-workers didn't know. She could dine out with them and have an occasional glass of wine. The church people didn't know. They just knew she was a divorcée.

Labels.

Ruby and Annette knew. But they accepted her as she was—skinny, elegantly dressed. Lara with the shriveled up insides. Lara with skin on her bones.

She didn't like food. She didn't like anything coming close to her mouth. But she would force herself. She had tolerantly dined in the best restaurants, here and abroad. None offered the relaxed, comfortable atmosphere of Annette's Kitchen, where Lara could enjoy the flavors and aromas of European and regional food, herbed teas, and exotic coffees.

This is life, she mused. *Rise. Have coffee. Dress. Work. Nibble lunch. Work. Force dinner. Watch a movie. Listen to a musical. Attend an opera. Read a book. Go to church. Sleep. Dream a nightmare. Rise. Have coffee.*

But Saturday was a time to be with her friends. Three women so different on the outside. Ruby was Ruby; what you saw was what you got. Lara was told she always looked terrific. Annette had managed to achieve perfection. . .in spite of the past. Now she even had a second chance at building a new life. Could she—had she—somehow managed to forget. . . ?

Would Annette tell Curt? If so, how much would she tell?

Chill bumps rose on Lara's arms.

Over her white silk blouse, she slipped on the bitter chocolate jacket of her pantsuit. The beige-brown belt and two-inch heels completed the sporty attire. Her dark brown hair lay against her cheek on one side and was brushed behind her ear on the other side and fell to just below her earlobes. The Lancaster 14K gold earrings set off the outfit nicely.

Was she really too thin?

That was only the doctor's opinion. Others complimented her—or her clothes. She'd even been told that she had a classic face, with her dark hair and eyes, long straight nose, and high cheekbones she knew came from some distant Indian relative. What exactly did that mean? Attractive? The doctor would probably say skeletal.

She abhorred that thought. She quickly strode from her master bathroom into the carpeted bedroom and picked up the purse that matched her two-inch heels. She retrieved her keys from a drawer in the kitchen and left by the side door to her car in the garage.

She backed her new car, this year's model she had bought last November, out of the garage and onto the quiet street. A studied quick glance around revealed the signs of spring coming to life in the flowerbeds. Many of the residents, mostly older retired couples who could afford a townhouse in the exclusive development, left the trees and shrubs to be tended by the gardener since maintenance was part of the development's package. Lara was one of those. She couldn't see herself on her hands and knees, ruining her manicure. She loved beauty but no longer created it, just enjoyed it.

With that thought, she drove past the gate bordered by boxwoods, heather, azaleas, and freshly planted pansies. She smiled appreciatively and glanced at the tranquility of the clear, light blue sky.

Driving away from the development, through the valley, and up and around the curved roads toward Annette's Kitchen, she felt skeptical about the future. She was basically alone, except for the closeness she had with Annette and Ruby. She looked forward to helping Annette plan her wedding. But what would that do to their friendship? Annette and Ruby were her only close friends.

Approaching the two-story white Victorian house and the inviting wraparound porch, she forced herself to concentrate on the happiness Annette and Curt might have together, not on the worm of loneliness and concern that crawled through her stomach, heading for her throat.

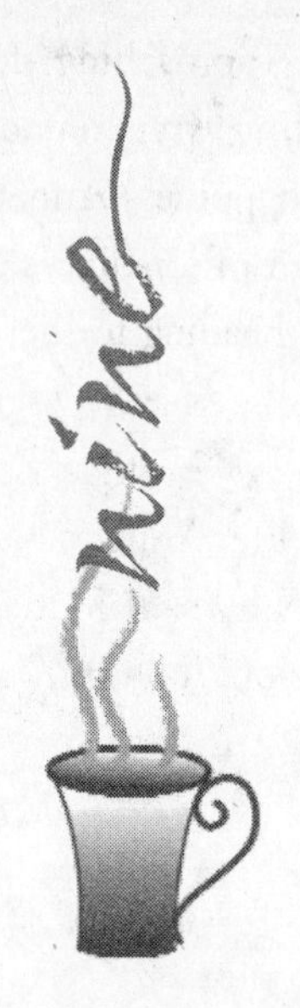

Although the three o'clock tea and coffee hours were Annette's favorite time of the day, she enjoyed the hustle and bustle of lunchtime. Most of her customers frequented the Kitchen regularly, especially during the winter months. Tourists were beginning to trickle in, coming to see springtime decorate the North Carolina mountainsides. This was spring break for many schools. Before long, tourists would come in droves to escape big-city life and enjoy the laid-back hospitality of the southern region.

She was having a conversation about the souvenir pewter teapots with a woman from Michigan when the overhead tinkling bell sounded and Lara walked in, looking like she'd stepped from a fashion magazine. Annette smiled at that. Lara had in fact been photographed wearing Lancaster clothes and featured in the company's fall catalog.

At a break in the conversation, Annette excused herself from the tourist and slipped her arm around Lara's waist as a brief greeting. The Saturday meetings were special. They rarely saw each other during the week, each being busy with work and daily living. They'd phone if a pressing matter occurred.

At each tinkle of the bell, she'd expected to see Curt coming to plead with her. She was rather disappointed that he hadn't. Nor had he called. She supposed he'd taken her seriously. That's what she'd wanted, but at the same time, she missed the attention of his giving a diversion from the sameness of the days, although she knew she had a good life and liked what she did. She had many blessings. Ruby complained about her big family, cats, and dogs, but that was surface talk. She was a wonderful mother, wife, and all-around good person. She cared about the troubled young girls who came to the church, seeking help. Lara lived a relatively solitary life. Annette had Tom and her customers.

That was good. That was enough. Curt had been a good distraction. It had felt good to be desired, loved. It was a good memory. She willed herself not to give in to the ache deep inside. She never should have allowed the situation with Curt to give her hope of a lifelong companion. She had adjusted to her lifestyle. She would again. She would keep telling herself that until it became truth.

"Come on into the Kitchen," Annette said to Lara. "Let me introduce you to my most recently acquired waitress, Marcella."

Annette introduced Lara as her friend. "Lara, Marcella is living with the Masons and going to our church now. She's been working for me a couple of days."

"Nice to meet you, Marcella," Lara said.

"You, too," Marcella said and complimented Lara on her outfit.

The tinkling of the bell drew Annette's attention. A couple she knew walked in. She should speak to them. "Go ahead and have a seat, Lara. I'll be with you in a minute."

"That's fine," Lara said. "We have to wait for Ruby anyway."

"Can I get you something while you wait?" Marcella asked

Lara didn't want anything but became aware of the mingling of lunch aromas of spiced teas, gourmet coffees, cooked meat, steamed vegetables, and fresh bread.

The young girl, who didn't appear old enough to work,

looked as awkward as Lara felt, so Lara ordered hot green tea with mint. Marcella smiled as if she'd been done a great favor.

Lara sat at the "reserved" corner table. Marcella brought the tea and set it on the table as if the cup and saucer might break, then nodded as if she were proud of doing something right. A young girl, new in town, living with a church couple aroused Lara's curiosity but also prompted her not to ask questions.

She added sugar to her tea. While sipping it and waiting for Ruby, she watched Annette move naturally from one table to another, one customer to another, making them feel welcomed. She looked comfortable in slacks and a simple white cotton shirt, with her hair pulled back, revealing her smooth complexion, which still sported a youthful glow.

Soon, the bell tinkled again. Ruby rushed through the room and flopped down in a chair opposite Lara, breathing hard.

"You didn't have to hurry, Ruby. We know you're always late."

"It's not just that," she said. "I've gained another two pounds, and it all goes to one place."

Before Lara could reprimand Ruby and tell her once again she wasn't supposed to look like she did in college before she had had three children, Annette stood beside Ruby.

"I heard that," Annette said. "You two start that way every time. Ruby, you're not as plump as you try to make everybody believe, and Lara, you're always a picture of perfection."

Leave it to Annette to always say the right thing. And she was right. Ruby was. . .Ruby. What you saw was what you got. She made everybody else feel good about themselves by putting herself down. She appeared to make life seem like a happy place full of humor. She was fun and funny and accepted as one who exaggerated.

Annette, on the other hand, made everyone envious. She seemed to weather every storm and come out a winner. She'd reacted to almost every situation with an aura of courage, strength, and renewed faith. Now she had a second chance of building a new life. That would give Ruby and Lara something to look forward to, help plan, be part of, talk about, rejoice in—like a good, strong cup of coffee after coming home from a cold, blustery, winter day.

"Let's eat upstairs," Annette said. "Tell Marcella what you want. I'll be right up. I want to speak to the Fossets."

Lara glanced at Ruby, who stared after Annette. Not too many things left Ruby speechless. However, it took a few seconds before she spoke.

"Lara, that look on Annette's face was not moonlight and roses. I have a sneaky feeling there's trouble in paradise."

Marcella brought up the glasses of sweet iced tea, silverware wrapped in napkins, and a basket of country French bread. Annette took real butter from her refrigerator.

Annette's son, Tom, soon brought up a huge round tray, which he balanced on his shoulder with one of his long-fingered hands. He set the tray on the island and began to bring the dishes to the round table.

"Haven't seen you around in a while, Tommy," Ruby said, using the name she'd called him from the time he was a small boy.

He set a sinfully healthy-looking plate of fruit surrounding Annette's special citrus yogurt sauce sprinkled with granola in front of Lara, who said, "And you're working!"

Tommy grinned, looking much like his tall, dark, and handsome dad, who Ruby had known and remembered from pictures Annette had shown her. "Mom makes me work for my money."

"Oh, ho," Ruby said. "You can't get any sympathy with that sob story. I have a teenage daughter who can wipe out a paycheck in one fell swoop. I'll bet keeping a kid in college, plus a car—"

He laughed and set Annette's Monte Cristo on the table. "Yeah, Ruby. But what are moms for but to feel worthwhile in these ventures? When I'm world famous, she can have the credit."

Annette laughed. "Now, Tom, how is going to the movies tonight going to make you world famous?"

He set Ruby's idea of a real lunch on the table—pan-fried seared chicken breast, hot on a croissant, with bacon, cheddar, Swiss, fresh tomatoes, and crisp lettuce. "Who knows? I might become a movie producer."

"The world could use some good ones," Lara said.

"See!" Tom left the tray on the countertop and started to leave.

"Hey," Ruby called. "Don't forget about dessert."

"Yes, ma'am. You ladies enjoy."

Ruby huffed and addressed Annette. "I was about to compliment you on raising him right, but that 'ma'am' business makes me feel old."

"Just a southern title of respect, Ruby," Lara said.

"Hmmm. I don't hear it too often in that context anymore."

Annette said the blessing, then Ruby pushed back her chair and stood.

"Something wrong, Ruby?" Annette asked.

Ruby wiggled out of her sweater. "It's warm in here. My, look at this fuzz-ball thing. No, don't look."

Lara sat back smugly. "You should take my advice and buy something from Lancaster's."

Ruby tossed the sweater onto a chair in the corner. "And where would I wear it? While I'm cooking and cleaning and yelling and washing and scrubbing and mopping? At church, I'm covered up by a choir robe. Anyway, I'm not the type for fancy clothes, hair color, and manicured nails."

Lara slid her hands off the table and into her lap.

Ruby felt like scum, but why apologize for the truth? She

took her seat and reached for the breadbasket. "Before we get personal, I want to know how Marcella's working out."

"Quite well," Annette said. "She's eager to learn and very sweet."

"Good." Ruby cut a bite of chicken and balanced it on her fork. "The Masons have to give her up. He's being transferred out west." She poked the forkful into her mouth, chewed, then pointed the fork in front of her. "I think Eunice might be the perfect one. She could homeschool her during the summer, and maybe Marcella could keep up with her grade in school."

Lara set down her tea glass and looked from Annette to Ruby. "What's your connection with Marcella?"

"This is a case that just came up this week. Marcella's parents heard about our outreach to single pregnant girls, talked it over with Marcella, and she wanted to come here. She felt too embarrassed to stay in her hometown. Several couples from the church volunteer to let girls like her stay with them. Karen and Joe Mason volunteered to keep Marcella."

"That project is working well, isn't it?" Lara asked.

"Very," Ruby said. "We've sent flyers to a lot of churches about it. Parents and young girls like the idea of Christian couples helping in this way. Anyhow, two days ago, Annette hired Marcella." Ruby put a bite of food in her mouth, chewed, swallowed, and continued, lowering her voice as if the persons downstairs could hear. "Marcella is only fifteen. She's not showing yet. She needs some good instruction and advice."

Lara nodded. "Eunice would be perfect for that."

"She's a good worker," Annette observed.

"Good of you to give her a job," Lara said between bites.

"For both of us," Annette said. "This job doesn't pay a lot since we're open only a few hours a day. The waitresses depend heavily on tips, too, and that doesn't bring in a lot. When the school break is over, she will work in the afternoons and on Saturdays."

"If we can just get this girl through the pregnancy, help her make the best decisions under the circumstances, then I think she'll be okay. Her state of mind is. . ." Ruby waved her hand, searching for a word.

"Precarious?" Lara said.

"Good word. She fluctuates between giving the baby up for adoption or keeping it. Her parents are willing to help all they can, but she doesn't want her church and friends to know. They think she's staying with a cousin in Florida for the rest of the school year." She turned to Annette. "Does she talk about it to you?"

"No, but she's not used to me yet. And of course I don't push her. She seems like a carefree teenager. But when there's a lull, I see that faraway or frightened look in her eyes."

Ruby nodded. "That's why I need to get her somewhere with somebody like Eunice. It's going to be hard when she starts showing." She shook her head. "Gives you pause. She's even younger than my Jill."

After a moment's silence of their eating, Annette spoke up. "How's your week been, Lara?"

"Nothing new. Except my family invited me to dinner tomorrow. So I won't be at church. This is one of those obligatory things, you know." She turned to Ruby. "Should I ask how things are with you?"

Lara and Annette laughed.

"It's the same. Except Charlie is going through midlife crisis."

They stared.

"In other words, I think he's wandering."

"Charlie?" Lara said. "Your Charlie?"

Ruby huffed. "Would I care if it was Charlie the Chipmunk? It started with him calling me 'honey.' Let me tell you what happened

Wednesday night, then again this morning."

She told them. Not waiting for a response, she added, "I'm just not going to go there. We're here to talk about Annette's future wedded bliss. Now give us all the mushy details about last night." She glanced at Annette and took another bite of chicken.

Annette washed down her food, then said calmly, "It's over."

Lara stared while Ruby chewed quickly, swallowed, then finally spat out, "Over? I thought last night was to be the beginning of the rest of your life."

Annette shook her head, then told them about Shelby's reaction and objection.

"You're breaking it off with Curt because his grown married daughter doesn't like it?"

"Exactly," Annette said. "I told Curt we would not continue with the relationship unless his family approved. Honestly, neither of us thought there would be any opposition." She took a deep breath. "But there was. I will do nothing to cause friction in that family. I don't want to take that on."

Annette's mind was apparently made up. "I asked God to close the door if I shouldn't walk through it."

Lara pushed a piece of fruit around her plate. "Sounds to me like Shelby closed the door."

Annette shook her head with a wistfulness in her eyes. "I will do nothing to intrude upon that family."

Lara laid down her fork. "How is Curt taking this?"

"He was disappointed, embarrassed, hopeful. But he hasn't called or come around this morning, so it looks like he's taking it just fine. Anyway, I'm content with my life. It's Shelby who needs to come to terms with hers. I suppose I sort of expected something to go wrong." She shrugged. "Shelby needs more time to get over the loss of her mother."

Ruby quipped, "How much time?"

They glanced at each other; then each looked down at her plate.

Annette took a sip of coffee because she needed to push down words in her throat that she couldn't allow to come forth. She swallowed. "I got over the loss of Louis. But it's hard, losing someone you love." They would know she was referring to Louis—just Louis.

Lara spoke. "Then if Shelby comes around, you and Curt will go forward?"

"I don't know. Our relationship seemed right, but now I'm unsure. I don't like being the cause of friction between Shelby and Curt. We need to pray for them."

"Oh, mercy!" Ruby slapped her forehead. "After you hear what I did in the closet, you'll never mention me praying. On Wednesday night, I was feeling kind of drastic, so I decided to pray on Thursday morning."

"What?" Annette said. "If it was so drastic, why did you wait 'til Thursday?"

Lara gave her a sideways glance. "You had to ask?"

Ruby started. "I can't pray at night. I fall asleep. Well, on Thursday morning I was doing the usual, cleaning up after everybody and watching *GMA* to find out what's going on in the world, as if I care. . .I have world wars in my own home. Anyway, when I think I'm about ready to flush myself down the toilet, I go into the closet to pray."

Annette and Lara glanced at each other with that what's-coming-next look and waited.

"You'll never believe what I did."

"Wanna bet?" Lara said, and Annette laughed.

"I mean, this takes the cake, even for me. Well, the TV was on. The overwhelming feeling hit me that I had told myself to pray on Thursday morning. *GMA* had gone off, and a talk show came on. I don't watch those things, but I was sweeping away. I'm hearing the host saying he wants the guest to pick out her long-lost sister from three young women they've brought in."

Ruby and Lara leaned forward, their forearms on the table as if they might miss something.

"She's never seen her sister. I'm fuming, fussing at the TV, saying how stupid, then realize I have to hurry and pray so I can get ready for work and not be late. So, I decide it's time to get in the closet. So I went."

She paused to take another bite of bread and butter, glancing at Annette and Lara to make sure she had their attention. She did. She chewed, then swallowed. "Now, while I'm pouring my heart out to the Lord, I hear the host say, 'Okay, now which one do you think is your sister?' I shot out of that closet, ran to that TV, and stood there watching this girl try and pick out her sister."

Ruby enjoyed the fact that Annette and Lara were having conniption fits and trying to catch their breath. She went on with her story. "I wanted to know if she picked the right one."

Finally Lara asked, "Well, did she?"

"She did." Ruby leaned forward without cracking a smile. "It swept all over me. I asked God to guide me but didn't stay in the closet long enough for that. Now how can I blame God for not listening to me if I left God for a girl picking out her sister?"

Ruby loved to watch Annette and Lara laughing. They were too uptight too often. "Anyway," she said, "I returned to the closet. I cried and prayed for forgiveness. How could I do such a thing?" She took a deep breath. "You still want me to pray?"

Five minutes later, in a tremulous voice, with tears of emotion streaming down her face, and refusing to look at the poker expression of Ruby or the frozen-laughter one of Lara, Annette said,

"I think we'll postpone it." She lifted her napkin and wiped her eyes. "Now, back to the business at hand. Any ideas what we can do for Shelby?"

"Yep," Ruby said between bites of fruit from Lara's plate that she'd pushed aside. "Take her a pie."

Ruby knew about singing in unison, reading in unison, but never before in her entire life had she experienced an entire congregation holding its breath for an eternal moment in unison on Sunday morning.

None of them expected it.

She sat in the choir, shocked. Her mind immediately reverted to the night before. She had refused to let Charlie get in her bed until he told her where he went Saturday morning. He said it was a called meeting and the announcement would be made Sunday morning. He could not divulge that confidence.

She'd wondered if he was going to resign. Was his ardor, once she let him in bed, a final five-minute aerobic workout for eighteen years of marriage? Was he going to resign and run off with the hen-warbling soloist?

When she asked, he rolled off the bed, laughing.

Now what kind of answer was that? Yes or no?

He just repeated, taking the covers with him when he got back in and turned on his side, "Wait 'til Sunday. . .honey." He even seemed sad about it.

She jerked the covers, turning him on his back. He gave her one of his what-in-the-world looks, sat up, folded his arms across his chest, and said, "Fix them the way you want them."

She did. He exhaled, slid underneath them, rolled his eyes back into his head, and turned on his side—away from her. He mumbled, "Good night."

Sometimes he could be so obnoxious.

She didn't feel like sleeping. He did. That's what aerobics did for him. She was hungry, so she got up and went to the kitchen. She wasn't in the mood for any chicken, not with Maybelle on her mind.

Now, sitting in the choir on Sunday morning, she understood where Charlie had gone Saturday morning and why. She wondered how the choir would be able to sing the final song. How could the congregation do it?

Henry Hogan had delivered his sermon. Most of the time, he had something lighthearted to say, often told a joke even if it was an old one, and had a quick wit that he could intersperse with his sermons. Today's sermon had been more serious. But that was nothing unusual. He had his moods and trials, too, and everyone understood that. He'd been the pastor there over two decades.

After the sermon ended, he paused, and instead of saying, "Let us pray," he said, "I need to make an announcement."

Ruby's first notion was, since Charlie and Maybelle hadn't run out together after her solo and Charlie hadn't resigned, maybe Henry was going to resign. She'd heard him make the statement many times that one doesn't resign from the Lord's work. He was a spry man in his mid-seventies with a quick mind. The church people loved him. Maybe it wasn't anything too serious. Maybe he wanted to call a deacons' meeting or something. Maybe he wanted to build a new building. Maybe he wanted Charlie to resign and Maybelle to quit hogging the solos.

Ah! She liked that one.

"I want to ask for your prayers," Pastor Hogan said.

He's ill, Ruby thought.

Then he began to talk about what the church and the people meant to him. About God, who was a miracle worker. He told them about God as if he were preaching another sermon. They already knew what he was saying. Maybe there was an unbeliever in the congregation, and he wanted to make sure that person got the message.

Not likely. Unbelievers didn't usually go to church.

Pastor Hogan talked about faith and miracles and eternal life but didn't seem to want to get to the point. Finally, he did. "A lot of you know Eunice had that bout with cancer years ago. She's been in remission since then. Well. . ." He cleared his throat. "It's come back." His voice trembled. "She's been given. . .six months."

The collective gasp followed by silence left a hush throughout the church. Pastor Hogan held onto the podium. He swayed. He asked for prayer. The associate pastor came immediately to stand beside him. She'd seen Henry Hogan crumble only once before. But she mustn't think of that. Not now.

The associate pastor held onto Pastor Hogan's arm as he walked down and sat beside Eunice on the front row. She laid her hand on his and looked like she always looked—like a saint. Her gray hair surrounded her face, which wore skin sinfully smooth. Normally, women had wrinkles and lines. Men had character marks.

Henry had them on his round pleasant face surrounded by close-cropped white hair. It closely resembled a crew cut except for the balding spot at the crown of his head. He was a handsome, well-built man who didn't look to be in his mid-seventies.

Eunice was one of those women who happened to get the character marks. She had lovely skin that looked like she'd just splashed cold water on her face and blotted it with a towel. She had soft, light blue eyes.

But Ruby remembered a time when they hadn't been soft. They'd been—

No! Don't go there.

She felt Annette's gaze tugging like candy at a taffy-pull. She couldn't resist, and their gazes stuck. Lara and Annette usually sat together, a little more than halfway toward the back and on the left side of the pew. Lara always sat next to the edge and saved a seat for Annette, as if she didn't want anybody else sitting beside her. Lara wasn't here. She and Annette would have to tell her.

Somebody—was it Charlie?—was saying they had a sheet for people to sign up for prayer times. You could volunteer to pray at the same time every day and night. They wanted a twenty-four-hour prayer vigil. God worked miracles.

Ruby stood along with the other choir members. She pantomimed the words of the final hymn, but her mind was stuck on one thought. When someone in church needed help, she, Annette, and Lara would ask, "What can we do to help?"

Now the thought, sticking like Super Glue was, "What can we do? Help."

After Eunice and Henry returned home from church, deciding not to go out to eat, the phone calls came. Church members wanted to make a list so they could bring food. She told them she would let them know when food was needed.

She took leftovers from the refrigerator. She wasn't incapacitated. How could she be granted a miracle when all the praying church members were behaving as if she were on her deathbed? She didn't mean to be unappreciative but wondered how many times her own "meaning well" had gone too far.

Henry and I need time to plan, to accept this.

"Are you going to rest, Eunice?" Henry asked.

"Yes, you go on to the hospital, Henry."

"I can stay here, Eunie. Everybody will understand."

"You don't need to stay here and watch me sleep. Now, go on."

The question and her response marked a change in their routine. Generally, on Sunday afternoon, the two of them would visit friends and church members in the hospital. But now, neither she nor Henry had any idea how to handle this new development with her health anymore than anyone else.

Eunice peeked through the aluminum mini-blind as Henry backed his car out of the driveway.

She and Henry hadn't yet talked about her option of perhaps

prolonging her life with treatments. They didn't have to talk about the funeral. Henry knew she wanted that lovely trio, Jeanie, Jean, and Larry, who called themselves Promise, to sing "It Is Well with My Soul" at her funeral.

They were each other's beneficiaries. The will and insurance policy were in the safety-deposit box. The only thing left to discuss was her option of taking treatments that might prolong her life.

When his car was out of sight, she made sure the front door was locked. She turned the sound down on the phone. Yes, she would rest her body, but not until she did what had been on her mind for quite some time.

This was not something she chanced doing during the week when Henry could pop in from church at any time and catch her in the closet underneath the stairs in the basement. She went down and moved several boxes marked "Christmas" with bold, black Magic Marker. Behind those were things they'd saved but would never use. She pulled out the box containing items she thought she might want to look at again. She hadn't since the day she packed them away. Henry might want to look at them someday.

She listened. No, that was just a car passing by out there somewhere. Returning to the box, she opened it, rummaged to the bottom of it, and pulled out a shoebox. Dread filled her mind as she tore away the tape and lifted the lid.

Reality and memory became one. She caressed the green item. With a sob, she held it to her heart. Her eyes overflowed with tears that wet her cheeks.

Since husbands usually died before their wives, she had thought she'd decide someday what to do with these items. But she could not leave the contents of this shoebox for Henry to deal with. She would wrap the black and green items in bags, put them inside another bag, and make sure they went out with trash.

She held another item, the official form, in her hands. What would she do with it? Henry had never seen it. Should he?

After replacing the boxes and discarding the shoebox, she went to her bedroom and picked up her Bible. Henry never touched it. He had plenty of his own. Yes, that is where she would put the coroner's report.

When she returned from the disastrous-as-usual family gathering, Lara saw the flashing light on her phone and checked her messages.

Annette's voice said, "Lara, call me when you get home. No matter how late it is."

Lara dialed her number. "What's up?"

Annette said she wanted to be the one to tell her. "Eunice Hogan has terminal cancer."

Lara found a chair and slumped into it. She already felt drained from having driven to Charlotte, endured her family's pretension of acceptance, and heard repeated comments about her need to get a real life before she got too old. She'd pretended none of their comments mattered, then had the return trip of a two-hour drive.

Annette would know how she felt after a visit with her relatives, and. . .now this. "I didn't want you to hear it from anyone else."

Lara managed to say, "Thanks."

"We'll get together soon. Will you be okay?"

"Yeah," Lara said. "I'm going straight to bed."

As soon as she hung up, Lara went to the medicine cabinet and took out the pills the doctor had prescribed for nights when she couldn't sleep.

Fortunately, by the time she changed into nightclothes, the fast-acting sleeping pill began doing its job admirably.

She refused to think. Her prayer was a repetition of, "Oh Lord, oh Lord, oh Lord," until blessed oblivion took over.

Reality returned when she went to work.

"The new spring-summer line is in," Sally, the manager, said. "Jen is out with the flu. See what you can do, Lara."

"I'd make a mess, Sally." Lara felt the reflux begin to crawl.

"Just put something on the models." Sally acted as if it were no big deal. "You couldn't do all that badly. Jen can change it if she wants when she comes back. But we need to get those clothes in the window."

Lara knew that. The new line had already been advertised. The window had to be dressed. She went to the back room where the new clothes hung on the racks. She moistened her lips and swallowed hard while picking out a few choice pieces and sliding them aside on a rack. That was the easy part. She could do it. After a deep breath, she went to the water fountain outside the rest room door and drank from it.

With an armload of clothes, she headed for one of the display windows.

Fingers trembling, she fumbled with buttons and scarves on winter clothes. She wouldn't look. She tried not to think.

She was a grown woman. She could undress and dress a manikin.

She removed the jacket. Just slipped it down the arms and laid it aside. She could do it. She unbuttoned the skirt and let it fall to the stand that held the manikin in place. Oh Lord, it wasn't wearing a slip. She knew that. She wouldn't look. Next came the blouse. She pulled the fabric away from the body to unbutton the blouse. She mustn't touch the body.

"Lara," Sally said, walking up to her. "You'll need to lay the manikin down or unscrew it from the base to dress it properly."

The intrusion into her concentration so startled her that

Lara's fingers touched the white cold plastic figure. She would have screamed had there been enough air. She couldn't. There was no breath. No air. The body. . .was moving, coming toward her. So was the figure behind the. . .manikin? Body?

She heard, "Lara, Lara. What's wrong?"

She flailed out at the cold white thing. She wouldn't look at its head. Its mouth. She dropped to her knees and covered her head with her arms.

"What's wrong, Lara?"

Somehow she managed to peek through her fingers and see shoes, pants, jacket, blouse, and Sally's face. "What's the matter?"

"Sick," she managed to say. Sally helped her to her feet. Lara hurried through the shop, her hands over her mouth, and didn't quite make it to her intended target in the rest room. After retching more, she cleaned the mess from the floor.

Not caring about her carefully applied makeup, she splashed cold water on her face and blotted it with a paper towel. Feeling reasonably capable of speaking, she went to Sally. "I think I must be getting Jen's flu."

Sally nodded sympathetically. "That's what I figured. Oh, you look awful."

"I feel it."

"You should go home," Judy said, while Holly stood beside her nodding. "I'll call Laura or Melissa or Lori and have one of them come in. We can handle things here."

Lara didn't have to be told twice. She left by the back door, although the front was closer to where her car was parked at the side of the building. For years, she'd managed not to look directly at those figures in the window.

Today she'd touched one.

Just as she reached her car, she felt a presence. Her head turned just enough for her to peek over her shoulder. One of them had followed her. The manikin was alive. She'd known that all along. That's why she hadn't looked. Now that she had looked, it was coming for her.

She tried to scream but choked on it.

"Let me help you," the thing said. It spoke. Its face came near. Its lips spread, and she knew it would laugh.

She tried to push it away. It came closer.

Her arms were flailing. She hit something soft. Her eyes peered into darkness.

Gasping, she fumbled for the light and knocked the clock off the nightstand. The alarm began its shrill ring. She found the lamp switch and turned it.

They were gone.

But it came up. The reflux was in her throat.

With her head in her hands, she moaned and cried and tried to calm her speeding heartbeat.

Finally she moved to the side of the bed, slipped her feet into slippers, and padded into the bathroom. She opened the medicine cabinet door and saw the sleeping pills. Even that wasn't keeping the nightmares away anymore.

She picked up another bottle, screwed off the top, and shook a little purple pill into the palm of her trembling hand. She lifted it into her mouth and washed it down with a mouthful of water from a paper cup.

Her eyes could not meet the ones in the mirror. She could only think what a sorry excuse for a woman she was.

I've lived with this for almost twenty years. Why can't I accept it?

The thought sent her trembling again, and she feared she'd lose control of her senses.

Lara always felt better when daylight came. She stayed in bed, dozed, rested, then rose and forced herself to eat a piece of dry toast and drink a cup of coffee. Even if she looked like death warmed over, she would go to work after lunchtime. That was better than staying home with nothing to do but think.

She allowed herself a brief review of her life, as if that might lead somewhere productive.

Her parents had approved her hasty decision to marry after only one year of college. Like kings of old, that meant their kingdoms would merge—the kingdoms of high finance. She would finish her studies in Paris.

Soon it became obvious her intentions were simply what she'd been led to believe was expected of her and what she'd parroted as her ambitions. She'd changed from her carefree years. She didn't fit in with her and her husband's crowd anymore. She tried forgiveness, prayer, and church attendance, but that didn't erase the past, and it didn't sit well with her husband and friends. She gave up church but didn't drink socially. She guzzled it down as if it would take away the sorrows she had failed to drown in any other way.

It didn't.

The showdown came when she totaled the new car and embarrassed her husband by being hauled off to jail on DUI charges.

After the divorce, she stayed in Paris for a while, living on alimony and trying to concentrate enough to graduate.

She heard often from her grandmother but rarely from her parents, except a postcard now and then about where they were traveling. Finally, she got a call from her mom, saying her grandfather had suffered a heart attack and it didn't look good.

Lara flew home.

After the funeral, Lara learned that her grandmother could no longer drive because of failing eyesight. The condition caused her to appear feebler than she would have been otherwise, having to be careful not to walk into things or stumble.

"We'll take care of her," Lara's mom said. "That's what families are for. Oh, Lara, I hope you can stay and help."

Lara was overjoyed. She'd returned a failure, a divorcée, a boozer, and other descriptions she cared to ignore whenever possible. Maybe these trials were bringing her family together, finally. She needed their love and approval.

However, as soon as her parents sold Grammy's Laurel Ridge mountainside home and got her settled in their house in Biltmore, it became imperative they travel abroad on business. First, they would spend a few days with business associates in the beach house at the Outer Banks.

"It's too dangerous leaving her alone, and you never know what kind of help you're getting," Lara's mom said. "Maybe we should put her in a health-care center."

Lara wouldn't hear of it. "I'll stay with her."

Lara's mom and dad praised Lara for her dedication to her grandmother and approved of the situation of Lara taking care of her grammy.

Two days later, Lara got the phone call. Her parents and the other couple were killed in a boating accident.

She would not make a trip to the Outer Banks. Her brothers, Stewart living in New York and Percival in London, took care of the arrangements. They decided on a private service with only a few of their friends invited. Lara drank herself into a stupor that worked so well she didn't care if others knew or thought her behavior was from grief or alcohol.

Wouldn't they be surprised to discover it was both—but not just because of her parents' death. Something else had once happened at the Outer Banks. She hoped she wouldn't tell them.

After the obituary appeared in the newspaper, Lara received many cards, mostly from Pastor Hogan's church. She did not get a card from the Hogans, however.

She was glad.

She knew Eunice would be the one to send personal cards.

She did get a card from Annette. "I'm sorry, Lara. Come and see me if you like."

She hadn't liked. Not until a year later, after Annette's husband was killed.

In the meantime, Lara had a rude awakening about her parents' financial situation. They weren't as solvent as they had led the family to believe.

Lara wondered if they had brought Grammy into their house so they could sell hers and increase their financial status. Any condemnation was short-lived. People did things for many reasons. Her own reason for taking care of Grammy was her love for her. But Lara needed those hugs from her grammy and to hear that someone loved her.

The house would be divided between Lara and her brothers. Percival wanted to buy it; Stewart was willing; but Lara refused to sell as long as Grammy needed a place to stay. Lara didn't want to put her in a nursing home. Although Biltmore was almost a thirty-minute drive from Laurel Ridge, Lara drove her grammy to Pastor Hogan's church on her good days.

Eventually Lara had to make arrangements for Grammy to be put in the health-care facility. She lost the last person who had really loved her. Maybe the first, too.

Stewart wanted money. Percival wanted the house. Lara sold her third of the house to Percival with the understanding that he and Stewart would make sure Grammy's bills were paid.

Lara put a down payment on the townhouse. She took a temporary job at Lancaster's while deciding what she wanted. Her brothers disapproved of the job. She should go abroad. She could open up an art gallery. Paint.

But Lara would not consider leaving Laurel Ridge as long as

Grammy was alive. Even when Grammy couldn't see her, she could hug her and say she loved her. No one else in the entire world had a hug for Lara. Yet the touch from the wrong person sent shivers up her spine. She needed someone to love. She had no one.

After Annette's husband was killed and the rumor was that Annette was fixing up the old Victorian house, Lara went to see her. It was one of the hardest things she'd ever done. She so wanted to do the right thing. Annette apparently had found a way to do that. She'd seen her at church but had not approached her. What was Annette's secret?

What a thought!

She knew Annette's secret.

What kept Annette on an even keel, in spite of the secret?

Neither mentioned it when Lara stopped by. Annette hugged her.

A hug.

Before long, Lara, with her flair for the artistic, was valuable in helping Annette decide on decor and furnishings for the house.

She stayed on at Lancaster's and alternated with other clerks in being top seller of the month. Many of her customers were people with whom she'd gone to school but with whom she would not have associated. Now she waited on them. A part of her thought about what might have been.

She knew what might have been. She might have ended up like her mother, who had occasionally attended the Biltmore Church, volunteered her home for special meetings and dinners, and given large donations to the church and to the needy at Christmas.

Instead, she chose to serve, which went against how she was raised. Oh, her mom or dad would never have told her she was better than anyone else, just "more privileged." And they had even quoted the Scripture, "To whom much is given, much is required."

She wanted the kind of peace Annette seemed to have. Like she'd done when Lara had been a college student and attended the Hogans' church, Annette asked Lara to come to the church.

Such a pleading look was in Annette's eyes that Lara realized Annette needed Lara, too—the only person who knew how she felt.

But Lara didn't want to go to the church where Eunice Hogan would look at her. She visited her grammy on Sundays. Then her grammy died.

Annette came to the funeral service and hugged her while they both cried. Lara began to wonder if she would live for the warmth of an occasional friendly touch or go to the bottle. Not the booze this time but the sleeping pills.

Then one day while Annette and Lara were upstairs having a cup of coffee, who but Ruby rushed in. "Ah ha!" Ruby put her hands on her hips like she'd done years ago when she was a cheerleader about to yell. "I heard you were turning this place into a restaurant. But I didn't expect counterfeiters."

Lara looked at Annette. Neither knew what to say. They hadn't seen Ruby in years, but here she was acting like she had before. . .

"Counterfeiters?" Annette said.

"Yeah." Ruby pointed toward the doorway. "Downstairs. That's what you call workers who put together kitchen cabinets. Counter-fitters. Get it?"

They laughed.

Laugh?

Oh, how long since she'd done that. She'd given polite, forced ones. This had the feel of being real. Corny, but real.

Ruby plopped down. "Can I have some of what you guys are having?"

Annette got up to pour her a cup.

The three of them together again. Could they make a go of it together?

She could try. Lara would even try church. Ruby had to go. Her husband was the new choir director. Was this reunion a blessing. . .or a bane?

She would try church again. She knew the Lord Jesus forgave sins. She'd asked. She was supposed to have received forgiveness. She could do no more than ask, plead, beg, cry, moan, groan, get on her knees, fall prostrate, bury herself beneath the covers of her bed, smother herself in a pillow, gag herself on reflux.

Then she would serve others—give money, help the needy, even pray.

What else could she do?

She knew.

She'd do what millions had to do. . .suffer the consequences.

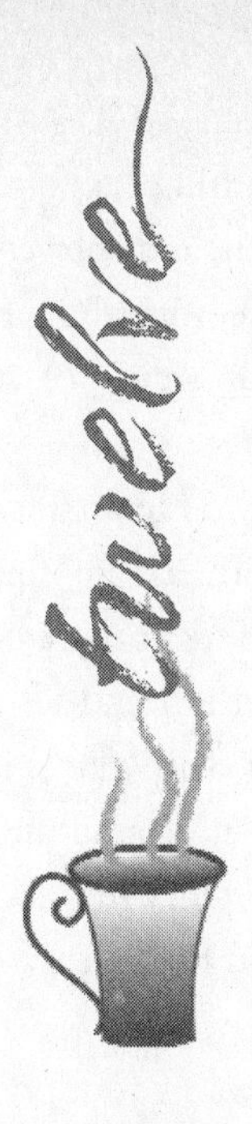

Henry came home from church for lunch. "I might as well have stayed home." He looked tired. "The meetings turned out to be about me and you. I guess that's the way it's going to be."

Eunice sighed. "They mean well."

"Yes. We show we care in whatever way we can." He bowed his head, and so did Eunice. His prayer over the food was brief. He didn't pray for health or that the food would nourish their bodies and their bodies would be used for God's glory. Somehow those words didn't seem to fit now. How easily they can be said. The Bible said to be thankful in all things. Did that include dying?

How many times she'd heard people say, "Oh, I want the Lord to come. I'm looking forward to the return of Jesus." Yet some of these same individuals now said they were sorry she was going to Him.

There was something about dying that began to put life into a different perspective.

"Do you want to talk about it, Eunice?"

"No. But we must, Henry. It's a fact. I need you to help me do this."

She felt like she could die on the spot when his chin began to tremble. His hands, holding his sandwich, shook, and he tried to poke his tomato back into the bread.

"But not now, Henry. I suppose you have gotten phone calls

all morning like I have. Let's talk about something else."

Henry nodded, took a bite of his sandwich, and chewed. She knew he was trying to think of something else, something good.

He swallowed and washed it down with a gulp of coffee. "Curt Crowder came by."

Curt? Yes, he would be a good one to talk to Henry. He'd lost his wife after her four-year-long battle with a rare form of dementia. Grief had taken its toll on Curt. He'd finally emerged from it and reached out. She knew he'd been a friend to others who lost their mates. He could help Henry with the grieving process, when it came to that. Would they sit around and talk about her? Sing her praises? She didn't want Henry to grieve, cry for her, be lonely, grow old alone. What would he do?

"How is Curt?"

"He said I could share this with you. He wants your prayers."

Eunice nodded. "Curt and his family have been on my prayer list for months, Henry. You know that."

Henry nodded. "There's another situation. You know he and Annette have been friends for a while. Well, it's become more serious."

Eunice wasn't as surprised about that as she was that Annette had remained single for so long. She could honestly say, "I think they make a good couple."

Henry's brow furrowed. "Annette called it off."

Eunice opened her mouth in surprise, but the surprise began to diminish when Henry talked about Shelby objecting to her dad's getting married again.

Henry shook his head. "Normally I wouldn't tell these things. But Curt thought you might talk to Shelby. She's always looked up to you."

Henry sighed and looked at the table. His voice was low when he spoke again. "Even though Curt is having his own problems, he wanted to let me know he's here for me if I need to talk, now or later."

"That's good, Henry. You need to talk to someone. I know you're not going to tell me all you're feeling."

"I might, Eunice. When I can feel again. What about you? Will it help for you to discuss what's going on with you?" He looked across at her. "With us," he added.

Yes, dear Henry would be going through whatever she went through. He was her better half. She reached for his hand and squeezed it.

"I don't know how I'm supposed to think about this, Henry. My death sentence is kind of like being in a plane that is going to crash. You know the plane could crash before you get on it, but you don't really believe it or you wouldn't have gotten on it. I don't feel it. Maybe it's the shock of it. I'm not afraid of dying, but the process of getting there. . ."

She tried to think of how to describe what wasn't really firm in her mind. "It's sort of like that last time we flew to the convention in Atlanta. Remember? We had turbulence. It was sudden. I was holding a cup of hot coffee. My concern was not about the plane crashing but about my spilling the coffee."

After Henry left to go back to church, Eunice turned off the sound on the phone. She leaned back against the pillows propped at the head of the bed and covered herself with an afghan. She thought over the conversation with Henry. She prayed for Shelby and Curt, that both would learn to accept what they must accept.

Attempting to be perfectly honest, she didn't pray for Annette. She remembered the times she had resented that woman when she married Louis. Others talked of it being a perfect marriage of two fine young people. They admired Annette's faithfulness to the church when Louis was called up to fight for his country. She lived in the Victorian bed-and-breakfast run by her parents and helped them with the running of the house.

Less than two years later, Annette gave birth to a precious baby boy who looked like his dad. Seeing the three of them together, the young man in uniform, the lovely Annette with her long auburn hair and sparkling blue-gray eyes, holding a little baby, wrenched Eunice's heart. She knew what she was supposed to feel, what she was supposed to say, how she was supposed to act.

She performed, not wanting the resentment, the hurt, the anger, the ugliness that stirred deep within her bosom. She prayed to the Lord. She couldn't tell Henry. He had enough to deal with. That was only a fraction of what she felt.

Another side of her, just as real, rejoiced in Annette's happiness. She wanted her to have a good and happy life. That was true. With time, all the bitterness would leave. If she prayed enough. Love is action, not feeling. She knew that. She would act with love.

She'd called herself all sorts of evil names. It had taken time, maturity, and listening to others relate similar feelings. Several women said they went through a period of hating their spouse for dying and leaving them alone. Oh, she didn't want Henry to feel a moment of that.

At the same time, she understood. The resentment and bitterness that swept through her, unwanted, was like a blister burned on the finger. The rest of the body could be healthy, well, feeling good, but the focus would be on the pain of the blister. She just had to apply the right medication, endure the pain, and wait for the healing.

Healing had come, but the memory of the pain surfaced at times. When Louis Billings died, he became a local hero. Annette became a martyr. Her parents moved to Florida, where the aging parents of Annette's mom needed their help. They left the crumbling Victorian house with Annette. She became a respectable businesswoman who used insurance money to turn the house into something productive. She was a single mother doing a wonderful job raising her son. She was a fine Christian woman.

Now, after all these years, a good man had fallen in love with her. But it wasn't working out.

How do I feel?

Eunice waited. Her file of bitterness did not appear. A question crossed her mind. Why should Curt and Annette find happiness together when she was losing her life and Henry was losing his wife? But that was one of those fleeting thoughts that were not her own. She'd come to recognize how evil thoughts slipped in to see what she would do with them.

She wanted people, even Annette, to find happiness in life. Most women would not take Shelby's immature reaction to heart but would do what she wanted to do, what she felt was right. No one would blame Annette or Curt. But Annette had the reputation of doing things. . .perfectly.

What had Annette felt during the past nineteen years? People were like a bunch of computer files. Even if they didn't open them all, the files were still there. They could erase the files, but the data remained on the computer's hard drive.

Did Annette's hard drive have the words Eunice had spoken back then? "I want the truth."

Eunice never asked again.

They never offered the answer.

thirteen

Curt felt the weight of the world on his shoulders. Talking to Henry—reliving Sybil's dying, Annette's rejecting him, and Shelby's problems—the extent of all he faced crashed in on him. Besides that, he was unable to leave the florist because of demands for flowers needed for a funeral the next day.

He remembered words he'd said through the years and after Sybil's death. Family comes first. He was the dad, the supposedly mature one. The one to make and keep peace in the family.

He didn't want to talk to Shelby, and at the same time he did. He understood the devastation she'd felt at the loss of her mom. He'd felt it. But a man had to act like a man. He had to bear up under it, and he hadn't let the family see him cry. He held back his grief until he was alone at night. He hadn't wanted his daughters taking care of things Sybil had done. At the same time, he had appreciated it. He'd let Shelby keep on taking care of him for too long.

He didn't know how to get through to her without hurting her feelings. He'd said some hurtful things to her. The entire family had.

He knew Shelby didn't understand. She was still grieving for her mom. So was he, in a sense. But he had grieved from the time the diagnosis had been made. He couldn't imagine what life would be like without Sybil. She was still his wife while he watched her illness worsen and the woman he loved regress from being a competent adult to slowly becoming totally incapacitated. All the family members had been helpful and supportive in physical ways. He'd dealt with the emotional and inevitable side of it in a different way than they. The hardest thing he'd ever done was to put her in a health-care facility when he could no longer get food into her mouth.

He'd become emotionally and physically drained. He'd hurt, he'd cried, he'd made final plans, he'd prayed, he'd grieved, over a period of four years. No one could understand unless they had lived with the situation. Although Annette could not fully understand, his friendship with someone who understood loss and grieving had been a tremendous help to him.

Shelby had her own emotions to deal with—what she'd lost, what she could never have. She and Sybil had lots of arguments before the illness was diagnosed.

Sybil had said, "Finish college before you marry."

Shelby hadn't.

Sybil had encouraged Shelby to continue in school after she married. Shelby had quit to take a job at an insurance company so she and Brian could save to buy a house.

While those should have been conversations in which two people had disagreed, it had become a matter of contention with Shelby. After Sybil died and Curt gave each of his children a sizeable amount of money, Shelby had seemed to want to make up for those arguments. She quit her job and returned to college. That's when she began to take over the household chores Sybil had always done.

In hindsight, he could see that Shelby's way of dealing with the loss of her mother was for her to become like her mother before the illness had destroyed her brain. She wanted to be a mom. . .like her mother. In doing so, if she wasn't careful, she'd lose her husband and the respect of her family.

He reasoned that she was young and couldn't think like he did. To her, he was an old man, almost fifty. To a twenty-five-year-old, that wasn't just over the hill, but halfway down the other side.

Curt didn't want to lose his daughter, didn't want this friction in the family. They had all gotten closer since Sybil's death. That's what family was for. He remembered Sybil saying the children had moved away from them mentally during their teen years. They'd begun to come back emotionally after getting married. The complete return had occurred after Sybil's death. Now it seemed their family life was crumbling.

He couldn't let that happen. Annette didn't need him as much as Shelby did. But he didn't know how to help her. How often he'd heard that communication is the key. He would try.

Curt left the florist around seven o'clock. He had no supper and missed going home and seeing Shelby in the kitchen with supper ready or having her call and say she would bring over a casserole or suggest he could go to her apartment and eat with her and Brian.

She opened the door without her usual enthusiasm at seeing him. She looked sad and tired.

"Brian home?"

Shelby shook her head. "He comes in for supper. We have a fight, and he discovers he has something to do. He has to grade papers. Or he has to do something with Outward Reach. Or he has to talk to Jim about plans for the youth group. He has to get something fixed on the car, usually air in the tires." She swiped at a piece of hair that was loose from her ponytail. "He finds some excuse to leave. Anyway, he's not here."

"What are you doing, Shelby?" He stepped farther in although she hadn't invited him. But he was the dad. He didn't have to be invited. He closed the door behind him and walked into the living room.

"What am I doing?" She didn't sit but stepped into the middle of the room. "I'm trying to work on a paper that's due after the break so I can get my education and get a real job. Seems I don't have even a part-time one now that you don't want me at the florist."

"That's not true, Shelby. I could use your help. The Sayers funeral is tomorrow. It's a big one."

She turned her head like she didn't know whether to laugh or cry or what. What could he say to help her? "Shelby. I love you." She made no move toward him, so he sat on the couch.

She turned and sat in the chair opposite him. She didn't respond verbally, but he knew how that was. It was hard making up after fighting with someone. But he had to try and make her understand his heart. She wasn't arguing, so maybe he could reassure her that he loved her. He knew she felt alone.

Shelby stared at her hands on her lap but seemed to listen. He tried to keep his voice kind and loving. "Shelby, I loved Sybil completely before we married. But I loved her more as the years went by. Love is something that grows."

He felt she was listening. "When Francine was born, I loved her with all the love I had. But it didn't divide into three pieces when you and Mike were born. It multiplied. The more we love, the more love we have to give. There's always room in the heart for another love."

Since she wasn't shouting at him, he felt confident enough to continue. "Don't you think if Brian died, you would love again?"

Her eyes met his. They flashed. "No," Shelby said. "I could never love another man. It's betrayal to turn to another whether your spouse is alive or dead."

Curt took a deep breath, reminding himself to remain calm.

"Didn't you have boyfriends, Shelby? Seems I remember them from even your kindergarten days."

Shelby moved to the edge of her chair. "Oh, Daddy, that was childish. Not married love. Aren't we taught that there's one mate meant for another? That marriages are made in heaven?"

"Yes, I've heard that. And I think if we lived in California, you would have found the perfect mate for yourself, and it wouldn't be Brian."

She folded her arms in a defensive gesture. "That doesn't make sense."

He leaned forward. "Sure it does. You think all the young men killed in war had a girl that God meant for them, but those girls are all to remain unmarried?" He answered the question himself. "No. Marriage is made in heaven means to me that God ordains it, blesses it, puts His stamp of approval on marriage as directed in the Bible. When you marry, you're to love that spouse, be loyal, serve God together, have children, raise them in the admonition of the Lord."

"You've done that, Daddy."

He sighed, his hands now on his knees. "Are you saying I did mine, so now I shouldn't have any of that again?"

"You have your children, your grandchildren, your home, your friends, your job." She spread her hands. "Good grief, Daddy. You have more than most, and you have wonderful memories of a good marriage."

He shook his head. He couldn't get through to Shelby. He hadn't wanted another argument. "Well, no need to discuss it. You made the decision for Annette."

Shelby sported a satisfied grin. "No, Daddy. Annette made that decision. You see, she knows it's wrong."

Curt looked at the floor and shook his head. Why argue with an immature, spoiled girl who thought she had all the answers?

"I'm sorry we can't agree." He rose from the couch.

"Before you leave, Dad. . ." Shelby stood. Her expression was stoic, matching her voice. "I have something for you." She walked out of the room.

He hoped it might be supper.

She returned with a foil-wrapped dish. "You can have this. I don't want it."

The dish felt cold to his hands. He was about to say thank you when her voice sounded colder than the dish. "Annette brought me this pie. She apologized for any trouble she might have caused. She promised not to go further with the relationship." Shelby sneered. "How's that for not interfering with our family? Try and look good and make me look bad. Oh, Dad. Can't you see what she's doing?"

"I certainly can." He took in a deep breath, then exhaled as he looked down at the crumpled foil. That's how his heart felt for the moment. He marveled that his daughter had taken the pie. Considering her frame of mind, she might have thrown it back in Annette's face. That's what her words were doing.

He set the dish on a side table. Walking to the door, he didn't hear as much as a "good-bye" from his daughter. His throat was too closed to say anything.

The phone call came the following morning around ten o'clock. Shelby had just finished with household chores, put a load of clothes in the washer, poured a cup of coffee, and resolved to get her essay finished. Normally she would ask Brian to critique it, but now she determined to handle it herself.

She reached for the phone. "Hello."

"Shelby?"

She recognized the voice. She'd heard it enough over the years. She knew what this was about. "Yes?"

"Your, um, test results have come back. You and Brian might want to come in and talk with me."

The "um" was the first clue. Come in and talk? About what? She and Brian had spent the last three years talking, being tested, being told that Brian's sperm count was fine, to try fertility drugs. Count days. Be intimate by clockwork. And relax! Then the final tests were done. Now. . .talk?

"Dr. Karber. Can't you tell me over the phone?"

"You may want Brian with you."

Why? He hates me. Must we tell him there's something else wrong with me? "I can't get pregnant, can I?"

"Shelby, I'm sorry. I'm sending a report of the findings. Then if you and Brian want to come in, we'll talk about it."

"Would talking change anything?"

She heard his breath. "No, Shelby. This is pretty much conclusive."

"Thanks," she said automatically. "Bye."

She walked over to the table, picked up the paper she'd worked on for weeks, tore it in half, then quarters, and shoved it into the trash can. Her gaze moved to the refrigerator. With a wry smile on her lips, she opened the door, took out the pie that had one missing piece—the piece Brian had eaten—and tossed it into the trash can.

Her feet led her to the second bedroom, the one that would have been a nursery. It would never be a nursery. She yanked the covers from the bed, threw the pillows on the floor, moved to the curtains, and grasped them in her hands. Her fists clenched. They locked. Her knees gave way; her hands slipped from the curtains as her body crumpled onto the floor.

No tears came into her eyes. Her sobs were dry. The great heaves from her stomach into her throat sounded hoarse, like some beast in agony from being trapped in a vise. She needed her mom, her dad, her husband.

After a long time, Shelby rose from the floor. She must go through the motions. She had to call Brian. Where was he? On this spring break they should have gone on a trip or planned the nursery or spent quality time at home together. But he was either at the florist helping her dad or at church helping the youth minister with the young people's part in the Easter pageant.

She called the church first. After a few minutes, he came on the line. "Brian, come home."

"What?"

"Just come."

Within five minutes, she heard him running through the house. He rushed into the kitchen. "What's wrong?"

She stood holding onto a kitchen chair. "Dr. Karber called."

He paled, looking like he might throw up. He nodded. "The news isn't good."

She shook her head. The tears came then, with the heaving sobs.

In an instant, he was holding her, crying with her. For a while they were one, feeling the pain, sharing the grief, needing each other.

The good moment passed, and he stepped back, wiping his wet face with the back of his hand. "We suspected it, Shelby. We've talked about the possibility."

She nodded. "But I didn't believe it."

"We had hope."

"Not anymore." *And it's my fault. I'm not a real woman.*

He pulled out a chair and gently led her into it, then pulled another one up and sat near her, their knees almost touching. He took her hands in his. "Shelby, now that we know for sure, we can adopt."

She jerked her hands out of his. How could he say such a thing? "I don't want a child that's not my own."

He looked like she'd hit him. "I want a son or daughter. You're sounding like a self-centered girl with room in your heart for no one but a blood relative. I guess I know where I am on your list of concerns. I'm not related to you." He stood and glared at her. "You try to run your dad's life, your siblings' lives. What about mine? You married me. What about what I want? Does that not count?"

Shelby jumped to her feet. "What you want is me to bend to everything you think is right. You want me to raise a child I can't love? You want me to pretend to be something I'm not?"

"No. I want you to have love in your heart for a child."

"That's not my own?"

"I would prefer that. But you can't have one of your own."

She grasped the chair, lest she fall.

His voice softened. "I'm not trying to hurt you, Shelby. I'm trying to make you see the light. You have this. . .obsession. . .this stupid idea that blood makes that much difference."

Her lips trembled. Her voice rose to a high shrill. "It does. That's what makes families. That's what makes parents and children. It's our own blood, our own DNA, our own genes."

"But you can't have blood children." He gestured with his hands, making a helpless gesture. "You want a test tube baby? A surrogate mother? What do you want?" He gasped for air and moved his hands as if leading an orchestra. "Okay. That's it. We're a childless couple. Let's get on with our marriage. How's that?"

"It's sarcastic."

"Then what? What do you want?"

"I want my own baby."

She watched his face crumble. "Does it occur to you, Shelby, that I, too, have just been told I can't have children of my own?"

Just as that fact began to register and she was about to reach out to him, he said coldly, "Except the one I'm living with."

The assault hit her like a bucket of cold water. Her wayward tongue spat out, “That can be remedied.”

“You’re danged right, it can!” He turned and strode out the door.

Had he said “danged” or something worse? But what did it matter? It was the tone he used that cut her to the depths of her heart. He was always careful about his speech. He had school and church kids to consider. But not her. . .

Shelby slid to the floor, wondering if that’s where she would spend the rest of her life. She felt like someone had kicked her into a gully. Now she was being trampled. She had lost her mother, could never have a child, and now was losing her family and her husband.

Fourteen

On Monday, Henry called and said he wouldn't be home for lunch. He was going out with Curt. As soon as he came home for supper, Eunice was eager to get a report. Had he wanted to talk about Curt's problems, or was Henry having a need to talk about her?

When Henry came home, he explained his reason for going out with Curt. "Brian's a big help to Jim, but he looked like he was coming down with something. I asked him, but Brian said he didn't want to bother me with his problems and off he went."

Eunice nodded. People were being kind and thoughtful. Then Henry said what she was thinking. "I need to let the members know I'm still the pastor. I am still the same person who wants to know what's going on with my members and help in any way I can."

"Are Brian and Shelby still at odds because of Curt and Annette?"

Henry sighed. "Curt is more concerned about Shelby than Annette. He's a little hurt that Annette is taking this so well. On one hand, he doesn't want to act like a whining boy, and on the other hand, he wants to get on his knees and beg her. But that's only the beginning of his problems. None of the family members can get through to Shelby. She's been sick all weekend, didn't go to church."

Henry took a bite and chewed for a long time before swallowing and glancing up at Eunice. "Shelby was tested to see if she could bear a child." He picked up his coffee cup and brought it to his lips.

"And?"

He swallowed, cleared his throat, set the cup down. "She can't." He shook his white head. "Curt's really worried about her."

Eunice closed her eyes against the onslaught of those words, empathizing with the trials going on in young Shelby's life. Suddenly, her eyes opened wide. "Henry!"

He startled. "What?"

Eunice laughed. "Oh, I'm okay. I just thought of something. The answer for Shelby and Brian is working at Annette's Kitchen."

His brown gaze questioned.

Eunice smiled. "You know Ruby talked to us about maybe keeping Marcella and helping her make decisions since the Masons are leaving. Now, of course, considering my physical condition, Ruby will have to make different arrangements for the girl."

She hated the look on his face when she indicated things like that. Somehow they both were going to have to accept it. "Don't you see, Henry? The perfect solution is for Shelby to adopt Marcella's baby."

She sat back, feeling smug. "God was working things out for Shelby and Brian before they even knew the problem." A bubble of happy laughter escaped her throat. "It's like God has dropped the solution in Shelby's lap."

"Let's have lunch, Shelby," Eunice said when Shelby picked up the ringing telephone.

Shelby breathed a sigh of relief. She'd hugged Eunice at church the day Pastor Hogan announced she was terminally ill.

She'd said she was sorry. But she had been so involved with her own problems, she hadn't given much thought to what was going on with Eunice, who had for years insisted that any adult should call her by her first name.

"I'd like that." Shelby would refuse if Eunice suggested Annette's Kitchen. "Where?"

"What about the Veranda?"

They decided to meet at one o'clock after most of the lunch crowd would have cleared out.

Shelby parked on Cherry Street, a block down from the restaurant. She arrived five minutes early. Eunice already sat at a side table next to the brick wall. She didn't look ill but as beautiful as ever. If anyone had ever grown old gracefully, it was Eunice.

Shelby wore flats with her stretch denims and turtleneck. She hadn't felt a need for a sweater today but noticed that Eunice wore a jacket over her blouse.

"Hi. How are you?" Shelby put her arm around Eunice's shoulders. Eunice touched her cheek to Shelby's.

"I'm all right, Shelby. How are you doing? We haven't talked in a while."

Eunice had taught Shelby in Sunday school before she married. After a few years, Eunice had given the class to a younger teacher, and she began to teach older women. Eunice had been mentor and teacher to almost everyone in the church. At least all the women. She had been a comfort to Shelby after her mother died.

"I'm not doing too well these days."

"Let's order; then we'll talk about it." Eunice looked up at the waitress. "Hello, Kayla. What do you have special today?"

Kayla rattled off the special—a toasted pimiento cheese on pinnani.

"I'll have that," Eunice said. "And the Hungarian mushroom soup."

Shelby chose the half sandwich of albacore tuna with gypsy soup. She hadn't eaten well lately. Now, amid the smells of bread and soup and seeing people communicating with each other, she realized she should not have stayed home moping.

Kayla returned with Shelby's mango tea and Eunice's ice water. While they waited for the order, the owner, Jeff, stopped by the table. He and Brian had known each other several years before when they worked together at one of the local conference centers. And of course, everyone knew Eunice both in her own right and because of her being a preacher's wife.

Shelby and Eunice mentioned their families. After Kayla brought their food, Eunice said the prayer. "Now tell me how things are with you, Shelby. I know it's hard without your mom."

Shelby surprised herself by being able to talk about the recent events while enjoying the meal. Eunice had a way of giving her undivided attention and letting a person talk. Shelby was able to relay the events about Annette in a calm tone of voice. . .even to the pie incident.

Eunice was finishing her soup. Shelby had eaten most of her sandwich. She enjoyed talking calmly about the situation. Eunice wasn't saying anything. "You think I'm wrong?"

Eunice picked up her napkin and blotted her lips. Then she looked across at Shelby. Her voice was kind as ever. Her eyes expressed sympathy. "If that's how you feel, Shelby, that's how you feel. But as far as Annette and your dad are concerned, I don't think it's your decision to make. If they want to pursue a life together, that's for them to decide."

Shelby didn't expect that from Eunice. But somehow it didn't have the edge to it as the night her dad brought Annette to the house or the days that followed when she and her family were at odds.

"That's just my opinion," Eunice said kindly.

A short laugh escaped Shelby's throat. "I asked for it." She took a sip of tea. "I'll think about what you said. Actually," she said, "that problem has been pushed into the back of my mind the last couple days." She sighed. "But you don't need to hear my problems."

"Yes, Shelby, I do. I'm not ready to talk about mine yet. If you are, I'm here to listen."

Shelby could have cried. Eunice was like a mom or a grandmother to her. She could always talk to her in a way she now wished she had talked to her mom. . .but hadn't. So many times she'd treated her mom like the enemy. She now knew she'd missed so much and would never have another chance.

She could hardly believe she could sit there, eating, telling anyone, "I'm not able to bear a child." Expecting sympathy or distress, she was surprised to see a sparkle in Eunice's eyes and a faint smile on her lips. She leaned forward, ready to speak as soon as Shelby paused.

"Shelby. God has the answer waiting for you."

Shelby sat in stunned silence while Eunice, almost glowing in her dissertation, told of a fifteen-year-old girl named Marcella who was pregnant and might give the baby up for adoption.

Kayla came to the table and asked if they wanted dessert.

"I'm stuffed," Shelby said, and Eunice agreed. At least they agreed about. . .something.

Eunice must have detected Shelby's sudden reserve. She opened her purse. "I've enjoyed this Shelby, but I must get home and take my afternoon siesta. I do need that."

"I'll pay," Shelby said.

Eunice shook her head. "No, no. I invited you. This is my treat." She laid a few dollar bills on the table for a tip. "I want to speak with Jeff anyway. I've eaten here since he bought this place. I've known him for years. He needs to know that I like those umbrellas he has as decoration up there along the wall."

Shelby laughed, glancing at the colorful array of umbrellas, then looked back at Eunice. "Thanks for inviting me."

Eunice stood and grew serious. "Think about what I've said, Shelby. You have a good day now."

On the way home, Shelby noticed that spring had made its way into her mountain town. Yellow came first—yellowbuds and pansies. The town seemed to favor the yellow pansies at the beginning of spring. She hadn't planted anything. The season of new life.

New life. She couldn't—

No, she wouldn't go there. Although Eunice hadn't agreed with her about Annette and mentioned what Shelby had no intention of doing—adoption—Shelby had felt good about talking with her. Eunice hadn't condemned her like everybody else did.

What would she do now? Go home and wallow in her tears on the floor again? What had that done for her? Some sense of reason seemed to settle in her mind. She was able to think about all this more clearly. Maybe it was the spring air.

Too, she felt good about wearing makeup, her hair loose instead of bound in a ponytail, wearing dressy-casual pants and top, and flats instead of sneakers. She felt more like a woman, although she'd been told she wasn't.

She forced those thoughts to stop, too. Would they ever?

When she pulled into her driveway, her plight of loneliness washed over her. Brian's car wasn't in the carport. They hadn't said two decent words to each other in two weeks. How long before he moved out? What if he didn't come home one night?

She could tolerate Annette with her dad, as hard as that might be. But that wasn't the biggest problem with Brian. He saw her as a cold-hearted, unfeeling, selfish person. Didn't her sister say so? Didn't her brother look at her and shake his head as if she were some alien he didn't understand? Didn't her dad blame her because she disapproved of his relationship? But he disapproved of some of hers in the past. And he'd been right. The tables had turned. He was getting senile. . .or maybe he was on the rebound.

Rebound!

Yes, that was it.

Being without Mom was difficult for him. Mom had taken care of him. Cooked, cleaned, picked out his clothes, shared his bed, borne his children, raised them, helped at the florist shop. Sure, he missed her. Shelby could understand that. But. . .bringing another woman into the family. . .that would be a mistake. His wife—her mother—was dead. They had to learn to accept that. . . together. They couldn't replace her with another person.

She looked at her yard. A few bushes displayed leaves with a touch of green. The beds lay barren, full of last year's leaves. She would buy flowers, plant them, put some color in her life.

With that resolve, she backed out of the driveway.

Eunice's words seemed to ring in her ears. *Let Curt and Annette decide their own lives.*

Okay. Okay. She'd go see Annette. Tell her she would stay out of it. She had problems that were much more pressing. Her personal life with Brian—if they had one anymore. Shelby was not going to let Annette Billings break up her marriage.

She could at least thank Annette for the pie. She hadn't thanked her the day she brought it by. She hadn't even invited Annette in but let her stand on the stoop, making her little speech. Then Shelby had taken the pie without a word.

Maybe after she talked to Annette, maybe then her dad, her siblings, and Brian would love her again.

Shelby practiced the words she'd say all the way to Annette's. She knew there'd be a lull between the lunch crowd and coffee and tea time, which started at three o'clock. The Kitchen wouldn't be very busy. The Victorian house was surrounded by a blaze of flowers—yellow jonquils, multicolored pansies, hedges of yellow-buds, and other flowering plants vibrant against green leaves.

Had her dad planted these flowers for Annette?

Well if he did, appreciate it, Shelby, she told herself. He was an expert with flowers. Determined, she stepped up onto the porch, made her way across it, went through the doorway with its tinkling bell, and stepped inside the gift shop. Her gaze went immediately to the dining area and to Annette, whose auburn hair was caught back with a clasp.

Immediately her gaze alighted upon the man facing Annette. Her dad was there, sitting at the table with Annette, even leaning over the table. Now, what did that body language say?

It said they had lied to her. They were not arguing or looking like a couple that had just broken up. Quite the contrary. They looked like two poets, drinking to each other with their eyes.

Annette had lied, saying she wouldn't continue the relationship. Her goodness was a facade. The pie was a ploy.

Her dad's startled gaze met Shelby's. He halfway stood, then sat again. "Shelby."

She walked forward.

"You want to sit down?"

Her dad motioned to the empty place at the table. Shelby knew Annette was looking up at her, but Shelby looked only at her dad. Maybe she could get the words out that she'd intended to say. Would they sound real? Or vindictive? Why did she think anybody really cared what she thought? Maybe she could be as two-faced as they were.

She would try.

Then she heard Annette say to the waitress who walked by, "Marcella, would you refill the tea glasses at the table down there?"

Marcella?

Shelby turned her head and looked at the waitress she'd never seen before. Was she the Marcella that Eunice had told her about? Shelby's eyes went to the girl's stomach. One normally wouldn't notice that slight outward curve. That little girl. . .could have a baby?

Shelby's mouth went dry. Her limbs felt weak.

"No." She turned back to Annette and her dad. "I just came to say. . ." She lifted her hand limply. Her words were weak. "Do what you want. I—" Then, before she could stop herself, she added, "You both lied to me."

She turned to go. The little girl was near her. Shelby stepped back, feeling she would faint dead away if any part of her touched that girl. She forced her attention away from the girl and commanded her feet to take her out of there. Were her dad and Annette saying her name?

Outside, she breathed deeply. She felt like the victim of a stoning. Once a stone is thrown, everybody else picks one up. Even the kindest woman in the world, Eunice Hogan, had thrown a stone.

On the way home, Shelby thought she couldn't stand it. Everybody was against her. Then she felt the anger. Little girls could have babies. Fifteen-year-olds who weren't much more than babies themselves.

I can't! It's not fair. God's not fair. He took my mother. He won't let me have children. My dad thinks I ruined his life. My husband hates me. I can't do what other women can do.

The next thought terrified her. Her breath seemed to stop.

What am I going to do with my life?

Take it.

Eunice needed to rest. First, she'd drive out beyond Asheville and stop by the Hope Center. She wanted some advice. She'd been told to call anytime. So she was calling—in person. Because she had five and a half months and was slowing down by the moment, she could not waste any precious time.

Driving along Interstate 40, she turned on the radio to the Billy Graham radio station.

She seemed to evaluate every word of a song, every action of a person. Life became more acute, taking on more significance now that she had so little of it left. It was not the same as just growing older. So many songs spoke of mansions and singing forever. Earth was a testing place, a preparation for what was to come for eternity, causing Eunice to visualize heaven as a place where one would still have abilities and challenges.

But she was still alive. That meant she had work to do on earth.

She took the Farmer's Market exit and thought of her conversation with Shelby, hoping she had been helpful to her. That young girl had so many years ahead of her and so many possibilities. She chuckled to herself. Just as energy was wasted on the young, hindsight was wasted on the elderly.

Seeing Shelby's problems so clearly and feeling she had counseled her correctly, Eunice now heaved a deep sigh. The words of a poem came to mind. "O wad some Pow'r the giftie gie us / To see oursels as others see us."

Yes, poet Robert Burns had expressed it in his Scottish accent and English of days gone by, but he had voiced a profound thought. How blessed we would be if God gave us the gift to see ourselves as others see us.

Eunice could clearly see the choices facing Shelby and the action she should take. Then, as if she had no insight at all, Eunice's own doubts and concerns rose to the surface. She'd already made her decision, yet her vehicle was heading in the direction of the doctor's office.

Driving past Biltmore Square Mall, she waited at the traffic light, then turned at Richfield, where she'd take the curves up to the right and park beside the brick building called the Hope Center.

Hope.

After parking, she took a few deep breaths of the warm spring air, observing resurrection in trees, bushes, and plants that had given the impression of being dead a short season away. Resurrection was the hope of all who believed in and obeyed the Lord Jesus Christ.

She had hope.

But. . .that fleeting thought she'd already dealt with began to surface. Should she take the chemo and radiation and spend more time with Henry? Would that perhaps be the method through which God might choose to work a miracle?

Eunice walked over to her left, was greeted by a girl who recognized her and called her by name. Yes, she would have the doctor or a nurse talk with her as soon as possible. Eunice took a seat in one of the sections decorated like a comfortable living room. A recent copy of their monthly newsletter lay on the table. She had received it in the mail that morning but hadn't yet read it.

She flipped through and stopped at an article entitled, "The Breath of Life."

She read of a woman younger than she who had lost her

husband to cancer a few months before, then was told she had that same dreaded disease. Eunice read about the woman's discovery, diagnosis, surgery.

The sound of her name being called pulled Eunice's attention from the article. She took the newsletter with her to the doctor's office and continued reading while waiting for him. The writer talked about her love of life and even thanked God for difficulties that taught her what life's priorities should be.

She read the sentence, "Dying is a form of healing if we have accepted Jesus into our hearts and lives."

Eunice knew that but found comfort in reading that from someone who had the same disease as she, who questioned, loved life, and wanted to continue on earth. She knew by experience that lessons in life were learned by trial and error. And by the time anyone learned a few things, it was time to go.

Before she finished the article, the doctor came in. She asked her questions. What should she expect if she took chemo and radiation? What would be her quality of life? Was it guaranteed to prolong her life? What would the quality of life be with or without prolonging it? If she were to go away for a few days, when should she do that before becoming too weak to travel?

When the conversation ended, Eunice had a prescription for VP-16. With that, she would be able to do what she had in mind. At the same time, her mind fluctuated from certainty to doubt.

Eunice felt the weakness overtake her by the time she reached home. Her destination was the bedroom. She found her copy of the newsletter and identified with the words, "Breathing and living become an act of worship, of realizing what is most important in life—and it's not my personal success, my bank account, or the size of my home. It is my relationship with my Lord and Savior, Jesus Christ."

Yes, she knew that, too. She laid the article aside. Her options were the same as before she'd seen the doctor. Treatments would not cure the cancer. They might give her a few days or weeks longer but with no guarantee of quality. The time the treatments might give her would be time spent taking the treatments. What kind of life was that?

She could choose not to take the treatments and have a shorter life in which to make preparations for her death with no guarantee except pain that could be treated with medication.

Pulling the afghan up around her shoulders, she turned her head until her eyes focused on the Bible. Other doubts and questions assailed her. Would hiding the truth from Henry be the same as lying? Would revealing the truth to Henry be the same as gossiping and destroying his faith in another human being?

Such questions could not begin to be answered unless she knew the truth for herself.

Would approaching those three women be some latent desire for revenge? Did she want to trouble and accuse them? Did she want to clear up this wall between them and her that they had pretended wasn't there for nineteen years?

Eunice recognized the questions in her mind as a time of doubt and lack of faith. She'd experienced enough years of such. It wouldn't last long. She knew how to find the answers.

As her eyes closed, she reprimanded herself. Doubt and fear had no place in a believer's life.

Eunice. Do what you have taught others, have counseled others, have done yourself. Ask God. He knows how to close doors and open doors. If it's a situation in which you're in doubt, don't do it. If you have peace or confirmation, then proceed.

Pray.

A peaceful feeling settled over her as her thoughts drifted into communication with her Lord.

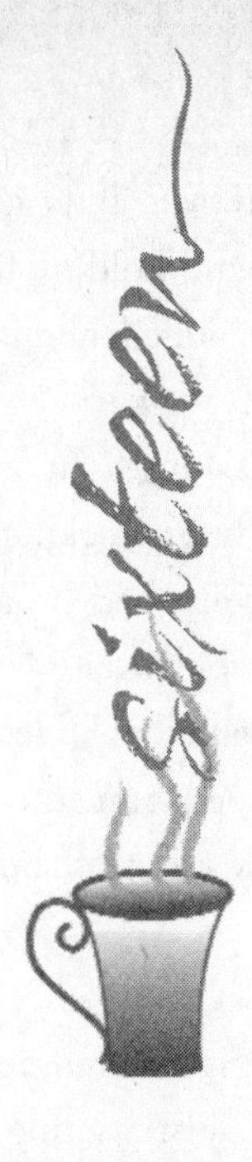

Annette sensed the pain Shelby was feeling. After watching her run from the house, she turned to Curt. "Curt, go make sure Shelby is all right."

His face clouded. "I'm disgusted with her. It's time she grew up. Live her life and let me live mine."

"She apologized, Curt."

"Halfheartedly. She didn't mean it."

"She tried. She feels I lied to her, saying I wouldn't see you, and here we are."

"We're not out together."

"No, but think how it looks to her. And Curt, you said she's just found out she can't bear a child. That's devastating."

He spread his hands. "What can I do?"

Annette shook her head. "I don't know. I just know she's hurting. Call and make sure she's all right and that Brian's home." Curt glanced away. She had to get through to him. "This is serious, Curt. And dangerous. I've been there."

He sighed and pulled his cell phone from his pocket. There was no answer from Shelby's apartment. He called Brian's cell phone. No answer. He called the church. No answer. He called Jim, who said he'd had lunch with Brian at the Chinese place. Brian had said he had some errands to run.

He stared at the silent cell phone in his hand. Annette reached over and put her hand over his. "Please. Let's make sure she's all right. If she is, you can drive me back. I won't go in."

He let go of the cell phone, turned his hand over, and caught her hand in his. She liked the strength of his hand holding hers. But she couldn't let the moment linger. She pulled her hand away. "Let's go."

When they neared the house, she saw the flashing light of the ambulance. Curt parked as close as he could without blocking the drive. He and Annette ran across the yard. Shelby was brought out on a stretcher and put in the back of the ambulance.

Brian stood looking helpless. "I couldn't wake her." He was trembling. An EMT grasped his arm and helped him into the ambulance. He looked out at them before they closed the door and repeated distantly, "I couldn't wake her."

No one knew or cared about the time—except it was moments, maybe hours, in eternity. There was no time, just waiting for someone to come and say everything would be all right. In the meantime, they all blamed themselves.

Francine and Mike had been called but hadn't arrived.

"I hate this," Curt said. "It all started because I wanted to get married. I should have realized that she was still grieving for her mother."

"No," Brian said. "This is about not being able to have children. And I haven't been the most sympathetic husband. She's going through a lot." He grimaced. "But I don't know how to help her. I guess I just wanted to escape it."

Annette knew Shelby's problems began with the loss of her mother. She was so young. She hadn't experienced it in the same way as Curt. Although she expected her mother to die, it would still have been a great shock.

Now the family members were feeling guilt. Annette recognized that. She'd lived with it long enough.

Am I to blame?

She tried not to ask herself that question. For almost twenty years, she'd tried not to hurt anyone, to never say an unkind word, never have an unkind thought. Just do what was right. She had been blessed. But then she'd dared think she could have married bliss with Curt Crowder. She should have known better. Such an attempt was like stirring up a nest of hornets. She should have stayed in her own safe world she'd made for herself. Not ventured outside it.

Now she stood in a hospital corridor with Shelby's family as if she were a part of it. They'd taken her side instead of Shelby's. Yes, she was a straw that weighed down the camel's back, if not the one that broke it. She needed to leave. Leave them alone to be what they were before she interfered—a family.

Leave?

She had ridden there with Curt. She couldn't ask him to leave. She would have to stay until they knew. What if. . . ?

No!

She walked over to a window. Her eyes stared into the sunlight, which burned like sand. She couldn't blink. She had to stop whatever thought followed "What if?" She wouldn't be able to stand it. She couldn't go through something like that. . .again.

She didn't turn when Francine and Mike arrived or even when the doctor came to give his report. She heard it. They knew what Shelby had taken because the EMT had told Brian to check around for medications when they were at the apartment. The empty bottle had been on the countertop in the bathroom, with the lid off, beside a paper cup next to the sink.

They'd pumped her stomach. She'd be all right, but the doctor wanted to keep her overnight, let her sleep it off because so much had already gone into her system. This would have to be reported. A psychologist would have to talk with her before she could be released.

Annette breathed a prayer of thankfulness. After a long time, she felt a comforting arm slip around her shoulders and Curt's presence next to her.

"You heard?"

Annette wiped at her tears with her fingertips and nodded.

"I learned something today," he said. "I've been upset with Shelby because of her attitude. I've called her selfish for wanting her own way, bemoaning the fact she can't have what she wants." He took a deep breath and lifted his eyes toward the ceiling for a moment. "But haven't I done the same thing? I've been angry because I want you in my life and she objects and you say no."

Annette turned toward him, feeling the warmth of his arm around her, his closeness. She looked into his eyes and sensed his sadness.

"I'm the older, mature one. I need to set the example for Shelby of one who can't have what he wants yet can go on with life." A wry laugh escaped his throat. "How much easier it is to give out good advice than to take it yourself."

At that moment, looking into his eyes and seeing the goodness of his soul, she felt that might be the moment she really fell in love with him.

Or was the feeling just because he had now agreed their relationship had come to a halt? He would no longer pursue her. She was alone. . .but safe. . .in the world of flowers she had built around herself.

By midmorning the next day, Shelby had become aware of what she'd done and thanked God she hadn't died. She hadn't really wanted that. She'd only wanted to scare Brian and her relatives enough to make them care about her—care if she lived or died.

She'd accomplished that. They all came, spoke softly, apologized for not realizing what she was going through. Her dad was so sweet. Brian was loving. Francine made no biting remarks.

Mike said he was glad she was going to be okay. Now that she'd gotten what she wanted, she felt guilty.

She wished she had behaved in such a way that they could like her, not have them come around because she tried to kill herself. She apologized for scaring them. They were so sweet to her, she cried, which made them even sweeter. She had a loving family—when they thought they'd lose her.

At her prompting, they all decided to go home and return later, except Brian. He said he'd be right back after going to the cafeteria for a cup of coffee. While he was gone, the psychologist came and asked all sorts of questions. She knew how to respond in a satisfactory way, acknowledging the blows to her life such as the loss of her mother, her dad wanting to remarry, and being told she was barren.

The psychologist agreed she'd been through a lot. Shelby told her she was sorry and really did want to live. She'd just wanted sympathy and realized how immature that was. She felt sure she'd convinced the psychologist she shouldn't be locked up in some institution. However, the woman said she would be required to meet with her weekly for a while.

After she left, Shelby fell asleep. She awakened and looked into the eyes of Eunice Hogan, who sat in a chair beside her bed.

Eunice held her gaze until Shelby's eyes filled and the wetness rolled down her cheeks. "I'm sorry."

Eunice's eyebrows shot up. "Sorry that you took the pills, or sorry you didn't die?"

Shelby was surprised. She swiped at the wetness on her face. She blinked, and her eyelashes felt heavy, drowned. Eunice, with her look, seemed to elicit the deepest truth from Shelby. "Both," she said. "I guess."

Eunice nodded. "I know how you feel."

Shelby looked away from her. "How can you?"

"Did you know I lost a daughter?"

Those words brought Shelby's head back toward Eunice. The older woman looked different. Not so sweet as she always appeared. Somehow she seemed to be Shelby's judge—rightfully so.

"I think I knew that. Not the details, but Pastor Hogan has mentioned it. I suppose that was years ago."

"Years ago and now!" Eunice said. "My daughter is gone. She can't be replaced. That tore out my heart."

"I'm sorry," Shelby said sincerely. "But at least you had one. I can't have a child."

"It seemed that neither could I," said Eunice. "Henry and I had been married for thirteen years. She was our miracle child when I was in my midthirties."

Shelby knew miracles could happen, but she also knew about reality. She tried to keep the acerbity from her voice. "You're saying that could happen to me?"

"No. I'm saying it's easier being childless than having a child and losing her. I want you to know, Shelby, that I not only sympathize with you, I empathize. You see, my daughter died when she was just a teenager."

Oh, Shelby thought she'd die. She heard the sorrow in Eunice's voice, she saw it in her eyes, she felt the pain in her own heart.

"I'm so sorry," Shelby whispered.

"I tell you this, Shelby, to let you know that I do know what you feel. I know it better than you do. I have lost grandparents, parents, and a child. Nothing hurts worse than losing a child. That is not to diminish your grief. But I was childless for thirteen years of our marriage and accepted the heartache of probably never having a child of my own. That heartache cannot begin to touch the grief of losing that child."

Shelby believed that, but it didn't diminish her own pain of what she was going through. Eunice had taught such in classes

Shelby had attended: You don't really measure trials by the size of someone else's. If you have a cut on your finger, that's what hurts at the moment.

"Count your blessings, Shelby." Eunice rose from her chair. "I'm not going to sit here and tell you how fortunate you are. How blessed."

"I don't feel that," Shelby said honestly. "How do I do it?"

"I can't do it for you, Shelby. But if you ever want to talk to someone like me who knows how you feel, I'm available."

While Shelby stared after her, Eunice turned and left the room.

Eunice called me," Ruby said after she, Annette, and Lara had their lunch set in front of them and Tom went back downstairs. Annette and Lara held their forks in midair, waiting for the next words. They lowered their forks to the plates when she added, "Eunice thinks Marcella is the answer to Shelby's problem and vice versa. She thinks it's more than coincidence that Marcella shows up pregnant just when Shelby finds out she can't have a child."

Annette told them what Shelby had done. "She's recovering from having her stomach pumped."

"I know," Ruby said. "So this may not be the situation for Marcella. Eunice said she could let the girl stay with her for a week or so if needed."

Lara turned to her. "How do you guys always hear things before I do?"

"Eunice told me," Ruby said. "I had to talk to her about Marcella. She's going to talk to Shelby some more. But I'm going to have to find a permanent place for her and help with her needs and decisions. Oh, this reminds me of a story. These two cows were standing together in the pasture. Daisy said to Dolly, 'I was artificially inseminated this morning.'

" 'I don't believe you,' said Dolly.

" 'It's true, no bull.' "

Lara almost choked on her food.

Ruby reveled in tickling Lara's funny bone. She took a bite while they laughed. Then she pointed her fork at Annette. "Marcella's doing really well here, you said." She looked around. "This is a big house."

Annette nodded, chewed a bite, then swallowed quickly. She stared at Ruby. "Oh, no. Don't look at me that way. I can't let her stay here. I mean, Tom still lives here, you know. I can't have a young girl under the same roof with my young son. It's just not the best of situations."

Lara laughed lightly. "Annette, she's already pregnant."

Ruby snorted. "That's not a legit argument, Lara. I've been pregnant three times, and believe me—"

"Oh, spare me the details," Lara said. She sipped from her cup and peered over the rim at the other two. After a sip, she said, "Don't look at me." She set the cup down. "I can help with money, but I'm not taking in anybody in my condo, especially not a young pregnant girl. Scares me to think of it."

"I might be able to," Ruby said, "if Jill will share her bedroom."

Lara lifted her eyebrows. "I thought you were about ready to toss Charlie out."

Ruby shrugged and grinned. "In that case, Jill and I will have to fight about which one of us shares our bedroom with Marcella. But you're right about the situation with Charlie. If he's not practicing singing for Christmas, it's Easter."

"Well, that's his job, Ruby," Lara reminded her.

Ruby nodded. "Sure, but I used to date him. His parents would ask why he came in so late, and he'd say he'd been out with friends. . .singing." She looked at the ceiling.

"What are you going to do about it?" Annette asked. Ruby knew she wasn't taking her very seriously.

"I don't have time or money to do anything right now. Anyway, too many people are having all sorts of problems. I think I'll postpone mine. Oh, look at that."

Marcella brought up cake and set it on the countertop.

"Bring it over here," Ruby said. "There's no reason why a person can't eat cake with the main course." She licked her lips as if the cake were already on them.

Marcella brought the cake, then left the room.

"This reminds me." Ruby plunged her fork into the cake. "Two Eskimos got cold while sitting in a kayak, so they lit a fire. It sank. That proves you can't have your kayak and heat it, too."

Ruby approved the cake, then returned to the main course. She wanted to slip in the rest of what she had to say and tried to do it as if it were the most natural thing in the world.

She waited until they'd stacked their dishes on the big round tray and Annette had poured coffee for each of them. Annette brought up the subject. "We need to decide what to do for Eunice. We have to acknowledge her somehow." She lifted her hands helplessly. "I don't know how to handle this."

Ruby looked up at her. "Charlie said Henry said Eunice said she didn't want people acting like she's dying until it's obvious that she is and unable to help herself or Henry." Just as Annette's and Lara's faces relaxed, she dropped the bomb. "She asked to see us."

"When?" Lara said quickly.

"When we were on the phone talking about Marcella. She said she would like for the three of us to visit her."

"Did she name us?" Annette asked.

Ruby shook her head. "She didn't have to. If she meant me and the children, that would be four of us. With Charlie, that would be five. The three of us is all she could have meant."

"What. . .do you think she wants?" Lara asked bleakly.

Ruby took a deep breath. "You know Eunice, bless her heart. She tries to make everybody feel comfortable. She knows all the church members feel like they have to do something. She tries to make it easier for everyone. I think she probably doesn't know what to do with company any more than company knows what to do with her."

Annette shook her head. "She always knows exactly what she's doing."

Lara took a deep breath before she spoke. "You can always take food, Annette. But. . .how can we see her and act. . .normal?"

Annette's voice was monotone. "We've acted normal for almost twenty years."

"Ha!" Ruby lifted her chin. "What do you mean, 'act'? How do you get more normal than being a redneck, harried, pudgy housewife with teenagers and an unfaithful husband?"

Thank God, Ruby thought, *for humor. Even sick humor. But that was better than just. . .sick.*

"I'm not going," Lara said. She picked up her cup. Her hand trembled, and her coffee spilled over onto the cloth.

Somehow, in the back of her mind, she heard Annette saying the perfect thing, like a perfect hostess, like a perfect woman with a perfect life. How could she be so calm? How could she stand it? Lara would go into her bedroom later and scream into her pillow. Muffle the sound. But nothing, nothing muffled the memory.

She knew Eunice would face death like a trooper. But Lara remembered the words Eunice Hogan had wailed. "I want to know the truth."

What did she want now? What could she want?

"Don't look so devastated, Lara." Annette laughed softly as she blotted the spilled coffee with a tea towel. "It's not the first time something's been spilled. That's why I chose white. Bleach will get it out."

"It didn't get that one out." Ruby pointed at the thin, shadow-like stain along the fold of the cloth draped over the round table.

"You would notice." Annette laughed uncomfortably. "There's always a stubborn one."

For a moment, Lara shut her eyes against the thought that jumped into her mind. *Yes, some are stubborn. Some are persistent. This one has been there for years. . .how many? Nineteen?*

"Don't mind me," Lara said. "I don't feel well. I've had something like the flu all week."

Ruby sympathized. "I thought you looked sick."

After a brief silence, Annette said the right thing. "She asked for us. You know we have to go. And what will she think if one of us doesn't go? That's going to lead to questions."

Lara nodded. There was only one thing Eunice Hogan ever wanted from them.

Did she still want it?

No. It was over and done.

Then why did its nightmare persist?

"We have to go see what she wants," Annette said.

Lara moaned. "And what if she asks us questions?"

Ruby admired Annette, who said with perfect clarity, "We don't have to tell Eunice any more than we told the police."

Lara looked like plastic, pale and stiff as one of those well-dressed manikins in Lancaster's windows.

Ruby wished she could think of a joke, a quip, something to make them laugh, or at least breathe again. Eunice Hogan was making a request that would kill them all, all over again. Eunice Hogan would be dying for months. The three of them had been dying for almost twenty years.

"What's on your mind, Ruby?" Annette asked quietly.

Ruby didn't intend this one to be funny, and she knew no one would laugh. "About these two fish who ran into a concrete wall. One turned to the other and said, 'Dam.' "

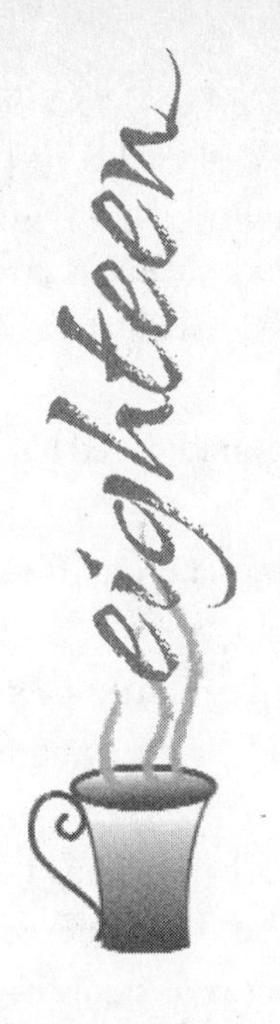

The Easter pageant was spectacular. Eunice knew it was the last one she'd ever see. Then she almost laughed at that. No, she wouldn't see human beings acting out parts. She would see the real risen Lord—Jesus Himself. The thought was overwhelming, as if it were new. Sometimes it was. She'd known and believed all her life, yet at times it struck her like a bolt of lightning. There really was another world, a spiritual world, a world of peace and beauty. She believed it all the time. She only knew it on rare occasions when the Lord showed His presence in such realistic ways.

Most of the time God seemed too big, too unfathomable. Occasionally He was as close as one's breath. In fact, wasn't He one's breath? Who could give themselves a breath of life? No one. Yes, she would see the Lord. She didn't think there would be pageantry. Just a welcoming home. What would it really be like?

Gates of pearl, streets of gold, stars in one's crown—those things didn't appeal. What appealed was freedom. How limited she'd felt through the years. Limited in ability. The mind could soar. But putting into practice what one visualized was another thing, often a disappointment. She would no longer be limited. What would she do for eternity? She didn't believe for one moment she would sprout wings and sing all day. Eternity. What great things God must have planned. A different world. A different life.

But she wasn't dead yet. And she didn't expect God to lead her into some new venture over the next months. Her health was failing. She felt it. She must continue the work she had started—with Shelby. And the work she had stopped—with those three women. And just continue to love Henry.

Shelby came up to her after the pageant and hugged her. She looked better than she had in weeks.

"I want you to know, Eunice, that I appreciate you. If there's anything I can do now. . .or later."

"There is," Eunice said and smiled. People didn't expect that kind of reply. Neither did Shelby. "Come and see me tomorrow."

"When they pumped my stomach, they must have pumped some of my stupidity out," Shelby said to her dad, then ducked her head. "Fortunately." She played with the pieces of stems he had cut from a pile of red roses.

"You're not stupid, Shel. . ."

"Oh, Dad." Why was apologizing so difficult? "I don't want to start anything again. It does seem to me that Mom hasn't been dead long enough for you to consider marrying again." She heard his sigh, so she hurried to say what she had to. "But I realize now that is your business. You've always been the smartest, the best, the most wonderful. . ."

She started to cry. He laid down his rose. Shelby went into his arms. "I love you, Dad. I'm going to try and trust you to know what you're doing."

He chuckled. "Now that's an improvement." He drew her closer. "You know I love you, baby." He spoke against her hair and patted her shoulder.

She nodded against his chest. After a moment, she drew back and sniffed, swiping at her eyes. "Forgive me?"

"Always."

She loved seeing a smile on his face and believed the moisture in his eyes was because of the kind of gladness she felt. "I'll let you live your life. Believe me, I have enough to deal with in my own."

"Yes, you do. And you've had a lot to deal with. I'm here for you. You know that."

She nodded. The tears started again.

After another hug, basking in the comfort of her dad's arms, she left to get on with her life.

With Brian's welcomed help, Shelby finished her report after two evening's work and turned it in after her eight o'clock class on Wednesday. She'd been exhausted physically and emotionally but determined to stay busy and go through the motions of being a responsible adult. She'd apologized to her whole family and to God. That was all she could do.

However, she now recalled her feelings during the Easter pageant. She'd seen Marcella sitting with Jill and Tom. If she hadn't known the girl's condition, she'd have thought Marcella was just another carefree teenager. That's what she should have been. She was young, not married. It wasn't fair!

The demon thoughts began to plague her again. Would she never be free of them?

Almost without deliberation, she turned the car in the opposite direction of her apartment complex. When she neared the brick ranch, she saw Eunice sitting in the sun on the front porch. Shelby parked in the driveway and walked past the wrought-iron railing.

Eunice rose to hug her and motioned to the other rocking chair.

Shelby thanked her and looked at the little round table between the chairs on which sat a pitcher of lemonade, two glasses, and a plate of cookies. "You look like you're expecting company."

Eunice smiled. "A preacher's wife is always expecting company." She returned to her chair. "Now tell me, how is school going?"

Of course Eunice or Pastor Hogan would have asked about her progress after that sleeping pill fiasco. Either her dad or Brian would have told them. Shelby poured herself a glass of lemonade and talked briefly about school.

The next subject was the weather. The lush green lawn stretched out in front of them, the flowerbeds Pastor Hogan worked in. "Your dad has been a big help to Henry with those flowers," Eunice said.

Shelby nodded. "When Dad gave up teaching to run the florist, everybody thought he was crazy." She and Eunice exchanged warm smiles. "But Dad loves it. He feels close to nature that way."

"Henry, too. He likes working with the earth."

Shelby sipped her lemonade. She set the glass down. "You asked me to come and see you."

"Yes," Eunice said. "In the hospital you asked me how you could accept your situation. I want to try and answer that. I can't tell you how to deal with your grief and the loss of your mother. I can't say you are right or wrong. There's one thing I can tell you that you must do."

Shelby waited expectantly. Listening to Eunice was easier than having listened to the accusing tones of her family members. She wished she had let her mom know she had heard her, even at times when she hadn't really listened.

"It's what Henry and I have had to do each time we took in a foster child. We had to be willing to give up that child. We've had little babies; we've had teenagers we've watched change from embittered, hurt kids to trusting children with a purpose in life. We fell in love with them. Not one ever, ever, could. . .or should. . . take the place of my daughter. But they had their own place. Yet the requirement was. . .be willing to give them up. So that is what you must consider. Don't adopt a child, don't take one in unless you first give that child to God. The Lord gives and the Lord takes away. If you think of others—whether it be a husband, a parent, a child—as being yours, your possession, your right, then you set yourself up for grief unbearable."

Eunice paused. Her tone of voice softened. "How are you dealing with your emotions?"

"Better," Shelby said.

"Better." Eunice huffed. "What does that mean? And be honest."

"Well, I got the sympathy I wanted from my relatives. Even Brian has quit calling me names. But it's like a guardian-child relationship. I think he thinks I'm going to slip any minute and try to kill myself again."

"Are you?"

"No. I wanted to scare everybody, make them sorry. I know that's immature. That's what they'd been calling me. I just couldn't stand any more. But you know, I've looked in that medicine cabinet, and there's more medication there I could have taken. I think in the back of my mind I didn't want to die; I just wanted somebody to see me, know I was hurting. I understand it better now, and I'm seeing the psychologist, who explains it, and it makes sense. I've had to admit some things about myself and that part of my grief is because everything wasn't settled between me and my mom."

Eunice looked down at her hands. "It wasn't between me and my daughter, either."

Shelby had difficulty thinking a relationship with Eunice was anything but ideal. "How did you handle that? I mean, did you feel guilty, like me? Did you. . .take something, like I did?"

"No," Eunice said. "I just beat myself up every day for a while."

She sort of laughed, so Shelby did, too.

"Did you ever get back to normal? Oops!" Shelby groaned. "What a question. You're the most normal person I know. What I mean is, how did you get over it?"

"Well, Shelby, it's easy to say just give it to the Lord. And there is truth in that. But then you have to do something yourself. If He were going to do everything Himself, He wouldn't have created us. We have to walk our walk, depending on Him. But we have to reach out to others. That's what I want you to do."

Shelby nodded. "You know Brian and I help with the youth at church. Besides that, when I hear about someone losing their mom, even though they're all older than me, I talk to them."

"That's good." Eunice smiled. She stared at Shelby for a moment. "There's something I want you to do for me."

Shelby wondered if she were in pain. If she needed a pill or something. "Anything, if I can."

Eunice smiled. "I want you to take Marcella into your home for a while."

Shelby was shocked, then honest. "I resent her."

"That's something you must overcome. And get over this resentment toward God."

"I never said—"

"You didn't have to, Shelby. Remember, I've been there. I know. But that is normal."

"How do I get over it?"

"You begin to show love to others. You don't have to feel it. Act on love, and the emotion of love will come."

Shelby felt that old rebellion rising. "You want me to adopt her baby. You think that will do it."

Eunice shook her head. "I want you to give yourself a chance to get rid of this feeling that you can't love a child. To stop resenting Marcella. Get to know her. Be a friend. I'm going away for a few days quite soon. Would you do this for me?"

"I'll think about it."

"Don't think, Shelby. The mind and heart debate each other. Just pray. You'll know what to do."

That evening, Shelby said yes when Ruby called and asked if she could come out and talk with her. Instead of hiding herself and her feelings, Shelby decided to face things head-on and be honest about her feelings but keep them in control.

When she told Brian about Eunice's wanting her to adopt Marcella's baby, she saw his initial look of hope fade. He took a deep breath, and she suspected he was counting to ten. His voice remained calm. "I would be glad to consider that, Shelby. But it has to be your decision, too."

He was still careful about his words and his actions. Maybe someday they could argue again without his wondering if she'd try to kill herself. That had been a terrible mistake she now regretted.

"But as far as helping her, I'm willing. You know we've been helpful to some of the youth when they had problems. Whatever you want to do, I'm with you."

She loved him for that and went to him. He held her tenderly. Both were so careful with their emotions. She missed the spontaneity.

The following morning, Ruby came at 10:00 a.m. They sat at the kitchen table.

Ruby got right to the point. "Eunice Hogan said she was going to talk to you about keeping Marcella for a while."

"She did," Shelby said.

Ruby opened the file folder she'd brought in.

"Brian and I talked it over. We might be receptive to that. But I have questions. Why is she pregnant? I mean, is she promiscuous? Was she drunk? On drugs? I mean, what kind of genes or

DNA or whatever is in that baby?"

Ruby bristled at what Shelby considered perfectly legitimate questions. "Why did God allow her to be pregnant? I'll tell you, Shelby. He allowed it because the girl and boy, children, partied too much. God didn't do it. He lets us make our choices, even when we're too young to understand. Sometimes people make mistakes, get caught up in emotions they don't understand and have never felt before. Really, Shelby, weren't you ever tempted to experiment with a boy?"

Shelby felt the color rising in her face. That was one thing wrong with knowing people from church. They felt they had the right to be personal. "Ruby, this is not about teenage emotions or. . . or. . .hormones. This is about whether or not I can be of help to that girl." She would be honest. "And about the fact that I can't have a child and that little girl can."

Ruby shook her finger at Shelby, emphasizing every word. "Oh-yes-you-can-have-children! There's a big wide world out there with children, newborn innocent babies, crying for a loving mother. You can have children."

Shelby turned defensive. "You want me to adopt her, like Eunice?"

Ruby shook her head. "What I want is some Christian person to help this girl. She considered abortion before she told her parents. They were mortified. Now they're supporting her in every way and trying to do what's best for her." Ruby closed her file folder and stood. "It's Marcella's choice what she does with her unborn baby, not what I might want. My job is to place her with someone who can help her make the right choice."

When Ruby reached the door, she turned back for a moment. "The other part of my job is not to determine whether Marcella is worthy to stay with you and Brian, but to find out if you are stable enough and good enough for us to let her stay with you."

Ruby's words cut deep. Shelby had recently been accused of being spoiled, self-centered, selfish. She was trying to see things from other people's point of view instead of just her own. That helped put things in perspective.

Am I not a good person? Unstable?

I know family can be brutal. . .but even Eunice indicated I wasn't all I should be. Now. . .Ruby.

Shelby did as the psychologist suggested: "Get in the shower and shout out your true feelings, or do it into a pillow, or go somewhere where you aren't concerned with being heard and do it." Shelby chose the shower. She didn't have to scream. She'd already screamed at her dad, her relatives. Now she cried out in low groans of anger and resentment. She attacked her mom for dying. She held animosity and bitterness toward God for letting it happen. If she'd been on better terms with her mom, if she'd known how to appreciate her, if she'd had time to tell her mom she loved her. . .

Shelby sunk to the bottom of the tub, her head on her drawn-up knees. She let the water fill the tub. *Mom, I'm sorry I didn't tell you every day I loved you. I thought you were just Mom, who had been there forever and would keep on being there. I didn't realize you were a person apart from being just my mom, always telling me what to do, how to do it, when to do it, what not to do, and I resented it.*

But Mom, what I know that is good came from you. It was you who taught me even when I didn't want to listen. I didn't want to believe you knew what was inside me, my thoughts, my temptations, my possibilities. You said you did, and I didn't like that.

I'm sorry. Forgive me. I know you loved me no matter what.

God, I'm not thinking straight, but I'm saying the words. I'm sorry for being such a pain. Forgive me. Help me.

Were those the magic words, or was it the chill of the water? What brought her back to the moment? Maybe it was the cold that cleared her mind enough for her to have a reasonable thought. *I will act like a good Christian, then the love will come. I cannot give it to myself. If God chooses to change my mind, He will have to do it. I can't.*

I will not focus entirely on myself, but another person in need.

I may mess up.

No, don't think that. Just. . .act. Eunice said God would honor that. If Eunice is an example of acting, she is also an example of God honoring her life. Eunice is not an actor. She is a saintly woman who witnesses, encourages, loves, helps, teaches.

Is it possible that I could be even half the woman she and my mom were?

A verse of Scripture she'd memorized years ago came to mind. *"I can do all things required of me, through the help of Jesus Christ my Lord."*

Oh man, I have a long way to go.

But I will take a step, even if it's a baby step.

Another thought. Was it Scripture? Yes, Eunice had taught it. *"She who is faithful in little, will be faithful in much."*

After supper, Eunice tidied the kitchen, then she and Henry went to the garden center for flowers. He would take the chance there'd be no more frost. Of course, the pansies could handle the cold, even snow. With the back of the car loaded down, they returned home. He went out back to get started while Eunice went inside to brew a pot of coffee.

Upon entering the kitchen, she saw the light blinking on the answering machine. She punched a button and heard Ruby's voice. "Eunice. This is Ruby. I'm calling to see what time would be convenient for me and Annette and Lara to stop by. We could come some evening or Saturday morning."

Ruby left her number. The phone stopped blinking, but the red one remained, indicating an old message.

Eunice took the coffee from the refrigerator, scooped out enough for several cups, emptied it into the filter, then poured water into the pot. This was her favorite pot. The only glass part about it was the thin rib with a little red ball that revealed the water line. The coffee brewed noiselessly. No steam escaped. After a short while, the coffee was ready. Only when she unscrewed the lid would the aroma and steam waft forward.

The red light went off. The coffee was ready.

Eunice poured a cup, put cream in it, and took it out to Henry. He was lining the beds with the plastic containers of flowers in the spots where they would go. Eunice approved the arrangement. He gulped down the coffee and handed the cup to her.

She went back inside. The old message needed to be answered. She dialed the number. One of Ruby's girls answered in what sounded like a struggle. Finally, Ruby said, "Hello," above the din in the background.

"I know you girls work," Eunice said after the preliminary greeting. "Some evening or Saturday morning would be fine with me."

Saturday morning.

Eunice laid the phone in its cradle and started the message again so she could press the DELETE button. After a few minutes, she went out back with a cup of coffee, afghan, and a house decorating magazine.

By that time, Henry was digging a hole beyond the patio and yard in the far bed. Eunice settled back in the lounge chair on the deck with the afghan to ward off the evening chill in the air. She sipped her coffee and wondered if the kitchen needed a new look.

A new thought occurred. Would Henry keep preaching, or would he retire afterward? The house belonged to the church, not them. Would Henry move? Oh my, they'd have to talk about such things, wouldn't they?

Time was flying. She took another sip and put the cup and the magazine on the table beside her. She lay back, enjoying the feel of the evening sun on her face. For a moment her eyes scanned the myriad trees with their new spring leaves softly decorating the mountainsides with a light red, yellow, and green hue. Her gaze moved to her beloved husband.

She had so much to do, to think about, with Henry and those three friends. The time was set. She could call it off. Before long, it would be too late. Did she really want to know—before she died?

She had terminal cancer.

Five months maximum to live.

She could even die in August.

A laugh of irony caught in her throat. It wouldn't be the first time she'd died in August.

God, do You want to give me a miracle and let me live?

Skepticism replaced faith.

God had supposedly given her a miracle eons ago. That miracle looked upon as God's favor hadn't been that. She was the only one who knew it.

Or. . .was she?

What about Henry? He never mentioned the truth. Did he know the truth that came about, not just nineteen but thirty-eight years ago?

Why had she done what she did?

Was it because she and Henry would likely never have a child? The doctor said there was no reason she couldn't. She didn't mention it to Henry.

Was there some latent resentment that led to what she did?

Eunice closed her eyes, and she was young again. Another town. She was not on a deck but on a concrete patio.

Avery had lost his wife and son in a car accident. He'd been driving. A terrible thing. He'd left that church and that city and become Henry's music director. Tears would come into his eyes. He and Henry spent time together. A healing time, Henry said. They'd sit on the back patio, and Eunice would serve him lemonade in the summer, hot chocolate in the winter by the fire in the study.

Avery had beautiful eyes. She was thirty-three and he was twenty-eight.

When the choir sang, when she sang, she was more aware of his blue eyes than the words of the hymns. She knew the songs by heart. She was learning his eyes.

A couple of years passed. The hurt in his eyes lessened. He was being healed. He and Henry had become close. Avery was a staff member. Always at the staff meetings. Always consulting Henry because the songs and the sermon needed to go together.

Another year passed. He learned to smile.

One Friday morning, Henry got a frantic call from his mother saying his dad had a stroke. As soon as Eunice could throw some things in a bag, Henry left in her car because his was almost out of gas. He would be back as soon as possible. Five hours later he called, saying his dad was in critical condition. He would let her know if she needed to come. His mom might need her more later on. He said she should let the church staff know there'd be no meeting at the house that night. The associate pastor might need to deliver the sermon on Sunday.

"Mom needs me to be here tonight. I'll call you in the morning. Don't worry. I love you."

"I love you, too."

Whatever happened to "I can't breathe without you. I love you so much." Whatever happened to the passion? When did it all become so commonplace that they could both say "I love you" like "pour me a cup of coffee" or "time to go to bed" because they were tired?

The first big church with more staff and more responsibilities?

Is that what did it?

Familiarity?

It was a good thing, wasn't it?

The heat inside her corresponded with the high temperatures. It came in waves like the flashes lighting the sky. To cool off, she stripped down to nothing but shorts and a tank top. The fewer clothes, the better. But she knew to take her beach robe with her. You never knew who would show up at a preacher's house. She'd grown used to it. She liked that, being needed, most of the time. Sometimes she wanted privacy.

She lay in the lounge chair and sipped lemonade through a straw and dared the lightning to strike her. It was far away. She wasn't worried about being struck. She just needed to cool off. A slight breeze stirred.

She lay back in the lounge chair.

She watched the clouds roiling, fascinated.

She heard the voice. She knew the voice. She felt the shadow as it fell across her. The patio had been alternately blotted with dark and light as the fast-moving clouds gathered.

"I knocked," he said. "I saw Henry's car in the driveway. The front door was open. I came on through the house and thought he might be out here."

He sure was talking fast.

She didn't jump up. Nor reach for her robe. Had she forgotten Avery would stop by to see if the songs he picked out coincided with Henry's theme for Sunday's sermon?

"That's all right," Eunice said. "A preacher's house is an open house, you know. Twenty-four hours a day."

His blue eyes, his beautiful blue eyes looked past her as if not sure where to settle.

"Pull up a chair, Avery."

He did.

She sat up then, on the side of the lounge chair. His nostrils flared slightly. Was he embarrassed?

She was burning up.

He had beautiful lips.

She'd watched them sing at practice, at meetings, in her home, on Sundays, in memory.

"Henry's dad had a stroke. Henry went immediately. He took my car since it had gas in it and the tires are better."

"Charleston?" Avery asked.

"Yes, he's going to call in the morning and let me know how things are."

"I'm sorry," he said.

She nodded. She realized he'd asked the location before he said he was sorry.

She felt a drop of rain. She saw a bead of rain on his forehead, over his upper lip? Was it. . .rain?

"It's been such a hot day." She looked up at the sky.

When she glanced at him, his eyes quickly averted to the sky. "The forecast says it's going to blow in, stick around awhile, and could cause some damage."

A warning.

Big drops of rain began to spot her legs, her tank top, her arms, her face, the patio.

He jumped up.

Eunice laughed, stood, and lifted her face to the faster-falling drops. "Oh, this feels good."

He laughed. He didn't do that often. His face relaxed. His blue eyes lingered on her face instead of moving away.

His eyes swept over her. "You're getting wet."

The downpour came. The lightning struck closer. The thunder crashed and rolled and threatened.

She jumped at the crash, picked up her glass and robe. "Oh, some of the windows are open."

"I'll help you," he said.

They went into the kitchen and closed the windows. "Others are open," she said. They hurried to the living room.

He closed the front windows. She, the side ones. She saw his car parked behind Henry's car.

He said, "Are the windows down in Henry's car?"

"Oh, probably," she said. "He doesn't like air-conditioning and sometimes forgets to roll them up."

Avery rushed out and rolled them up.

He came back in.

Eunice closed the front door just as a spray of rain came in. “Oh, you’re soaked.” He was dripping on the hardwood floor.

A loud clap of thunder sounded quite close. She automatically reached out and touched his arm.

“Maybe you have a towel.” His hair was dripping into his eyes.

“Come on.” She led him to the bathroom, switched on the light, got a towel, and began to blot him.

She looked up. “It’s a beautiful storm,” she whispered.

“You’re a beautiful woman.” His eyes swept over her. His blue eyes. His beautiful blue eyes.

“Here, let me dry you,” he said, although she hadn’t done more than blot his light blue, short-sleeved shirt he wore with slacks.

His eyes were burning her flesh. This was a wet T-shirt night. The towel roamed over her arms. His blue eyes found hers. Then the towel brushed over her top, down to her waist, down her shorts. He knelt and the towel roamed over her legs. At the same time the crash of thunder sounded right at them, the lights went out. Lightning flashed at the windows, giving glimpses of him.

He tossed the towel aside and his lovely hands. . .

They were alone. No one would come in the storm. The door locked automatically when it closed. The storm was to last awhile, he’d said.

Yes, she hoped it never ended. What a beautiful storm. Full of beautiful blue eyes admiring her. You’re beautiful. I want you. Hands in the dark, with an occasional glimpse when the lightning shown against the windows.

Blissful desperation as if they were part of the storm itself. Such abandon. She hadn’t been swept away like that in. . .ages.

Being one with the storm.

His moans, matched by her own.

What a beautiful storm.

She lay on her stomach finally, her energy spent, listening to the storm, the rain against the windows, the thunder crash, the wind, and she felt a coolness settle over her, drying the perspiration.

She reveled in it. . .did not open her eyes, simply lay on her stomach and let the perspiration evaporate into the air, cooling her. She did not wish to hurry the feeling away. Let it subside with the storm. She relaxed into the storm, exhausted, spent, satisfied, pleased.

Then came the silence.

Everything was still.

Her eyes opened to the darkness. No light shown from around the window. Something. . .lay on her. She felt it. Yes, it seemed to be the bedspread from the other side of the bed. She did not feel hot. Rather, she felt, even beneath the coverlet on a summer's night, quite. . .icy.

Her nakedness had been covered.

She heard a sound.

She must have dreamed it all.

Making sure the coverlet stayed on top of her, she turned toward the doorway. Faint light shone from somewhere down the hallway. She must have dreamed it.

Then a silhouette appeared in the doorway.

She must still be dreaming.

"I. . .have to go," his rich voice said, full of uncertainty.

"Are your clothes wet?"

A short laugh. "That's okay." An intake of breath, then, "I don't know what to say."

She hoped he wouldn't say he was sorry. She didn't want to say it. A million excuses hung in the balance on the scale of truth.

She would think about it later.

She pulled the cover up to make sure it covered what he

claimed was beautiful, where he had. . . It never happened.

The silhouette seemed to nod, as if agreeing.

It turned away. It walked toward the faint light and disappeared. A soft click sounded, followed by the car starting.

Clutching the spread in her fists, she sat in the darkened guest room. A guest in her own home. An unwanted guest, thinking of *The Fall of the House of Usher.*

It hadn't happened.

After he left, that phantom, that figment of her imagination, that dream, that fantasy, Eunice slipped off the bed, found a robe in the closet, and shrugged into it.

The blinds in the kitchen were open. No homes were really near. Their house sat on a corner, a little higher than the neighbors. If anyone had looked, they would have seen Henry's car in the driveway. It was still there. Just his. No one else knew he had left town in her car. Nobody needed to know what time he left.

Anyone passing by, looking, would think Henry and Avery had been discussing music and sermons.

The electricity was off. The electricity had played itself out. She couldn't make tea.

She walked into the living room and looked out the window. Far down the valley, she could see car lights, like eyes, crawling along the mountainside.

Was that. . .him?

The eerie light of evening turned to darkness. She stumbled in the dark, seeking a candle. The trembling oval led a shadowy path to the bedroom. She set the candle on the dresser, where its flame flickered as she wadded the bedspread and her clothes into a bundle. She must take them to the washing machine. Instead, she dropped them to the floor and ran out into the hallway, where she leaned against the wall as if trying to press herself into it and hide.

Without electricity, she could not wash away the stains. . .of sin.

No. It never happened.

The next morning, Henry called and said, "My dad died."

She might have said, *He's not the only one. In a moment of such passionate living, something in me died, or was it something begging to live?*

I can sin.

I am a sinner.

I enjoyed that sin.

I can never again be sure I won't sin. Oh, I won't sin that way again, but there are millions of ways.

"I'm sorry, Henry."

"I'll let you know when we have any details settled here. Call Jerry and let him know I can't be there Sunday, will you?"

"Of course."

Yes, she'd call Jerry. He would tell the other staff. She would drive to Charleston. . .no, she would fly. Then she could drive back with Henry. He would need her.

His dad died.

That was an anniversary she would remember, marked indelibly on hers and Henry's minds, on their mental calendar.

That's the day Henry's dad died.

And so did I.

Her mother had raised her on the saying, "You make your bed, you lie on it."

Eunice read it in the book of Isaiah. He wrote about there being no place of refuge. The bed one made was too short to lie on. The blankets were too narrow to cover you.

Accusations were all through the Bible. You reap what you sow. The Lord Almighty is a wonderful teacher.

Yes. . .just as she'd heard through the years that a good preacher, a good teacher, steps on your toes, wrenches your heart, she knew the Lord Almighty is a good teacher. She learned a lesson from a wonderful teacher. . .never to be forgotten?

Her mind was in constant debate, eventually acknowledging she had no excuses or reasons.

She'd heard the "Why?" questions time and again.

Why did God let my son die?

Because he took that overdose of drugs.

Why did God let her be run over by a drunk driver?

Because the driver had freedom of choice and chose wrongly and your daughter was in his path.

Why this?

Because I did what I wanted to do in that frenzied moment.

I knew. I was no innocent child. I played with temptation from the moment I looked into those blue eyes and saw the challenge. I could have admitted it, not smiled at his glances.

There have been others whose eyes have questioned and my attitude or words said no, we don't go there.

You're lovely.

Thank you and move the attention to something else.

With him I said, "Thank you," and smiled and let my gaze linger a second. That's all it takes. A fraction of a second.

The eyes are the mirror of the soul. Play with fire. I didn't intend to play with fire and get burned.

Yes, the Lord is a wonderful teacher.

Don't commit adultery.

Don't play with fire.

Make your bed.

Sow. . .and reap.

Put your hand to the plow and look back and you're not fit for the kingdom.

Nothing can separate you from the love of God.

I thought I was getting old at thirty-five. I was young when the storm began.

I was old when it ended.

I grew wise.

Know yourself!

I do.

So I know others.

I am weak, but He is strong.

Jesus keep me from all wrong.

I have to let Him. I must call on Him when storms approach. Before they approach. Don't stand out in the rain.

Or the lightning.

Or the thunder.

He promised never to leave me. Never to leave me alone.

She no longer knew the definition of "unfaithful" and "adultery."

She'd known it all her life. . .before. But now, she searched her heart, her life, the Scripture. God called Israel an adulterer. He called Israel unfaithful. And yet, King David committed adultery, his punishment was that his baby died, but David repented and he was still a man after God's own heart. David had sinned. He did not continue in his sin.

Israel continued to disobey God, to turn to idols, to disobey. Unfaithful and adultery seemed like words used to describe a lifestyle, a continuation of turning from God. She had not done that. She sinned. Once. Well, her heart and mind led up to it by remaining in a tempting situation. But the act, the sinful act, occurred once. Only once. She was sorry. She begged forgiveness. She returned to Henry, the man she loved. God's chosen for her. They belonged together. She never doubted that. The other had been. . .what? A temptation she hadn't yielded to as a teenager.

She'd been tempted as a teenager? The unknown. The forbidden. The great experience that was so precious one saved themselves for it. The one great forbidden thing that so tempted and taunted mankind. . .they risked marriages, families for it. They abused others for it. It could become so overwhelming that some even murdered and killed for it.

Even preachers, called servants of God, who knew the temptations, the penalties, lost families, respect of their followers, because of becoming involved in a sexual experience. . .not love, but sex.

That was something Eunice never yielded to as a teenager, as a young adult, as a maturing woman. Not until she was halfway between thirty and forty. Why? She had wanted him. He had wanted her. They both knew it.

They played with fire.

She got burned.

Her and Henry's sadness could be explained. His dad had died; her father-in-law had died. Church members had storm damage such as downed trees, parts of roofs blown off, damaged homes. Henry's beloved flowerbeds were demolished.

But Eunice knew. The girl, the wife, the woman he'd known wasn't there. She went through the motions, automatically doing the things she'd done for years. Only her heart was missing. His tender, loving, brown eyes turned sad. He turned quiet and thoughtful. They both did what they had to do but watched TV in silence, not even commenting about the condition of the world.

Then one day when there seemed not a cloud in the sky, the rain came. Her eyes flooded. "Is anything wrong, Eunice?" he asked kindly.

"No, Henry," she said. That wasn't a lie. Anything wasn't wrong. Everything was wrong.

With the hurt of the world on his face, he reached out and took her hand. He led her to the bedroom, where they lay on the bed while the rain beat against the roof and streamed down the window panes.

"Let's talk," he said.

No, Henry, her whole being shouted. *Divorce me, but please don't make me talk.*

She waited.

"I've been thinking, Eunice. When I had that staff meeting here at the house the other night, you said you wouldn't be here but would be going to visit Mrs. Hawkins in the hospital."

He said it kept going through his mind that she wouldn't be there to answer the doorbell, greet the guests, welcome them in, serve them coffee and a piece of cake.

He told himself he could do that, of course. It's just. . .she'd always done it. It was a habit, a ritual, expected.

He looked at her when she was ready to leave and did the usual. He went up to her with his arms open wide. She came into them, and he gave her a peck of a kiss.

That was habit. . .and a ritual, expected.

He'd gone to the window, lifted a slat of the aluminum mini-blind. He looked at her walking to her car. The girl he married was a beautiful woman. He'd known it, accepted it, taken it for granted.

Like some habit. . .or ritual.

The meeting wasn't as jovial as usual. Maybe because of the talk of the storm, the damage. One of George's trees was uprooted, a limb fell on electric lines, and he was several days without electricity. Some of the roof tiles blew off of Jerald's house. A shutter came loose from Don's. No damage to Avery's apartment. He looked like he wasn't feeling too well, but he stayed.

Henry thought himself fortunate. No storm damage to his

house, or cars, or trees, although his flowerbeds were demolished. They could be replaced.

The meeting hadn't been the same without Eunice, although she didn't get involved in their discussions. She just served them, made them smile, and they in turn brought a light into her eyes, made her smile, made her feel important about the cake, the cookies, and the coffee.

That was the first time since they had married that Eunice wasn't by his side at a meeting like that. She was always home with him, his helpmate, his support. . .because. . .he was the preacher.

Was this going to become a habit. . .a ritual?

"I've taken you for granted, Eunice. I'm sorry. Forgive me."

She felt the wetness in her hair from the tears that ran down the sides of her face. "No, Henry, it's—"

"Please," he said. "Let me feel the guilt. I'm human. Not above those who look to me as if I know all the answers. There's danger in that, danger of pride. I need to remember that the Holy Spirit guides the ladies in the nursery. Their changing a baby's diaper is a ministry, just as important as the ministry of one who stands in the pulpit commenting on God's Word. Keep me humble, aware. Love me."

"I do love you, Henry. More than anything."

He'd held her. Close to his chest. He was her comfort, her strength.

The next thing she knew, she was being awakened by Henry calling, "Eunice. Come look."

He took her hand and led her out on the porch, then into the yard. They stared into the sky. Eunice could hardly get her breath. A rainbow haloed the earth with the most glorious colors she had ever seen.

"God's promise," Henry said. "There will never be a flood again. No storm like that."

"Yes," Eunice agreed.

They stood with their arms around each other's waist, looking into a sky from which the rainbow faded. But it remained in her heart, in her mind, and she would never forget God's promise. Such a storm would not occur again.

She had asked, and He had forgiven.

She was pure. Clean.

She lived the words of the song that said sometimes God calms the storm, sometimes He calms me.

The hymn was all about being washed in the blood of the Lamb, garments being spotless, white as snow, and it implored that one be washed in the soul-cleansing blood of the Lamb.

Her blood stopped four months ago.

When she'd begun to show, Henry said, "Can we tell the congregation? Can we tell them about the miracle that God has granted us? Would you want to tell them?"

Her emotions crumbled. Her body slumped. He held her against his chest. She sobbed. "Oh, Henry. I love you so. Don't ever doubt that. You haven't, have you?"

"No," he said and smoothed her hair until she thought it must surely be plastered to her head. "You are my love. My only love from the moment I laid eyes on you. I asked God to send the right woman to me, and He did. I've never doubted that. You have taught me so much."

What, Henry? Not just to preach about forgiveness, but to do it? Do you know? But she dared not say those words.

She was forgiven, but there were still consequences to human behavior, their choices.

Finally she lifted her face to his without looking into his eyes. "You tell them, Henry."

"Yes," he said.

She moved away. She started to turn, but he caught her arm. With his big, gentle hands, he tenderly wiped the wetness from her cheeks, from under her eyes. She looked up at him through soggy eyelashes. He smiled. He wiped away her tears, not bothering to wipe away his own.

He put his hand on her abdomen. "I will tell the congregation."

Now, still, Eunice sang as she had done all of her life—her previous life that is. In the choir, she sang, never meeting those blue eyes but knowing them.

And yes, her robe was clean. It covered everything. One choir member looked no different from another. One couldn't judge them according to their shape or size or what they wore. They're in uniform. All wearing clean robes. They just opened their mouths and sang, all looking the same. Choir members have said they felt like the congregation stared at them. The congregation said they felt like the choir members stared at them.

Now she knew.

It was just her, staring at herself. She saw her soul, her life, as God saw it, and it wasn't pretty.

You're beautiful.

No. I'm a sinner.

Saved by grace.

Yes, but I feel the guilt. I am a hypocrite.

Don't the pastors all say that churches are full of saved sinners?

Yes, but that was past. We were sinners before we were saved. After being saved, we're to obey, obey the rules and commands. The Holy Spirit in us is to prevent our being like unbelievers.

Did you call on the Holy Spirit. . .when. . .before. . . ?

No. That's not what I wanted.

Learn. . .about the Holy Spirit.

I know enough. . .the Bible says you can quench the Spirit, grieve the Spirit, refuse to listen, refuse to obey.

Yes. . .could you do that if the Holy Spirit were not in you?

No. I know the Holy Spirit is in me. I also know. . .I am weak.

I am weak, but thou art strong. Jesus, keep me from all wrong. I've sung it. I thought He would. I took Him for granted. I thought I was. . .above. . .the weak, sinful, hypocritical, saved sinner.

"Know yourself," the Scriptures admonish.

Oh my, I've learned. I don't like it. But God, You know I did like that night while it was happening. While it was leading up to it.

You knew it was leading up to it?

I didn't let myself believe it, but I thrilled at looking into those blue, blue eyes. I thrilled at watching his mouth form the words. At his voice so rich and resonant. At his handsome face. I sympathized at his aloneness, his being young. . .he was young to me because I was five years older, midthirties. His being widowed, having lost a wife and child, I told myself it was his pain I responded to. And it was. It was. But I responded to him as a man who was needy. I liked to think he found me attractive. I, on my way to forty.

I was like two people. The one that housed the Holy Spirit and had right motives. I was also the one who was tantalized by temptation, by worldly thoughts. So I found him attractive. Didn't people, good Christians, go around saying just because you're married doesn't mean you're blind? You know a good-looking man when you see one. And they'd laugh. Innocently.

She could laugh as innocently as anyone else, but she never said those things. She had to be above them. She was the preacher's wife. The one they came to for counsel, to listen while she taught the revelations of God from the Bible, who told them how to live, how to overcome temptation, the right things to do. She was the teacher. The above-the-run-of-the-mill Christian. She was strong. Somehow, more spiritual than the others because she was the preacher's wife.

Henry had preached that the word *hypocrite* came from the

Greek word meaning *actor*.

She was an actor.

She had to play the part.

Henry looked around at her in the choir, then turned back toward the congregation.

"I have an announcement," he said before beginning his sermon. "Eunice and I are expecting a miracle child in about five months."

Congratulations came in the form of Nettie squeezing her right hand. Marge patted her left forearm. Eunice reached into the pocket of the robe for a tissue. They all knew to keep certain things in those pockets because their purses were locked in a choir closet, but they might need glasses, or a tissue, or a cough drop.

She got the tissue and swiped at her eyes, which were moist from the joy of carrying what Henry was describing as a miracle child.

It never happened.

She glanced out at the congregation. All eyes were on her. She was sure her eyes met each one, and a smile, or a nod, or a congratulatory look came into their eyes. She looked and saw. . .except she did not look into the blue eyes on the front row.

That was a silhouette sitting there, looking at his hands as if they were strange, with one laid over the other on top of the Bible. He didn't turn to the Scripture when Henry gave the book, chapter, and verse. He usually did. He had lovely hands, long fingers, smooth skin, like a creative person should have. She had thought he made beautiful music. He could play the piano. He could conduct a choir with a baton in one hand and the other hand empty.

Beautiful eyes. Beautiful hands. You're beautiful.

It never happened.

She didn't know what Henry preached about that morning. She closed her eyes to look like she was praying. She tried to concentrate. She had stopped reading his sermons and making suggestions. She had no right. He was the preacher. He was the called one. She wasn't called. What did she know? She didn't want to play the hypocrite any more than necessary.

Choir members stood. She was only a fraction slower than they. She stood, too, because those in front of her stood. She could hear the squeaks of the chairs behind her when the men stood and the seats were pushed back with their legs.

"I'm standing on the promises of Christ my Savior. . .standing. . .standing. . .standing on the promises. . . ."

She looked at the songbook. The hands and arms of the silhouette were moving, back and forth, up and down, in time with the organ and piano, and the voices responded automatically. She pantomimed this one. Her heart was too full to make sounds. They wouldn't possibly come out right.

Oh, Lord. Oh, God.

It never happened.

Otherwise, the silhouette couldn't be up there. . .standing. . . with his arms moving in time with the organ and piano and the voices.

That proved it.

Afterward, she was swamped with well-wishers. She was the heroine of the day. . .the year. She was going to be a mother.

Henry was going to be a daddy.

They were having a miracle child.

What a wonderful day.

The silhouette didn't come into the choir room. He usually did and told them what a great job they did. They liked hearing that. His praise encouraged and brought them back for practice after practice. Be worthwhile. Accomplish something. Serve the

Lord. Give glory to the Lord. He must have gotten stopped by someone wanting to chat.

It never happened.

A few weeks after he announced to the congregation that he and Eunice were pregnant, Henry came home for lunch. He didn't always do that. Sometimes he went out with staff. Sometimes he went to a fast-food place and sat where someone he knew would come in, and they'd talk.

She fixed them both a sandwich. He said, "Avery talked to me this morning."

She thought her baby gave a mighty leap, kicked, warned. *No, don't mention it. It's nerves. An unborn baby doesn't know things. . . like that.*

What did Avery talk about? Why did Henry come home to tell her? Henry didn't reveal what others came to talk to him about in private. He did not reveal his congregation's secrets or sins. When someone was ill or needed prayer, he would tell her. He did not tell about their problems. He might say, "Pray for Jim and his son. Pray for Mary and her situation." He did not say what the situation was.

Sometimes Eunice heard about it from another church member but never from Henry. He was loyal. He was. . .faithful. . .to his calling.

She glanced at Henry, who glanced at his sandwich and took a bite.

She didn't ask. Just waited.

Henry chewed, swallowed, washed it down with a gulp of coffee, then spoke. "He has an offer from a big church up in Philadelphia."

"Philadelphia?" She looked at him.

Henry glanced at her, then back at his sandwich. "Yes. A

friend he went to seminary with is the pastor of the church. Their music director left. He asked Avery to come visit and see what happens from there."

"You think he. . ." She didn't want to say Avery's name. "Wants to go?"

Henry nodded. "Yes. Otherwise he wouldn't have mentioned it to me. He's preparing me. I think he wants to do the right thing. He, um, seems to think this might be it."

Henry ate a little more. Eunice waited. She chewed slowly.

"He's discontented," Henry said. "I could see it in his eyes, hear it in his voice. He needs a change. I think it might be a good thing."

Eunice felt that, too. She mustn't say it. "We'd have to find someone to. . ." She started to say, "to take his place." No, no one took another's place. "To fill the position."

"Yes," he said. He got up and took his cup over to the pot. Normally, he would hold out his cup and ask her to pour him another cup. Since she became pregnant, he did much more for himself and for her.

"You want more?" he asked.

"No, I still have mine."

When she felt another leap inside her stomach, Eunice's hand shook. When she lifted her cup again, she saw a small curve of brown had stained the tablecloth. Without thinking, she touched it with her finger. It was wet, and the simple touch made the stain spread farther.

She quickly set the cup over it. When she picked it up again, she wondered if Henry saw the mess she'd made.

If he did, he didn't say anything about it.

Eunice had wondered how people lived with themselves after something like she'd done. Now she knew. Just. . .don't accept it. Live in denial. Eventually be able to ask God's forgiveness and believe the sin has been thrown into the deepest ocean.

Hadn't Henry preached about sin? He said things like the real you being your lifetime, your lifestyle—not the failures but the successes. He said focus on the years you have loved and served the Lord, not on the times you have disobeyed and betrayed Him.

Eunice must focus on the years she had been faithful, not on that one stormy night.

Many times she wondered if he suspected, if he knew. But she never had seen a moment of doubt in his eyes. Never a moment of accusation. How could she hurt him by telling him? What would that accomplish? Pain!

No. If the child came deformed, maybe she would tell him she was being punished. She would accept the punishment. She would take the blame.

The child was born. . .perfect.

A perfect little girl was born to a crippled mother.

Eunice had thought of naming her Charity. That was another word for love.

Henry said no. Her name should be Dove. She was a gift from heaven.

The dove was a symbol of the Holy Spirit. Henry had given up hope of having a child. When he said Dove, she knew that was her name.

She was a special child. She was Henry's miracle child. The light of his life. Dove, he said, sounded like love. "And she came from the love of my life, Eunice," Henry had said softly, looking at her with tender eyes.

Dove became the light of his life. After she was born, he no longer had church staff come on Fridays but handled all church business in his office away from the parsonage.

Eunice never again had a personal conversation with Avery, nor did they make eye contact. Not even that Friday evening when she walked out of the nursery with the baby, not realizing Avery was there.

The moment she saw a flash of blue, she stopped in the doorway of the study and focused on the baby. Avery stood and made some kind of apology about disturbing them, but Maria had laryngitis and wouldn't be able to sing the special song on Sunday.

Eunice knew he had to be polite and come over to her. His back was to Henry. He reached out and touched the baby's soft pink cheek with his long, graceful fingers. She heard his breath.

Maybe she felt it. She kept her eyes on Dove.

He whispered, "She's. . .m—"

Eunice stopped breathing. What was he saying?

He finished the word. "She's music."

Was she? Or was she thunder and lightning? At three weeks old, she already displayed a temper.

"Dove," he said.

Fearing he would ask to hold her, Eunice walked around him and placed the baby in Henry's arms, which outstretched when she neared. His face was sunshine. The time for her feeding was near. Henry said that a mother feeding her baby was one of the most beautiful pictures in the world.

Avery must have sensed he was an intruder. He didn't return to his seat but said he had to be going.

He never gave any clue that he had anything to say, to ask, until the night of his appreciation reception on Sunday evening in the church fellowship hall. He would be leaving for Philadelphia the following morning.

Eunice had taken Dove into the nursery to change her diaper before going down to the hall. When she came out of the nursery, she saw Avery in the hallway alone. She felt he had known where she was and had waited for her. Laughter and talking sounded from on the floor below them.

She headed for the stairs. He fell in step.

She felt the blue. She would not look.

"Is she mine?" he whispered.

Like lightning, the blue disappeared, and she saw the back of him step ahead of her and rush down the stairs when she replied, "She's mine."

Dove was the most beautiful baby anyone had ever seen, including mothers with their own babies. People used to say to Dove when she was a toddler, "Where did you get those beautiful blue eyes and that blond hair?"

Henry would answer, "Oh, I think there are blue-eyed blond beauties in most families somewhere along the line."

Eunice just laughed lightly as if that were a rhetorical question. She supposed it was, since Dove couldn't tell them. She began to teach Dove to say, "God gave them to me."

The little girl with platinum-blond fine hair like strands of silk and brilliant blue eyes stole the hearts of any who saw her. Any flaw that might have been in her went unnoticed by those blinded by her beauty, which rivaled the young woman written about in Song of Songs. Her brilliant blue eyes sparkled like jewels in the sun. Her cheeks were the blush of a ripe peach. Her lips were young rose petals opening to the morning dew. She had a golden voice that radiated like the sun on her hair.

Eunice raised her the best she could. She was Daddy's girl. She rode on his shoulders. They wrestled on the floor. They planted gardens and watched them grow. They planted flowers and brought bouquets to Eunice. They lifted their faces to the rain in spring and stomped in puddles. Henry never missed a chance to credit God with blessings and made sure Dove knew about her Creator and the Sustainer of Life.

Henry taught her fun things. Oh, Eunice was in it, too, but she was more the disciplinarian, the teacher of responsibilities and chores. Eunice returned to teaching school after Dove started kindergarten. She taught Dove to cook, and they'd have surprises for Henry when he came home from church—either a special dish Dove had made or they'd go out to eat.

They had resisted allowing her to be in beauty contests as many encouraged. In high school, however, she was elected homecoming queen each year. Her beautiful face graced the school yearbooks, the local papers, and she shone like the sun even in black and white.

She had a following and was loved, like Henry. Although tall like Eunice and well endowed, she had an air of innocence about her that attracted.

She was a good girl. She sang solos, attended church every time the doors were open, made the community and church proud that a girl could be both a Christian and a beauty. She signed a pledge during a program for abstinence from sex before marriage.

But Eunice detected a rebellious streak in Dove. Henry thought it was normal teenage behavior, and perhaps it was, but that was no trivial matter. That's the time when young people made mistakes from which they might never recover.

She worried when Henry accepted the pastorate in Laurel Ridge. What would such a change do to a girl starting her freshman year in high school? She needn't have worried. Very fine Christian girls, Annette and Ruby, became her closest friends. Then Lara, who had come only occasionally with her grandmother, became a regular attendee and a part of their foursome.

Henry said, "Train up a child in the way she should go and when she is old she will not depart from it."

But Dove had a lot of years between seventeen and old.

Eunice hoped and prayed Dove would get through her young years and go into maturity without having made wrong choices that would bring her guilt and dishonor. But how could Eunice tell Dove how vulnerable a person could be? If she told her what she did, even as a mature, thirty-five-year-old preacher's wife, then Dove would question.

"How do you know, Mama? Did you sin? What did you do? When? Oh, you were an exemplary teenager? You never submitted to temptation? Then what makes you think I would? Huh?"

Once, after Eunice had reprimanded her for staying out late,

Dove laughed. “Mama, haven’t you ever been seventeen?”

Eunice couldn’t say, “No, not until I was thirty-five.”

Dove knew right from wrong. She knew the Word of God. She’d proclaimed Jesus Christ as her Savior and Lord. She was kind to others. She loved others.

Eunice wondered about herself. Had she been too sheltered as a young person? Had she not allowed herself to be young enough, have fun enough? Had she been too serious? Was that the reason. . . ?

She trusted her daughter. Henry trusted their daughter. She was his sun, moon, and stars.

Their years with Dove were good, wonderful.

She began to move away from them physically and emotionally, but that had to be. How else could she ever make it on her own?

She often stayed overnight with friends after starting college. Her grades dropped some the second semester, but she still made Bs and Cs. Eunice suspected. . .no, she wouldn’t let herself suspect. She only suspected not because of Dove but because of what she knew had lain in her own realm of possibilities.

Dove, over eighteen then, still asked permission to go to the beach after that first year of college. They needed a break. And she was going with her three friends. She’d spent nights with them before right there in town, so what was so different about a six-hour drive to the coast?

They were all over eighteen, good Christian girls. Annette was the smartest of them, a leader, pretty and popular, active in church. Lara had a classic face and the figure of a model, quite artistic, very confident, the granddaughter of a woman whose generous financial gifts were known to all the church members and likely the townsfolk, too. Ruby was the life of any party, a straightforward girl with no pretense. She always joked and laughed and said she was a professional cheerleader who made no money, but as long as she got to jump up and down and yell, that was payment enough. Ruby made others feel good about themselves because she was always talking about being able to do nothing with her hair or explaining that her mouth was too big but it needed to be because she usually had both feet in it. Ruby was a good, strong alto. She sometimes sang with Dove.

Charlie was already a member of the choir, recognized as being one of the better singers. He sometimes sang with Dove and Ruby. When Dove went through a troublesome time she wouldn't talk about, she didn't sing. Ruby and Charlie sang together. Those girls were Dove's friends. Why shouldn't they go to the beach together?

Afterward. . .

Afterward. . .Eunice felt someone needed to pay.

Those friends who were there but claimed to know nothing didn't deserve to have happy lives, did they?

Why did they come back when her child didn't?

Why didn't they save her child?

Why didn't God save her child?

For a while she thought Henry wouldn't be able to stand it. He suffered. He cried all the time. In his sermons, he said the right things. He said the scriptural things. He sounded so good, so right, and his faith was unshaken. But sometimes, he couldn't even hold back the tears in the pulpit.

Henry cried it out. He openly sobbed at home. He would get on his knees. He would get in the closet. He would cry out to God. He shouted, "Why?" He shouted, "It's not fair!"

Eunice would walk through the house or wash the dishes, her face getting more soaked than her hands, and it's a wonder her face hadn't shriveled up like a prune.

She would nod.

Then she would hear Henry crying out to God for forgiveness. He would say he understood how life was. He knew the Lord gave and the Lord took away. He knew people made their choices. He knew Dove was in a better place. But he wanted her here, now, forever.

Eunice did not nod when Henry told God it was all right.

It wasn't all right with her.

She felt cheated.

She harbored resentment in her heart.

And for the second time in her life, she kept a secret from Henry.

She did not tell him about the note she had found the night before the funeral, underneath Dove's pillow.

Eunice lived in a fog for a long time. Summer passed, and she returned to the classroom and her other activities. She went through the motions and did her duties automatically. Winter came, as if it hadn't already ruled and reigned in her heart for months. Yes, she begged the Lord. People said they didn't know how people could get through things without the Lord. She did. They could find escapes with drugs or drink or activity. They could cease to care about anyone, even God. They could live in misery.

She credited God for getting her through it, although she knew it was an endless river and she was forever walking in it, unable to get to the other side. Life flowed around her while she stood still because she didn't want to dishonor Henry or the Lord. They sustained her. . .but for what?

She did not want the bitterness, the resentment and was afraid of what she might do or say when she confronted those girls who were supposed to be Dove's friends.

Guilty ones look away when you stare at them, she'd heard.

They all did. At the funeral, she'd said, "I want the truth."

They never came to give it. She didn't trust herself to ask again for a long time. She could not speak of it. By the time she found her tongue, the girls had begun their happily-ever-after lives, while her precious Dove lay cold in the ground. It was as if they danced upon her grave, trampled her memory. Did they not care? Did they not suffer? Shouldn't they suffer?

For what?

That's what she needed to find out.

But Lara left the church, married Jared in a ceremony at the church her parents attended in Asheville. Eunice and Henry were invited. Henry shook his head when he saw the invitation, and tears welled up in his eyes. Eunice feared what she might say or do, so they didn't attend.

Lara and Jared honeymooned in Hawaii, then went immediately to Europe, where he would operate the successful business his dad had built up. Lara would study and become a famous artist.

Then there were two—Annette and Ruby.

When each married, Eunice felt a sadness, a jolt to her heart that her daughter would not have that happiness. Hardly before Eunice realized it, summer had ended. Her heart hurt when the engagement of Ruby and Charlie was announced. He was the kind of man she thought Dove might have married.

Henry performed the ceremony in the church parlor with family and only a few friends because they couldn't afford a big church wedding, and they were going to seminary. Eunice could have attended since she was the pastor's wife, but she didn't.

Then there was only one—Annette.

Eunice couldn't very well question Annette when she was planning her church wedding to the young man who had been her sweetheart for years. The wedding would take place in October, and Henry would perform the ceremony. The reception was held at the big Victorian house her parents left to her. Eunice felt obligated to go. She ate cake and drank punch and stood back like others, observing the happy pair so in love.

Then there were none.

Someday. . .

Someday.

She told herself to let it go, let it go.

Would Dove have married someone like Louis Billings? He'd been an exemplary young man, active in church, during his high school years. When he got a four-year scholarship to Western and stayed on campus, speculation was that his attentions might focus elsewhere. However, he came home many weekends and all holidays and entered into activities with his college-aged friends.

After he and Annette married, they lived at the bed-and-breakfast. He commuted the almost two-hour drive daily, and Annette dropped out to help her parents full time. A couple of months later, her parents moved to Florida.

They left the house to Annette. Some of the church people even helped when Louis and Annette began repairs on the beautiful but old place. Everyone knew their situation. Louis's parents had given him the money they'd saved for his college for a wedding present. After Annette's parents left, however, that amount began to dwindle quickly. She took a job at a local restaurant. Not long after that, she announced her pregnancy.

Louis graduated shortly after Tommy was born. He took one of the several jobs offered him at a computer firm in Asheville. Still military minded, he joined the army reserves.

During that period of Annette's happy family life, Eunice walked into Laurel Ridge's most exclusive women's apparel store during one of their big sales on to see if she might find something reasonably priced since her Sunday school class had given her a Lancaster's gift certificate for her birthday.

Eunice was looking through the blouses when she heard a cultured voice that had a familiar ring to it. "Can I help you with anything?"

She turned around. Her gaze met the shocked eyes of Lara Sharpton. No, she'd married Jared Gerard. Could she help Eunice? Why would Lara ask such a question? Sure she could. . . if she would.

"What. . .do you mean?" Eunice said.

Lara paled except for the deep red on her neck as if the blood had settled there. She swallowed hard, and her words came out stilted. In fact, her entire demeanor looked stiff. "I. . .work here."

Eunice felt her eyebrows shoot up.

Lara works here. She wouldn't ask why. That girl had been in her house many times. She'd been Dove's friend. She'd married well and had gone off to live happily every after. She was the kind who shopped at Lancaster's—not worked there.

Eunice lifted a blouse from the rack. "This one's pretty." As if the others weren't. Well, she wouldn't stand there and talk about blouses with the likes of Lara Gerard. She slipped the blouse back onto the rack. "How is your grandmother, Lara?"

"Not getting any better. That's one reason I came back. She said you'd been to see her."

"Yes. And are you back to stay?"

"I don't know," Lara said.

"Is your husband with you?"

"We're divorced."

Eunice should say she was sorry. But she really didn't know if she was at all. She didn't know the situation. She turned and pushed first one blouse aside, then another.

"Just. . .let me know if I can help you."

Eunice's hand stopped dead on the shoulder of the blouse. Her head lifted, and she looked straight ahead. Just let Lara know. . .if she could help. She'd tried that years ago. Lara never volunteered a thing. Slowly, Eunice turned to face Lara, who took a step back and looked as if she were thinking the same thing. Lara walked away. Eunice flipped through the blouse rack, determined to do what she came in here for in spite of Lara Gerard.

Divorced!

She'd returned to Laurel Ridge.

Now there are two—Annette and Lara.

When his boy was four, Louis joined the army. They would have a Realtor handle rentals for the big Victorian house that had been a bed-and-breakfast. Annette and Tommy would join Louis after his basic training, wherever he would be stationed. They hadn't reckoned with the Middle East nor the expanding uprisings.

Louis looked so handsome at church in his uniform and with his perfect family. Annette and Tommy stayed in the big house alone. When Tommy started kindergarten, Annette again became a waitress at the restaurant. Less than a year later, Annette was a widow. Tommy would never know his dad except in pictures and from what his mother would tell him.

Lara's and Annette's lives had not turned out so well.

Then Ruby returned.

Now there were three again—Annette, Lara, and Ruby.

Ruby's return prompted an old saying to occur to Eunice. Criminals often return to the scene of the crime.

What criminal? What crime?

Why such evil thoughts? Why any suspicion? She did not know what to be suspicious of.

Was it instinct?

What kind?

Of what?

She did not know what, and that was the problem.

Deep in her heart, she believed those three girls knew.

Eunice knew Ruby from the time she was a freshman in high school, when Henry had begun his ministry at Faith Church. Why was Ruby so uncomfortable after their return? Why did she never sing a solo or a duet with her husband. Was she angry with him? Or herself? Why could she not worship the Lord freely? What held her back? What secret thing did she harbor in her soul that prevented her from using her natural talent for the Lord?

Eunice asked Charlie if Ruby had sung solos when they were in Texas, and he said yes. She was just so busy now with the toddler. She felt her voice wasn't as good. She hadn't exercised it enough, and it faltered.

Eunice tried to accept that. Okay, that might very well happen in a solo, although she doubted it. But why not sing a duet with her husband? Ruby used to do it. She used to be so happy. So much changed after Dove's death. Could Ruby not get over the loss of her friend?

If not, why not?

Why were those three friends so uncomfortable around her?

The three of them were together again. Fixing up the Victorian house. Lara coming to church occasionally.

Eunice considered approaching them.

Things kept getting in the way. Lara's grandmother died. Ruby was pregnant again. She didn't work but stayed home to take care of her children, which Eunice admired. Charlie's salary wasn't all that much. They lived poorly. Charlie took a part-time job as a DJ at the local radio station. When Jill had appendicitis, the church took up an offering to pay the deductible on their insurance.

Would that have been her daughter's plight? Would Dove

have had children so close together that she became busy, poor, couldn't take care of her family without help? Why did Ruby let herself go? Why did she let herself gain weight? Would Eunice's daughter have done that? Was her daughter spared a life of hardship?

Why must she compare her daughter with those girls?

From all indications, Ruby was a good mother. She had no time for anything else, and there was nothing wrong with that, but she never taught a class at church. She was there all the time but never giving of herself. She had been asked to do many things but said she couldn't. She was simply supportive of her husband.

Eunice understood that to a certain extent. When she was Ruby's age, she'd felt her primary role was to be supportive of Henry. He was a messenger of God. She had accepted being childless through the years because her calling was to be a helpmate. She'd taught school for a while. They were her children. She taught Sunday school. She headed up the missionary society. Led prayer groups. Counseled young women who felt she could better understand their particular problem than Henry.

They were her children. She taught young women, ages seventeen until they married.

She'd taught the single young women.

Until the. . .accident that took her daughter's life.

Accident? There had to be a cause. You don't just drown and call it an accident. There's a reason. There's a reason in a car accident. A drunk driver? Speeding? Taking a curve too fast? Losing control for a reason? Inattention? Falling asleep? Fatigue?

Yes, it could be an accident. But there would still be a reason.

She didn't know the reason.

I want to know the reason.

Those girls know. They were there. Why won't they tell me?

A flash of green passed before Eunice's mental eyes.

The green was not the result of a sick woman's imagination or medication.

She still had it. Taped up in a cardboard box in the basement with other memories.

Would she have to show it to them to get the truth out of them?

She could.

The item had dried. But as easily as bringing up a file on a computer, her mind remembered the image as clearly as if this were nineteen years ago.

Green. Wet.

Dozing off and on, Eunice's mind reverted again to the past. Her attention to those girls' lives was diverted when she had been diagnosed with cancer in her pelvic area. She was in her sixties, middle-aged, supposedly in the prime of her life.

She would never say that all illnesses and trials are a person's fault or punishment. However, she knew one's state of mind affected his or her health. She must change hers. She must rid herself of guilt and resentment. She must let go of the past. There was nothing she could do to change the past. She didn't expect her recovery to be an easy journey.

She didn't have the desire to hang onto the burdensome depression that had caused a disease worse than cancer in her mind. She was young enough and had always been healthy. She went through the tests and treatments with faith, hope, joy, and Henry's insistence upon a miracle-working God.

He was so right. If God could cure her misery, guilt, and resentment, that would be a miracle.

After several months, she was considered cancer-free, in remission.

She could resume life. . .as usual.

No, it mustn't be as usual.

She would have to put feet to her prayers.

She empathized with others who lost loved ones. When unborn babies died and twice when little children had been killed. A church member's six-year-old boy on his new bike he'd just learned to ride flew out of the driveway right in front of a car that couldn't stop.

She and Henry had tried to console them, admit they, too, had lost a child. She and Henry quoted Scripture. They prayed.

Maybe it was when Dove's friends had losses that she began to realize her daughter would have gone through trials. Oh, yes. And Henry's heart would have been shattered if he knew about the note. Sometimes it wasn't good to tell all you knew.

Henry stopped grieving. He missed Dove. He talked about her and wondered whom she would have married. If he would be a grandfather. He had a special love for Dove's three friends and for Ruby's children.

Eunice had to fight a sense of satisfaction as she watched Lara return as a divorced woman. Her marriage had failed in less than three years. Although Eunice didn't verbalize it, something inside her felt that Lara didn't deserve happiness. Dove couldn't have it; why should Lara? Oh, that was a fleeting thought, yet it condemned her and the bitterness still in her heart.

When Ruby returned and let herself have one child after another when she couldn't afford it, and let herself go, and wouldn't sing, something in Eunice fleetingly said it served her right. Dove would have had more sense. Dove was a sensible girl. . .until. . .no, she mustn't go there.

Eunice had to fight being such a sinful woman. She understood it. She'd lost her baby. Her life. Henry had lost his heart. No, he hadn't, and that upset her, too. He got over it. He accepted it. He would look at Dove's picture, remember something, and tell the story. He even told stories about her in church. But he didn't know. . .everything.

And neither do I.

She knew what had happened to Avery.

She and Henry got a Christmas card each year after he became music director in Philadelphia. He stayed there three years, then left to travel and sing with a gospel group. Later, he married and became a choir director in a big church.

Each Christmas through the years, he sent a card addressed to Pastor and Mrs. Henry Hogan and Dove. It was signed Avery Firman.

Later, it was signed Avery and Betty Firman.

Two years later, it was signed Avery, Betty, and Daniel Firman.

Four years later, it was signed Avery, Betty, Daniel, and Kristin Firman.

Seven years later, it was signed Avery, Betty, Daniel, Kristin, and Douglas Firman.

She never sent a card. She never wrote a letter. Henry would look at the card and say, "Well, well, looks like Avery got married. Well, well, looks like Avery has a boy now. Well, well. Well, well." He never asked if she wrote to them. He never asked if she sent a card. Was Henry so caught up in the present, in his life, in his current responsibilities that he let go of the past, no matter how good it had seemed? Did he suspect?

If so, he never let on.

During Dove's funeral, a car stopped. A man got out and stood on top of the hill, silhouetted against the gray sky. He didn't move when a light rain began to fall. After the graveside ritual ended and people began to move around, he got into the car and drove away.

Henry didn't seem to notice. He didn't even wipe his tear-stained face, just accepted the handshakes and the hugs and the kind words and let his face get rain and tear soaked without attempting to conceal his grief.

Eunice hurt too much to cry. Her body was one big ache. She doubted that it would ever go away. What would she and Henry do now? They had no child on whom to concentrate. Henry had his work, his calling, his church. What did she have? What would she do?

She looked at the mound of red dirt covered with a tarp. She would like to fall upon her daughter's casket and let them shovel the red earth on top of her.

Already, she felt like a truckload of it had been dumped on her.

What she wanted that day was the truth of why her Dove lay dead in that coffin.

That was not the time to speak of it.

But she would.

She would.

Ten years later, the Christmas card from the Firmans had only one signature. "Avery thought so much of you two. I just wanted to let you know he died in his sleep in September. I thought you would want to know. Betty Firman."

Avery. . .was gone.

Eunice handed the card to Henry. He read the note. His brow creased. He shook his head, then he sort of nodded as if to say, "That's too bad," then, "That's the way of things."

She handed other cards to him, and he began to look through them and make comments. He never spoke of Avery through the years.

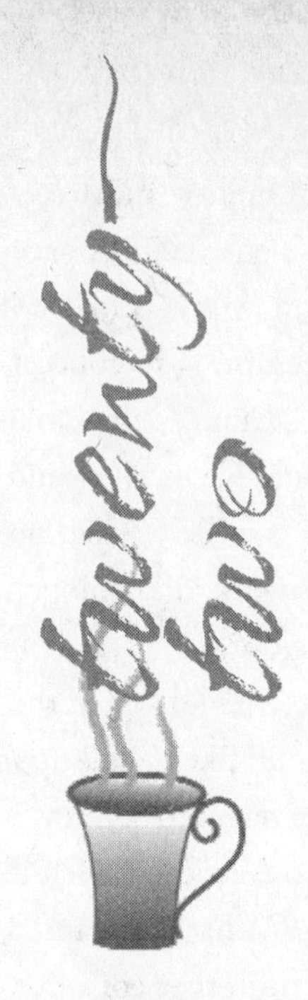

On Saturday morning, Lara wore pants with matching jacket over a knit, mock-turtleneck tank. The color was whisper, similar to the bluish tint of a tranquil morning sky. Maybe she could quietly blend into the scenery. No amount of talking had convinced her that Eunice Hogan wanted to see them simply because they'd gone to her church off and on for over two decades. Hundreds of people had gone to that church over the years, and not for one minute did she believe they were all invited for some kind of final good-bye.

She parked in back and walked onto the porch and around to the front to enter the gift shop instead of having Annette come to her entrance. She might still be getting ready. However, after entering, Lara spied Annette and Ruby, early for once in her life, sitting at a table. She walked over.

"Another new outfit," Annette said. "That is gorgeous."

"As usual," Ruby said.

"Thanks," Lara said shortly, hardly acknowledging the compliment. "But are we really going to see Eunice?" She took a deep breath, feeling like she could hyperventilate. "What will we say?"

"We've already been through this," Ruby said. "I'm going to talk to Eunice about Marcella and tell a few jokes." She motioned with her hand. "Annette is going to be the picture of composure while graciously presenting a pie."

"And me?" Lara said.

"Just stand there looking gorgeous."

Lara hated this. If she were complimented on her clothes, she would say thank you and then what?

Ruby said Lara's clothes would get messed up in her rattletrap of a car that was perpetual transportation for three girls in various stages of irresponsibility. Annette had to hold her pie, so Lara drove her car.

At least it gave her something to do with her hands other than wring them.

Sitting in the backseat, Ruby kept telling them jokes. Lara glanced at Annette, who laughed at the right times, but her eyes looking ahead held a distant expression.

"Stop," Ruby yelled.

Lara braked in time. She'd almost passed the stop sign at the four-way intersection. "Sorry."

She needed to stay calm. But she saw the steeple of the church rising high in the sky. The parsonage was next to it. When they'd discussed this before, Ruby and Annette had said they should act normal.

Okay, her normal came with several options. She could scream, gag on reflux, or throw up.

She didn't want to do this.

The last thing Eunice Hogan had said after the funeral, in the rain, was, "I want the truth."

She couldn't have it there at the funeral in the rain.

As soon as possible after that, Lara married Jared, honeymooned in Hawaii, then left for Europe. She'd hoped marriage and three years of study in Europe would give her the life she longed for—as far away from Laurel Ridge as possible.

"Slow down and turn," Ruby said.

Lara obeyed. She pulled up into the driveway, behind Eunice's car in the carport. The long brick ranch was nice. The lawn immaculately trimmed. Boxwood shrubs flanked by azaleas not yet in bloom bordered by yellow jonquils and multicolored pansies made a lovely array of spring. The groundskeeper at church also took care of the pastor's yard. But they all knew that Henry Hogan loved flowers. He was known to often putter around in his beds.

Ruby rang the bell.

After Lara came back from Europe, she and Eunice had talked at church. They'd talked about her grandmother, who Eunice asked about and visited in the nursing home. For a while, she'd asked if Lara was painting. Lara said no. Eunice stopped asking. They spoke through the years. They smiled at each other. But they always seemed to be waiting.

Eunice was waiting for a response to her statement.

They never gave it.

Why were they here now?

Eunice opened the door. She looked as lovely as always, not like most seventy-year-olds. She had a good figure she kept in shape by walking around the lake many summer evenings. At times she had joined exercise classes, even water aerobics. She'd been an active, healthy woman.

Now. . .this.

"Come in. It's so good to see you girls."

Girls. That's how she greeted them years ago when they came to meetings here or a party or special event, some kind of church activity, and later to pick up Dove. Lara always drove because she was the only one with her own car. The others had to ask parents for their car.

If it wasn't for that statement of Eunice's nineteen years ago, this would seem a reversion to the years when they came happy, young, carefree. This was a comfortable home where they'd felt welcomed. The only one who hadn't liked it was Dove. They figured she pretended that. How could she not be perfectly at ease with her wonderful dad and gracious, beautiful mother? But they understood her desire to be out from under their control. Dove always complained that everyone expected her to be perfect, being a preacher's daughter. She wasn't, but she adored her dad, and he adored her. There was friction between Dove and her mom.

Eunice thanked Annette for the pie and said they would have to stay for a piece of it. She took it to the kitchen, then led them into the sunroom, a glassed-in portion at the back of the house where plants abounded on tables and hung from the ceiling. That was the handiwork of Henry. Caring for flowers was his hobby.

They sat in the room being warmed by the morning sunshine. Lara felt that symbolized what awaited them. Eunice's demeanor was one of sunlight, but she hadn't invited them here for the first time in nineteen years just for them to feel the warmth of the sunlight.

Ruby talked about speaking to Shelby about Marcella.

"How did she react?" Eunice asked.

"Like somebody who's afraid of heights and water being asked to hang-glide from the top of Mt. Mitchell and land in Lake Junaluska."

Eunice laughed. "Oh my. Well, I told Shelby I'd like her to give it a try, let that young girl stay with her for a few days."

Lara knew when Eunice asked something, most people complied.

Eunice turned her attention to Annette and mentioned how proud she and Henry were of Tom's participating in the Easter pageant and being such a fine boy.

Lara knew this chitchat was preliminary to something. Then Eunice's eyes met Lara's.

Lara felt the crawl in her stomach.

"You're lovely as ever," Eunice said, to which Lara said,

"Thank you." That's all anyone ever had to say about her. And it wasn't she who was lovely; it was her clothes.

Eunice took a deep breath, but before she could say anything, Annette quickly asked, "How are you doing, Eunice?"

Eunice gave a brief report on her condition. She could tell she was getting weaker and needed her afternoon naps but was able to do whatever she wished without pain.

Lara could have slapped Annette when she said, "Is there anything we can do?"

Lara felt like she could mimic Eunice's words as she would say them. She would say, "Why yes there is; you can tell me the truth." Lara braced herself for it. She kept one hand over the other on her lap. She stared at her painted toenails below the strap of her cognac-colored high-heeled sandals that matched her handbag.

But Eunice didn't say that. Eunice was more vindictive than Lara could ever have imagined. How could she suggest such a thing? How could she want to do such a thing? Had she planned this for nineteen years? Just to punish them further?

Eunice began her request—no, somehow it was more than a request. It was a demand, a command. How could they live another nineteen years saying no to a dying woman? She began, "It's admirable how you three have remained friends all these years. Now, there is something you can do together. That's why I asked you girls to come here today."

Then she said it.

No way!

Lara felt she had to get out of there. That is, if her eyes would become unglued from her toes and if her hands became unstuck from her pant legs.

Never!

When Eunice said she admired how the three of them stayed

friends, Ruby thought of a conversation she and Lara had one time, sitting in Annette's tea and coffee room. Annette had asked them what they would think if she and Curt got serious.

Ruby had said, "If you get any more serious, you're going to have to wear a lampshade to hide the light he's turned on inside you."

They'd laughed, then Annette had been summoned by a customer. Ruby sighed. "Other than losing her husband, she's had a pretty good life."

Lara nodded. "She attracts people. I suppose it's her way of seeming to have everything under control."

Ruby leaned forward with her elbows on the table. "If she's so perfect, why does she have two friends like us? You're divorced, heaven forbid. And I'm fat and gray-headed."

Lara didn't take it as a joke. "That makes her even more perfect. Even if her hair color does come from a bottle, she still associates with her imperfect friends. That's loyalty to be admired."

"Friends." Ruby sighed. "Would we be friends if it wasn't for. . . ?"

Lara's quick intake of breath and her widened eyes stopped Ruby from saying more. Would she have said it? They never talked about it.

After she and Charlie married and went away to seminary, Ruby wanted to get as far away as possible.

Ruby remembered when she left Laurel Ridge. Friends, church members, and Charlie himself praised her for being so supportive of her husband when he wanted to go to seminary to study for a music ministry. Like the famous Ruth who said to her mother-in-law, "Wherever you go, I will go. Your God will be my God. Your people will be my people," Ruby even quit college to go and took a waitress job in Texas. Yes, he went to the seminary in Texas, clear across the country, and Ruby was glad. The farther away, the better.

They all thought she gave up her education, her friends, her church, her dreams, her hometown, her family, to be supportive of a man called of God.

She might have been willing to do all that because she fell in love with Charlie's curly hair and dimpled cheek. But after. . .that night. . .she had to do anything to get away, and Charlie had proposed. He couldn't back out, because how would that look? He was a fine, Christian man, three years older than she, and the two of them often stood up in church and sang duets together.

Well now, she did all those things, but her motive had been escape, not some divine sacrifice. Yes, she could go through the motions, laughing, telling jokes like she'd learned to do early in life when she found out she made friends that way. She'd be invited to parties, so she had to start memorizing jokes. She was happy in Texas, working her fingers to the bone, being praised by Charlie and the world—the little martyr. Having children just added to the joy because she didn't have time to think. Live the life of a martyr, and let Charlie shine.

After all, she'd had the experience of four years in high school and one in college as a cheerleader. Cheer for Charlie! Not that it would be so difficult. What more did a girl need in marriage than a good-looking fellow with curly hair and a dimpled left cheek?

It didn't take long before she began to shout, "Smile, Charlie, smile!"

After seminary, she couldn't beg Charlie not to return to his home church. That was his dream. He prayed. That was God's answer to his prayers. It was Charlie's will. The will of the church. The will of God.

Ruby prayed, "Don't make us go back."

But plans went forward. She prayed no, but all along she knew God wouldn't answer her prayer. Not that one.

He would make her pay. She had to pay. She had to reap the consequences.

At least. . .at least. . .He wasn't sending them to the Outer Banks.

They returned to Laurel Ridge, where Annette had stayed. She was married to a military man who was away most of the time. She had a little boy. She had stopped running the bed-and-breakfast at her husband's request. He said he feared for the safety of his young pretty wife and little boy.

Annette began to fix up the Victorian house. Lara, the divorcée, had returned and was helping Annette. How could Ruby not come and offer her services? Everyone knew the three of them had been friends in high school, at church, in college. What reason would they have for not remaining friends—through thick or thin. . . ?

So Ruby said Annette could experiment with her cooking. Annette and Lara could remain thin, but Ruby, already thickening, would become official food taster.

A couple of years later, Annette's husband was killed.

The whole town sympathized. Ruby's martyrdom was over, and Annette's began.

The past, the college years, would have dimmed in the minds of the people of Laurel Ridge. If they talked now, it would be about Lara the divorcée, Ruby the fatty, and Annette the martyr.

Eunice had welcomed Ruby and Charlie back like they were old friends. Only a flicker of a glance from that beautiful, elegant, middle-aged woman said they had unfinished business. But she never asked. Ruby never volunteered anything.

Now. . .Eunice was. . .asking? No, just saying what she wanted. If they said no, then Eunice undoubtedly would say, okay, let's get to the subject at hand right now.

She couldn't. Ruby had to think. She'd have to talk to Annette and Lara. They'd have to decide what to say.

Ruby could have kissed Eunice's feet when she said, "I know this is sudden. You can think about it while we have a piece of Annette's pie."

Great! Ruby had the time it took to eat about four bites to choke back any protest clawing its way up her esophagus into her throat. Maybe she'd have two pieces. She'd had nineteen years to think about all this but was no better off and didn't know what she might say. Now she had a few bites of pie-time to come up with some explanation she hadn't had in nineteen years.

While Eunice cut the fresh strawberry pie with a big knife that looked like a saber, Ruby wondered if the older woman would stab them if they said no.

While Ruby and Lara held onto the backs of kitchen chairs, Annette, bless her heart, took four plates from the cupboard and began making excuses in her perfect way.

Annette took the plates from the cupboard as if she were taking dishes from her own cabinets in her own place of business. She'd done it for years, for the Hogans when they came, Louis's family when they came, former friends who returned to the area. Somehow, at times she could shut out the world and focus on one thing.

That came not only from the survival instinct but also from her early training from the time she was a toddler. Swimming had been an activity the family had done together. In the summer, they'd go to a public pool, and in the winter they'd go to the Y.

Comments began to be made that Annette was a fish in water. Lessons began. Her parents, who owned the Victorian bed-and-breakfast, had a swimming pool put behind the house. With the pool as a gathering place and with her becoming a member of a swimming team, her popularity increased. Even Lara, whose family was most prominent in the area, found it advantageous to be friends with Annette at school and at church.

Lara's grandmother attended frequently, and Annette got Lara to start coming to Sunday school and church activities.

In college, when Annette was nominated for president of the student Christian union, she nominated Lara for treasurer. No contest. Everybody knew she'd be honest with the money. Her family was rich.

Ruby was a friend to everyone, but being in the same church as Annette and Lara, their friendship was closer. Ruby didn't want to be elected to anything except cheerleading.

Annette became the fastest swimmer on the team that second year in college. The coach didn't know her speed resulted from her trying to get away from it all. Other swimmers were the demons trying to pull her under. She wouldn't let them. She'd outswim them. She did. She broke her own records, won medals, ribbons, and trophies.

She felt like she'd swum around the world several times. Louis said, "I love you. Let's get married." She jumped at the chance. She'd loved him. She supposed that was love. He thought she was the most wonderful person in the world. He would take care of her forever. Wasn't that better than swimming yourself to death while demons continued to chase you, grinning insidiously, knowing eventually you would tire?

She was tired.

She married. He thought the beach would be perfect for their honeymoon. She said no. She'd been to the beach before. So had he. They went to the Grand Canyon.

Then her tall, good-looking husband put on a uniform and became the area's pride, especially after he was killed.

Annette had dreaded Lara's return. But after Lara told her how she'd tried to fit in with the European crowd and it hadn't worked and she wanted to try Annette's way, the relationship became closer. Then Ruby returned. They all knew it wouldn't look right if they didn't resume their friendship. Why wouldn't they? None of them wanted any speculation.

They were under a microscope. Lara came from a wealthy family; she became like her mother she'd so resented. She had to prove she was decent and would faithfully attend church. Her donations were listed in the church bulletin frequently along with others because she always donated "in memory of" or "in honor of" or bought a poinsettia at Christmas, with the proceeds given to youth projects. That proved she was a good Christian woman.

Ruby had to behave fairly reasonably since her husband was choir director and known by the area as the Christian disc jockey at FROM radio station—"Friend 'round our mountains." She could tell her jokes, act like a scatterbrain, but she'd better be in that choir on Sunday morning.

Annette had to walk the straight and narrow, being a young widow. She had the swimming pool filled in, didn't swim anymore. She saw that plates of food were set before her patrons.

Now she set Eunice's plates on the kitchen table without breaking them. She thought Lara and Ruby might break the chair backs. With her eyes, she motioned for them to sit. They did. Eunice was wielding her sharp-edged knife. She put a big chunk on a plate. Ruby took it.

"Just a little piece," Lara said.

Eunice cut a thinner slice.

"Where you've asked us to go could be cold this time of year," Annette said.

Eunice slid the small slice over to Lara. "I'm not worried about the cold."

"Do you need to get a doctor's approval to make the trip?"

Eunice stopped cutting and looked over at Annette, as if that were a foolish question. She took a deep breath, then said, "No. When you have a short time to live, you don't ask the doctor; you do what you want to do and what you feel like doing."

They all tried to laugh lightly. Weird noises that sounded more like a dog growling with a sore throat.

Annette accepted her pie and sat. Eunice followed.

They all took a bite. After swallowing, Annette said, "I shouldn't have a problem getting away, but Lara and Ruby have bosses, you know."

"Pray about it."

Annette slowly glanced at her friends. Ruby was tackling her pie, Lara picking at hers. Annette lifted her fork in unison with Eunice. She could play the game. . .for a while.

But the expressions on Ruby's and Lara's faces reflected what she felt inside. . .like one of those fish of Ruby's that had run into the concrete wall.

The downpour drowned gardens recently planted. Dirt washed over the roads, making mud like quicksand. People along the overflowing creek banks were evacuated. Buses couldn't run on flooded streets, so schools were cancelled. The sides of roads washed away. Mud and boulders slid down the mountainsides, blocking the only road between North Carolina and Tennessee.

Whoo-hoo!

Ruby felt like singing in the rain.

Nobody could be expected to go to the Outer Banks in that deluge.

Maybe it was divine intervention. After the storm left the mountains, it was reported to be heading for the coast.

Even Eunice wouldn't want to drive to the Outer Banks in that kind of weather. . .would she? Knowing Eunice, however, she might not care if they drowned on the way to the beach. She was dying anyway and didn't seem to mind it.

If Ruby had the faith of Joshua, who asked God to make the

sun stand still, and He did, she could avoid this trip. All it would take was faith the size of a grain of mustard seed. She wondered if half a seed would have any effect.

Oh foot! By Tuesday she hated the weatherman and the itsy-bitsy spider that could go up the waterspout again because the sun came out and dried up all the rain. The intensity of the storm decreased, and it would go out into the ocean.

Okay, she didn't have that excuse anymore. She knew she could get away from social services. She'd worked overtime often. They'd be glad to have her gone.

Ah ha! Surely Charlie would forbid her to go. How could he have an affair if he had to run the household? That would put a kink in his activities.

On Tuesday morning after breakfast while he was having his second cup of coffee, she decided to take a ten-second break. She sat down and said to Charlie, "How could I possibly leave kith and kin and go to the Outer Banks?"

He shrugged. "Ruby, you know good and well if Eunice wants to get away for a few days and wants you to go with her, half the church will come and stay with the children."

"I don't want half the church here."

He scratched his curly head. "Well, in that case, I guess I'll have to do like Henry said and take a few days off from church. The girls will be in school while I'm at the radio station. I'll be home at night."

Ruby tried any excuse she could find. "The house will be a wreck."

His eyebrows rose. "Is that anything new?"

Frankly, no. That's what she fussed about all the time.

"What if temptation overtakes you if I'm not here to threaten you?"

He screwed up his face as if he were trying to come up with

a good answer. He tapped on his cheek with his finger. "Hmmm," he said. "I guess if the Lord isn't enough to keep me on the right path, there's not much you can do about it."

She reckoned that was true. At least he wasn't being a hypocrite about it. That was the same as admitting his affair with Maybelle. And there he sat, grinning like the hyenas in *The Lion King* movie. One of these days, she was going to throw him out—if she ever got the time or the energy. In the meantime, she had to clean up from breakfast, check to see what she needed for supper, go to work, go to the store, come home, cook. . . . Oh man! She could sing that song about bringing home the bacon and cooking it, too.

On Wednesday night, the whole church had heard that Eunice wanted to go to the beach. Eunice must have told it herself, but that didn't matter. Gossip always twisted things, and it was a done deal by the time Ruby had been there two minutes.

At choir practice everybody began saying how sweet it was of her and Annette and Lara to be taking Eunice to the beach. Maybelle was particularly gleeful, all gushy-gooey, and she even offered to help with the children.

Ruby wasn't sure how mad wet hens got, but they couldn't have been madder than she was by the time she got home. Later when Charlie appeared, she laid down the law. "Don't you dare let that woman near my children."

"What woman?"

What woman! "You know what woman. The one who was so eager to get into this house and take care of my. . .children." Ruby felt like her head had a rubber strap around it and somebody on the floor was pulling and letting go, the way her head wouldn't stop bobbing. "The one with the voice so beautiful, you just can't get enough of it, that's who."

"Oh." He had the nerve to stand there and act as if he didn't know exactly whom she meant. "You mean two-thirds of the choir members who offered to help while you're at the beach or one in particular?"

"The ding-dong of spring, that's who. Miss Maybelle! You let her near this house and I. . .I'll—"

"Divorce me?"

She exhaled a deep breath. "The word I'm thinking of, Charlie, is not divorce. It's murder."

He laughed. She had to look away. He was the cutest thing. And of course he didn't take her any more seriously than anyone else in the world. Well, when she got back from the beach, if she got back from the beach, she would show him how serious she was.

Right now, however, she had to go to the Outer Banks.

Did Eunice want them to suffer all over again?

Or. . .did she have something else in mind?

Ruby had to sit down on that one.

Was this revenge?

Was this to be. . .a replay?

If I'm good enough!

I care about other people just as much as other people do. Maybe more. Haven't Brian and I helped with youth? Gone on trips with Jim and his wife as chaperones? Gone to camps? Other churches?

It wasn't as if she and Brian would have minded taking off by themselves and going to Hawaii, or even Pigeon Forge, or any other area attractions. This was a tourist area.

They'd helped with the youth because they cared about them. Not too many years ago the two of them had been teenagers. They could identify. Shelby had especially enjoyed watching kids like Ruby's Jill and Annette's Tom grow physically and spiritually through the years.

But for a week, she'd lived with that statement of Ruby's that sounded much like condemnation. Shelby had talked it over with the psychologist. "She implied that I might not be good for Marcella."

"Shelby, she's in a position much like a judge in a custody trial. He sees only what's on paper—not the hearts or intents of the adults. He tries to make a decision by what's best for the child."

Shelby recognized Dr. Elesha's attempt at tact, but that analogy didn't apply here. She raised her hands in a helpless gesture.

"Ruby has known me for. . .I don't know. . .twelve, thirteen years or so. She's trusted me with her own daughter for years. Now her second one is coming to youth activities."

Dr. Elesha smiled benignly. "That's before you attempted suicide. Shelby, that attempt might be taken into consideration if you ever plan to adopt."

Shelby was mortified. She didn't plan to adopt but realized anew the consequences of a foolish, rash act. She felt hot tears sting her eyes.

Shelby leaned forward, but the doctor raised her hand. "Let me finish. I know you didn't really want to die and that you had many problems going on at the same time. But look at it from Ruby's point of view. She must be objective. It could appear you would be resentful of Marcella."

Shelby's hand moved to her forehead. "I don't resent that little girl. I resent not being able to have a child of my own. It's the situations I resent, not. . .her. I'd like to help her. A lot of girls have talked to me about things like drugs and drinking and sex."

Dr. Elesha leaned back against her leather chair. "You're an outspoken young woman. You spoke out against your dad's remarrying. That caused you problems. You say you want to change everyone's opinion of you. So why not speak out about your willingness to help Marcella? After all, Ruby trusted you enough to come to you about Marcella. Did she not?"

Shelby sighed. "Yes. But I ruined it with my. . ." She grinned. "My outspokenness."

On the way home, she thought about Dr. Elesha telling her to think of the positive things, not the negative. Yes, Ruby had come to her, even after that foolish pill episode of hers. Eunice had approached her about Marcella. Brian had always said she was good with young people. They seemed to like her.

She could at least say she would let Marcella stay with her a few days while Eunice went to the beach. If it didn't seem to be working well, then Marcella could stay with Eunice until Ruby found the right home for her.

Shelby was glad Eunice and her friends were going to the beach for a few days. The fact that Eunice chose Annette as one of them was sort of a thorn in the flesh when she first heard it. The more she thought of it, the more she remembered that Annette was a good person—good enough that her dad wanted to marry her. She gave Marcella a job. Without a husband, she'd raised her son to be a fine, Christian young man.

Shelby's recent attitudes and actions overshadowed whatever good she'd ever done.

Eunice had said that love is action. Perform the acts and the feelings will come.

That could very well be the last request Eunice ever made of her. But Ruby was right about what she said. If she couldn't treat Marcella with love and respect, then the girl would be better off going elsewhere.

Jesus said love others as you love yourself. She could certainly do that much. She hadn't loved herself very much lately.

"It doesn't mean I want her baby."

Shelby wanted to make sure Brian knew that. She saw the light of hope in his eyes when she told him she would be willing to help out with Marcella if he agreed.

"I think that's wonderful of you, Shel. You know the major responsibility will be yours. I don't know anything about this stuff except what I've heard about morning sickness and all that."

"You don't need to. Francine has fully indoctrinated me on morning sickness. . .and all that stuff."

They laughed together. It had been awhile. He came and enfolded her in his arms, holding her tighter than he had in a long time. His gaze was tender. "Here's that beautiful girl I married. I think this is great, Shel. But be sure you want to take this on. I know we've had teenagers here for days at a time. But don't do this to try and prove something to us. If we take her in, her needs have to come first as if she were our daughter."

That bothered Shelby. Was she capable? "I do know that, Brian. And I'm not old enough to be her mother. I can only try and be a friend."

"Our apartment could get crowded."

Shelby nodded. "If you don't feel right about it, then it's best we don't."

He looked very serious. "I'll tell you this, Shelby. If she takes up more than half the kitchen table while I'm grading papers, she's out."

They both laughed. It sounded like a done deal. However, they went out to eat and discussed it, then continued far into the night. Much had to be considered. They would need to talk with Ruby.

Brian made the concluding observation before they allowed the discussion to end. The church had become known for not only speaking out against wrongs, but also for starting a ministry to help people get back on the right track. How could they talk about love without showing it? How could they speak out about abortion, then not give young girls any other option? How could they call themselves Christians and not respond to a need that was within their grasp?

"I'll call Ruby tomorrow," Shelby said. "I know you've seen Marcella at church and at some of the youth activities, but would you like to have lunch at Annette's Kitchen tomorrow and see Marcella at work?"

"Annette's?"

"I want to apologize to her."

The next day, Shelby asked Annette if she could speak to her alone before she and Brian went to the Kitchen. Brian began to look at items in the gift shop while Annette took Shelby upstairs to her private quarters.

"I'm sorry I've been rude to you," Shelby said after being seated. "I really wish I'd handled things differently. I didn't know how." She felt self-conscious.

Annette's shake of her head and smile helped ease Shelby's discomfort. "It's all right. I don't blame you. You can't help how you feel."

"No," Shelby said, feeling warmth in her face. "But I can help how I act. Or I should be able to. I've made such foolish decisions lately, I have no right to criticize others. I'm. . .trying to learn."

"You do fine. It's better to let others know how you feel than to keep it bottled up. You can lose friends that way. But not if they're truly your friends. I would like to be your friend, Shelby."

Shelby picked at the fabric on the couch. "I can see why Dad. . .likes you so much." She looked up and spoke the truth. "I'm not objecting to you two seeing each other."

"Thank you, Shelby." Annette stood.

They hugged each other and went downstairs. Shelby felt good about herself. The way Brian looked at her, she had the idea he did, too.

Seeing Annette with her customers and thinking about her having given Marcella a job made Shelby think. If she was ever going to be a strong Christian witness like Eunice and Annette, she'd better get started.

Curses were a part of superstition that Lara knew she wasn't supposed to believe in, but her relatives vowed the place was cursed. After the first tragic event, a relative broke his leg water skiing, another's engine failed and those aboard were adrift all night before being rescued, then Lara's parents died in a boating accident. The beach house was left to her. She told her relatives they could use the beach house any time, but none were interested.

Lara hadn't been there since. . .that night. She didn't intend to ever go again. She didn't want to think about it, just have the Realtor handle everything and send her the payments or the repair bills.

Yet didn't she know this day had to come? Hadn't she seen it in Eunice's eyes all these years? Hadn't she felt it in her heart? Hadn't it been like a noose tightening around her, Ruby's, and Annette's necks? The curse had drawn them back together, wouldn't let them go. It had to be revisited.

She didn't know how long they would stay.

Eunice said, "A few days."

One thing about it: She didn't have to return. The Outer Banks had been crooking its finger for nineteen years, beckoning, compelling, demanding they return. She'd escaped. . .except emotionally. . .and now she would return. Maybe the ocean would have its way this time.

She didn't get out of the car at Eunice's. She felt stuck.

Henry brought out Eunice's suitcase, extolled them for taking Eunice, wished them all a wonderful trip, said he'd be praying for them. He drew his wife into his embrace and kissed her soundly on the lips.

Lara looked away. Vexing saliva gathered beneath her tongue. She swallowed and cleared her throat.

"You sit in front, Eunice," Ruby said. "Everybody knows it's polite to put the oldest person in the death seat."

Lara looked askance at Annette, who simply lifted her eyebrows as if to say, "That's Ruby. She's nervous again."

Eunice laughed, put her tote bag on the floorboard, and climbed in.

Six hours.

Lara didn't want to drive. Ruby's car was a junk heap, and Jill would need it anyway to take herself and the younger girls places. Annette wasn't used to driving on long trips and didn't feel comfortable with it. They couldn't very well ask Eunice to drive in her condition.

When they were all settled in the car, Eunice reached over and laid her hand on Lara's arm.

Lara remembered another time when Eunice had touched her. Lara had been standing in the receiving line at her grandmother's viewing, thanking someone for her sympathy. Then she'd looked at the next person in line. She'd nearly jumped out of her skin.

Eunice had said, "I'm sorry, dear. I didn't mean to scare you," and their gazes locked. Lara thought she couldn't look away. Eunice's eyes were hypnotic. But Eunice was saying what others had said, offering sympathy. The words were right, but the message in her eyes said something else. The gaze. The accusing gaze. The questioning eyes. That statement of just wanting the truth was in her eyes. *No, no, you don't want the truth.*

Eunice's husband had preached, "Be careful what you want; you might get it."

Now Lara struggled not to jerk away or scream. She didn't like to be touched. Not by Eunice, anyway, and particularly not when she was trying to keep her wits about her.

Eunice seemed not to notice. "I'm not worried about your driving, Lara. If I was going to go in a car accident, the Lord wouldn't have given me a six-month notice."

"Don't you two worry," Ruby said. "If we have an accident, it's not the driver's fault; it's not the back-seater's fault. It's the asphalt."

Lara breathed a sigh of relief. She should have known Ruby would come prepared. She had a collection of jokes on every possible topic, ranging from old age to sayings of southerners and rednecks to miscellaneous.

That exhausted, they began to tell of embarrassing moments of which Ruby had no scarcity. Even Eunice added her own brand to a moment. "I had this pair of expensive shoes that zipped on the sides. I was all dressed up and spoke to a women's group of several hundred at a conference center. I looked down and saw that one of my shoes was unzipped." She shook her head. "I felt like an embarrassed man."

Ruby kept them laughing about antics at home with her family. She was trying to teach them correct English and at the same time discipline them for fighting, so she said, "Go lie on your bed until you can come out and be civil to each other."

After a few minutes, they came in. Jill said, "We all did what you said, Mom. We lied. I told Carley she wasn't the biggest brat I've ever known."

Carley giggled. "And I told Jill and Kristin they were pretty."

They exhausted the family jokes and moved to old age. Eunice told about the time her stove timer went off and she answered the cell phone.

Lara happened to remember one she'd heard at work. "Middle-age is when you're wise enough to know that life throws us curves, and you realize you're sitting on the biggest ones."

Lara didn't have that problem, but they all laughed.

When they moved to children, Ruby said, "Angst is when you look at your know-it-all teenagers and think, 'For this I have stretch marks?' "

Annette joined in. "This jumper cable came into the Kitchen. I said, 'I'll serve you, but don't start anything.' "

Ruby wondered if Eunice wasn't any more eager for the seriousness of the trip than they. Ruby tested the waters with her jokes. Before long they were all laughing and talking as if they'd been friends for years. Actually, they had not been enemies with Eunice. Just cautious never to mention the unmentionable. But they had never tried to be a close friend to her. She was a teacher, a mentor, an older woman. The age of their mothers. Dove's. . .mother.

For three hours, they kept it up, then stopped for lunch, used the rest room, walked around for a little while. Eunice took her medication.

After they returned to the car, Eunice said she would need to lay her head back, close her eyes, and rest for a little while, but their talking wouldn't disturb her. The medication made her sleepy.

Annette suggested they listen to music.

Lara pushed a couple of buttons on her CD player and out came Mozart. She looked up at the rearview mirror. "I saw that," she said. Ruby and Annette were looking at each other with grimaces on their faces as if something smelled like a skunk. "You guys don't know how to appreciate good music."

"At my house, any of the religious music is about Jesus-freaks. Is that sacrilegious?"

Annette shrugged. "I don't know what Tom listens to. He says it's contemporary Christian music, but I can't understand a word. I hope it's not blasphemy."

Eunice leaned forward and rustled in her tote bag next to her feet. "I brought a few contemporary CDs I thought you might like if we needed some noise on the way. See what you think."

Lara put one in. It had a great beat, and the words were understandable. "My kids have that one," Ruby said. She began to sing along. Eunice sang one or two songs, then seemed to doze off.

Lara continued to play the upbeat contemporary CDs.

The land flattened out considerably. High mountains had turned to rolling hills and finally flat land that spread into the horizon. Tall oaks, leafy maples, flowering dogwoods changed to a scene of scrawny pines and palm trees. Visibility stretched to a distant horizon. Curved roads became long, straight stretches.

The music stopped. Silence permeated the car. Lara looked into the rearview mirror and saw the starkness of her friends' faces, reflecting what she felt. "You guys need to look at that map and make sure we're okay. I haven't done this in a long time, and nothing looks familiar."

"How long since you've been here, Lara?" Eunice asked.

Lara took a shaky breath. She hoped her voice didn't reflect it. "Nineteen years," she said.

"Oh." Eunice was silent, and so were the two in the backseat. After a moment, Eunice spoke again. "You do suppose the place is still here?"

Lara smiled. "Yes. I've had Realtors handle things for me. They rent it out."

Eunice spoke as if to herself, "I suppose I should have known. . . ." Her voice trailed off.

Yes, she should have known.

Would it have mattered?

Lara thought not. This had always hung between them, waiting to happen. Eunice had been determined. She would have asked them to come even if the beach house had rotted away. It wasn't so much the house she wanted to see. . .but. . .the spot.

They went to the real estate office, which was still there, but agents had come and gone through the years. Lara had known them only by names written on official papers. Now Mr. Case handed her the keys to the house.

"I haven't been here in a number of years," Lara said. "Can you give me directions? Everything's so built up."

He nodded as if he knew she hadn't been there in nineteen years. "I'll do better than that. I'll lead the way, and you follow. That way, if everything's not in order, I'll see that it will be, pronto."

"Thanks."

Lara felt relief that she could follow the man instead of having to look at everything. She didn't want to see the house and particularly not the beach and ocean. It was creeping again—the reflux. She needed a purple pill.

She could have laughed at that were it not so devastating. No pill could help her now.

Mr. Case led the way. Three-thirty in the afternoon, the sun was high. The land became sandier, the palms sparser, the houses fewer. She didn't want to recognize anything, just follow the car ahead and stop listening to the persistent voices in her head. She wished the others would talk.

They spoke softly as if on hallowed ground. It wasn't hallowed. It was horrid.

Looking now at the beach house, Lara shuddered, remembering nineteen years ago. She tried to concentrate on the changes. Mr. Case said there'd been storm and hurricane damage through the years. There'd been a new roof, new floors, the porch replaced.

He said they'd aired out the house, anticipating Lara's return. There had been no renters during the winter, but some were booked to come soon. Of course, that could change if Lara—

"No, we'll only be here a short while," Lara said, having no idea how long Eunice wanted to stay. She did not want to spend the night here. There would be no sleeping.

But. . .Eunice hadn't come here to sleep.

Mr. Case asked if he should open the windows, let the cool breeze in. "Yes, thank you."

The last time she was here, there were four. Now, there were four again. They stayed close to her as she followed Mr. Case. He tried the water, the electricity, flushed the commode, turned on the fan, said the fireplace worked but no cold weather was expected, however it was nice to have a fire sometimes anyway. After she assured him all appeared well, he left.

As if they were invited guests, Lara told Eunice she could take the bedroom with the private bath. Ruby and Annette could take the one that had a bath adjoining the third bedroom. Lara wasn't about to sleep with anyone.

She wouldn't sleep anyway. And if she couldn't stand it, she wouldn't have to. She'd heard the beckoning of the ocean's voice for years, as clearly as if she'd been holding a shell to her ear.

Eunice took her tote bag into the bedroom Lara indicated. She had the vague impression of a spacious, nicely furnished pastel room with a breeze blowing a curtain from the open window. None of that mattered. Eunice sat on the side of the bed, setting her tote bag on the floor. She felt the soft, seashell-colored bed covering beneath her hand.

Did my little girl sit here? Sleep here? No. . .there had been no sleep that night for Dove. She and her friends had left early that morning.

"They're here," Henry had called through the screen door.

He'd been sitting in the porch swing. Eunice came from the kitchen as Dove exited her bedroom with a suitcase. Eunice followed her out onto the porch and lifted her hand in greeting to Ruby and Annette in the backseat of the red convertible. Lara was opening the trunk.

Dove set the case down and hugged Eunice hastily.

"You girls be careful, now."

"Yes, Mama." She hugged Henry a little longer.

"Have a good time, baby," he said. "I love you."

"Love you." She broke away and reached for her suitcase.

Oh, in such a hurry to get away. But that was normal. She'd finished her first year of college. She was young and on vacation.

"Call when you get there," Eunice said.

She seemed to resent that. "Mom," she said, "you only get calls if we don't arrive."

"I just want to know you're all right."

Their gazes held for a moment. . .like. . .no, those were not Dove's eyes. She seemed to be thinking. Then Dove looked down, and her eyelids closed over her big blue eyes. "I'll be all right."

She hurried to Lara's car. Her long fine hair swayed gently past her shoulders and shone like the golden sun. Lara opened the trunk and helped her lift the bag inside. Did Eunice's admonitions embarrass Dove?

Perhaps not. As soon as she and Lara got into the car, the four smiling girls waved. She and Henry waved until the car backed down the driveway and out onto the neighborhood road. Eunice and Henry watched as splotches of red appeared and disappeared around the curves and through myriad trees.

Like the phases of one's life. So many changes—from an infant to a toddler, learning to walk and speak; starting school; learning to dance, play the piano, swim; sleepovers; parties; friends; dating; graduation; college.

And now she was eighteen. Another phase, another change. Something else to accept and adjust to. Eunice turned to Henry. He looked at her and smiled, then put his arm around her waist. They went inside to begin their daily responsibilities.

Eunice didn't mean to be overly protective. She just wanted her daughter safe. When in bed that night, she remembered Dove saying you don't get calls about safe arrivals.

She'd be all right.

Eunice remembered Dove's words again when the doorbell rang in the middle of the night. When she looked at the clock with hands indicating 3:52 a.m. She didn't want to go, but the bell insisted. Henry awoke, sat up, and turned his head toward her like a phantom in a darkened room. She couldn't see his eyes, but she knew them. Dear Henry, with his soft brown eyes.

Anyone might be at a pastor's door in the middle of the night.

Sometimes, however, you just know.

She knew.

Hadn't she known for nineteen years?

Did Henry know? Is that why he didn't tell her to stay in bed and he'd see who was at the door? Who needed help in the middle of the night? No, he didn't say that. He switched on the lamp by the time she had reached for the robe she'd laid across a chair before going to bed. Preacher's wives had to be prepared for anything, anytime.

Henry put his arm around her waist as they walked down the hallway; the only sounds were the persistent ringing of the doorbell and the padding of their house slippers on the carpet. If there'd been any doubt, it left when Henry unlocked the door and saw the faces of the police officers, one of them a member of their church. Brad tried but choked on the words he couldn't say. He blinked, but tears streaked his face anyway, and he just shook his head.

The other officer, whom they also knew, said, "There's been an accident." He tried to clear his throat. She felt sorry for him. Could have told him he didn't have to say it. She knew. She didn't want to hear it. He forced the words. "At the beach."

Eunice felt Henry's arm tighten around her waist. He asked a foolish question. "My daughter?"

Both officers nodded.

She heard the starkness in Henry's hoarse whisper. "What happened?"

"She. . .drowned."

Eunice ran then. She jerked away from Henry's embrace. She ran through the living room and down the hallway. She went through a doorway leading where she didn't know. She had to escape. She found the back door, but hands were pulling on her, voices were chiding her. They wouldn't let her go but forced her into a kitchen chair.

Someone had switched on a light. Two men in uniform stared at her. Henry said, "Call Phil and Dee." The officers nodded and hurried from the room. Henry put his arm around her shoulders and agonized, "Eunice, Eunice. Eunice."

Her body bent until her forehead lay on the table along with her forearms. Her fists beat against the table. The sound coming from her insides was like something that had been caged up for years. It was loose. She couldn't control it. She had to. She grasped for anything. The lament came forth with each pounding of her fists against the tabletop.

"Absalom! My son, my son Absalom."

She felt the agony of King David when he'd been told his enemy-son was killed.

"Eunice, Eunice, Eunice."

A realization struck. Straightening up, she turned to look at Henry, who had pulled up a chair next to her. His eyes were red.

His face was wet. She had shed no tears. Suddenly she laughed and put her hand on Henry's face. "Don't cry. It's not true. This is ridiculous. Sometimes in your dreams, you know it's a nightmare. I know this. I went to sleep worried." She shook her head. "This isn't real."

Brad and the other officer—she couldn't think of his name—who had invaded her nightmare appeared in the doorway. "They'll be here as soon as they can. They'll take you down there."

Henry's next words proved this wasn't real. "What about the other girls?" If this were real, he wouldn't have thought of them.

"They're okay. Their parents will be notified."

Henry nodded, then turned to Eunice. "Let's get dressed."

Brad said something that could only happen in dreams. "I've gotten permission to pick up my wife, and we'll drive down there in case the girls or anybody needs us."

The officers stepped aside as Henry took hold of Eunice's arm and led her into the bedroom. She looked at Brad and what's-his-name and almost giggled. In dreams, did characters who looked like real people have feelings? Or did only the one dreaming it? She'd have to investigate that.

When Dee came, Eunice said, "So you're in it, too."

Dee had with her a sleeping pill and a pillow. Eunice didn't protest. Dee was a nurse in real life, and it didn't matter in a dream. But. . .could one go to sleep in a dream in which one was already asleep?

It's not real.

She quickly took the pill.

Several hours later, Dee was shaking her. Eunice opened her eyes, closed her mouth, and lifted her head from where it lay against the pillow in the back corner of the car. Henry and Phil were getting out of the front seat in a parking lot at the back of a hospital. Brad and Sara got out of their car.

The sun was shining. Brad had radioed ahead. A man came up to them. He held open a door for them to enter. He looked solemn. Brad said something. The man's voice was solemn. The corridor was solemn. It smelled of disinfectant, cold steel, and souring mops. The man opened a door, and they walked into a solemn room. One table dominated the center of the room. On it was a white sheet covering. . .something.

"These are the Hogans," Brad said to someone. He indicated Henry and Eunice with a movement of his hand.

"I'm sorry," said a voice that sounded as cold as Eunice felt. "We need you to identify. . .her."

Hands were trying to move Eunice closer so she could look. She saw Henry's head moving from side to side. He didn't want to look. She couldn't. Oh, sure she could. But even in a dream, she didn't want Henry suffering. She put her hand on his arm. Then his arm came around her waist, and they took a step closer.

The man wearing white moved to the other side. Reaching his arm across, he carefully took hold of the edge of the sheet like a maid in a fancy hotel might do when turning down the bed covers. Slowly, inch by inch, the covering was lowered.

A monotone voice spoke. "Can you identify this. . .young woman?"

Eunice didn't want to look. She wanted to stay in a state of disbelief, oblivion. With only a little effort she could go there. But if she did, she would babble. Oh, what would she say then? She mustn't. She had to face it. She had to be there for Henry.

Nobody spoke for an eternity.

Somebody said, "That's Dove Hogan."

"Sir?" The man in white said, looking at Henry.

Eunice saw Henry nod. How could he? That was not Dove Hogan.

Dove's hair wouldn't be clumped and matted like straw. The eyes staring into space. Those blue, blue eyes aren't hers. They are—

Eunice clamped her hand over her mouth. Even in a dream she mustn't say that. Her daughter's face wasn't pasty but wore the blush of youth. Her daughter's mouth wasn't pale and stretched over teeth and gaped that way. Her daughter had lovely, moist, glossy, full lips that smiled. Her daughter didn't lie silent. She laughed and breathed and loved life.

"No!" Eunice shook her head. Of course she knew, but she had to hang on to something. That thin thread of disbelief was all she had. . .except that Absalom feeling again.

Then Henry moved forward. His arms went over that fake person, and he put his face next to it. He began babbling like Eunice mustn't. Garbled words that sounded like "Baby, wake up, oh my honey, don't, please don't be, this can't be, oh God help us. Oh my baby, I love you, I love you, don't do this, wake up, I can't, I can't, get up, get up," and he was pulling on the sheet and shaking her shoulders.

That thing's eyes just kept staring at the ceiling.

"Sir, sir." The man in white was trying to keep the sheet in place while the other man came forward. Hands were all over Henry. Eunice felt hands on her, too. "What was that?"

"Ma'am, we were required to perform an autopsy."

Eunice screamed. "You cut my baby?"

Henry began to gag. "I'm sick."

The men took him out. Dee and Sarah were holding both her arms as if they were a straitjacket and she insane. She would be if this weren't a nightmare.

This couldn't be real.

Henry wouldn't fall apart. She needed his strength. They

wouldn't cut her baby. "Autopsy?"

"Yes, ma'am."

"Why?"

"We had to rule out foul play," said the man who had been standing back.

"Foul. . . ?"

"There was none, ma'am. It's been ruled accidental drowning."

She would touch her. She would slowly reach her hand out and lay it on that pasty cheek. Maybe that would wake her up.

It did.

By the time Henry returned from the rest room, apologetic for coming apart that way, she had in her hands two items. One was the medical examiner's report he'd intended to give Henry. The other was a two-piece bathing suit in a plastic bag.

"It's all right, Henry," Eunice and everyone else assured him. Eunice envied him for accepting this. Why didn't she break down and cry for her daughter?

Her eyes were dry.

With Henry in front with Phil, both Dee and Sara sat with Eunice in the backseat of the car. Brad followed a police officer who was leading them to the private beach near the Outer Banks.

Eunice's mind kept repeating the same words. "Foul play." The man said there hadn't been any. Why would they suspect it? She opened the envelope and read the report. Cause of death: accidental drowning. Her eyes scanned the rest of the official document. For a moment she clutched it close to her chest. When Dee and Sara began to describe whatever they saw outside the windows, Eunice looked at the official document again. She folded it, had to ask about her purse. Dee had it. Eunice put the document inside and snapped it shut.

After a while, they drove onto a section marked No

TRESPASSING: PRIVATE PROPERTY and to a beachfront house past some boulders on an incline about forty feet from the shoreline.

Questions entered Eunice's mind when she saw the police cars. A policewoman stood near the three girls in shorts, seated on the front steps. When the three cars pulled up, the three girls stood. They didn't move as Eunice, Henry, and the others advanced.

They volunteered nothing.

"How did this happen?" Eunice asked.

Who was saying what, Eunice didn't exactly know. The girls talked over each other, started, stopped, started again. They trembled, they cried, they had the look of horror. Eunice could almost feel sorry for them.

Dove was. . .on that slab?

The policewoman stepped up and spoke for them. She'd talked to them for hours. Had all the details. The four girls had gone for a swim. Dove went out too far. Undertow took her farther. They tried to get her. They had difficulty. One of them, the redheaded one, yes that was Annette, finally managed to bring her in, but Dove had drowned.

That's all.

The three girls clung to each other and wailed, "I'm sorry. We tried. I'm sorry."

Dee and Sarah hugged the girls, tried to soothe them, and they all cried except Eunice. She gazed out at the ocean. It looked so calm. The sun shone on it as if it were warm. It sparkled like a jewel. Golden swatches of sunlight danced on white foamy tips. The tide gently caressed the shore.

Her gaze moved off to the right, toward the outcropping of rock.

Then Eunice saw something. . .green.

A gentle knock sounded on the bedroom door. Eunice looked up and saw Annette standing there with her suitcase. "Come in."

"We were wondering if you want to eat out or cook here." Annette set the suitcase by the bed. "We need to buy groceries regardless. There's nothing here to eat." She straightened. "Or do you want to rest?"

"I'm fine," Eunice said. "We can all go. Just let me unpack a few things."

"We need to do that, too," Annette said.

Eunice hung some shirts, shorts, and pants in the closet. She'd had to pack as if going on a few days' vacation with friends. Henry had been concerned about her coming to this particular place but said if that's what she needed to do, then she should do it.

She realized this was not the closet from which she'd taken Dove's clothes that day. So this had not been Dove's room.

Nothing had made much sense back then. Had it been disbelief? Grief? The sleeping pill Dee had given her? One simply didn't want to believe something like that. At the same time, Eunice hadn't wanted to make Ruby, Lara, and Annette any more distressed than they were.

Looking back, Eunice thought of her shock. That had been more shocking than the first time she had cancer about ten years after Dove's death or a few weeks ago when she got her six-month notice. One's child was not supposed to die before her mother, before her parents. And Eunice had to try and help Henry. She didn't know if she could survive the loss, but what about Henry?

Dove had been his miracle child, his heart. Dove was her love, too, but in a different way. Dove was the personification of her guilt, her sin, her weakness, as well as her mercy, her forgiveness, God's presence. To him, Dove was not a part of the past. She had been his ever-present joy. His joy was gone. Eunice had to think of him. Help him. He was God's choice as shepherd to His people. She must be a helpmate in the most troubled time of his life.

Other things. . .could wait.

They waited.

Nineteen years ago, Eunice had gone into this house, taken Dove's clothes that the girls offered. She took the makeup case, the purse, the shoes, and packed them in Dove's suitcase. On top of it all, she'd laid the green item, then looked up at those girls, first one, then the other.

Without blinking, their eyes had stared at the item as if they were speechless before their executioner come to claim their heads for the guillotine. Lara raised her hand to her mouth and turned. Ruby and Annette made a strangling sound. All three girls ran from the room.

They were in no condition to speak of it, and Eunice could wait.

She'd waited.

For nineteen years.

All she could say at the funeral was, "I want the truth."

She would not leave here until she got it.

While the others were making phone calls to their families, Lara stood on the porch, grasping the banister. The motion of the waves was like a giant hand, palm up, unfolding its fingers, then slowly beckoning as it pulled back, then reached out again, repeating the process over and over.

She knew it could look innocent, appealing, inviting. She had thought so nineteen years ago. But it had been a demon. A glutton. It seemed placid; then it would grab your ankles, knock you over, play with you until you trusted it. Then it laughed, and it opened its cavernous mouth. It rose above you like some menacing being clad in a robe of deep blue outlined in white as if it wore a silver lining. You laugh; it's only a wave. So each time it came, it grew larger, higher, wider. But it's your friend. You can trust it. Until. . .

It turns on you. Won't turn you loose, rolls you over, pushes you under. . .and out. . .and you can't breathe. . .you can't see the moon hide behind a cloud. It doesn't care. . . . It's in and out, too. You want to live. . .but it's too late. . . . You fight it. . .all the while hearing its sinister laugh that is a roar. You can't open your mouth. . . can't allow your nose to open. . .there's only water. . .your eyes are open but blind. . . . What is it pushing you. . .is it the wave. . .or is it. . . ? You feel hands on your head. . . . Can a wave do that?

You grab and the wave has flesh. . .it has hands grasping

you. . . . You fight. . .you pull on the wave, shoving yourself up, and gasp and feel the salty wet air in your lungs, but it's air. . . . And before you can hold it in and take another, the hands are on your head again, then your neck. . . . You fight, you surface, manage to let the air out in a scream that is unlike any sound you've ever heard. It's like an animal trapped. Then there are more hands. You feel them pulling your arms. Legs are tangled up with yours. Then it hits your face. You're on your back; someone's arm is around your throat. They're going to kill you. No, you're going to die from coughing, spitting up water, being choked, but you're on your back, and your stinging eyes see the man in the moon peek out, grin at you, and hide his face again.

Then she was on the beach, being rolled over on her stomach. Hands were pushing into her back, and she was throwing up water in the sand. Ruby was screaming at her to talk to her.

"Get. . .off. . .my. . .back."

Ruby did. Lara got to her knees, coughed, and gagged. Finally, she raked away the sandy hair sticking to her face and peered up at Ruby. "What were you. . . ?"

The look on Ruby's face changed, and the sheer terror alarmed Lara. She looked in the direction Ruby was staring. Annette was pulling Dove from the ocean, calling, "Help me!"

They ran and helped drag Dove from the ocean's edge.

Annette called Tom, who said lunch, then coffee and teatime went as usual. No problems. Nobody missed her. He laughed then and said he'd worked harder than usual, being supervisor while she was away. He said he was kidding but for her not to worry and have a good time.

She started to tell him the same but thought better of it. "Be sweet," she said. "I love you."

He said he loved her, and they broke the connection. Annette took her phone in to Eunice, who had neglected to bring her own cell phone. She was grateful and said she wanted to call Henry.

Ruby was laying down the law, talking to first one, then another of her girls and asking all sorts of questions. She sometimes held the phone in front of her, looking at it askance as if the person on the other end could see her.

Annette walked away from the women talking on the phones and went in search of Lara. She stopped at the front screen and stared at the back of Lara, gazing out ahead of her. She seemed so forlorn. She had looked that way years ago when she came to church with her grandmother. That's when Annette approached her and invited her to church activities when they'd been sixteen.

Another time had been the morning after that awful night. After the rescue squad and police came, they'd watched as Dove was taken away. Then they'd been questioned as if they were some kind of criminals.

The police were still there when the Hogans and their friends came. One of them was a policeman, too. She knew because he and his wife were members of Pastor Hogan's church. That morning, Annette's parents came. Later, Ruby's parents arrived. After talking with the Hogans and the police and being told there was nothing more anyone could do there, Ruby crawled into the backseat of her parents' car.

Annette's parents said they should go, too, but Annette saw the starkness on Lara's face and told her parents they couldn't leave her there like that. Lara said her family members couldn't come. Her parents were out of the country. Her grandmother had enough on her hands taking care of her ailing husband. Her brother couldn't get away. Another brother couldn't be reached. "I can't stay," Lara said. "I'll just drive to my grandmother's."

Finally it was decided that Annette's parents would take Lara to her grandmother's. Brad's wife would follow in Lara's convertible. All the way back to Laurel Ridge, Annette felt like her eyes would not stay open, but she couldn't sleep. Neither she nor Lara spoke a word, and each time she glanced at Lara, Lara looked as if her eyes would pop out.

Annette put her hand on the screen door, then withdrew it. Another memory assailed her. That same morning before her parents had arrived.

Eunice had turned and slowly walked away from them toward the ocean. No one knew why. No one questioned. It didn't matter. This was not a time for doing anything one might call sensible. Just not losing your mind completely was hard enough. If that's what Eunice needed to do then—

But she began to walk faster. Then she broke into a run. Henry bolted and ran after her. Phil and Dee looked at each other and hurried after them.

Lara, Ruby, and Annette stood frozen in their tracks, watching. Eunice ran to the outcropping of rock and bent over. She picked something up, straightened, and held it out. Then she crushed it to her chest. She screamed. She looked toward heaven, yelling, "Why? Why? Why?"

Henry reached her, put his arm around her, and let her cry against his chest. He cried, too. Phil and Dee reached them and cried. Lara, Ruby, and Annette put their arms around each other and blubbered incoherently.

They turned loose when the voice of Henry reached them. "This is good. It's the first time she's cried. It's good to get it out." His face was completely wet.

Then the three of them saw it at the same time. Lara knew Annette and Ruby saw it, too, by the way each of them took in a breath that caused their throats to make sounds like panic.

Eunice turned toward them, her eyes filled with a question.

What she clutched in her hands, shoved against her chest. . .was green.

As if nothing more than that was on their minds, they shopped and kidded about who would pay for what. "That depends upon whether we have to pay Lara for rent and utilities," Eunice said.

"No way," Annette said. "I paid for the gas."

"Being adept at housekeeping," Ruby said, "I can clean up after supper, so I guess that leaves Eunice to buy the groceries."

Lara scoffed. "You're always complaining that your house is never clean."

"Right. I have to clean it so the girls and Charlie have room to pile their new junk all over it."

Their letting her pay for the groceries pleased Eunice. She hadn't wanted to be treated like some sick old woman or someone they tiptoed around. If they maintained a relaxed attitude, perhaps they could get through the difficult time that lay ahead of them.

How long would that take?

Until it was over.

They managed a congenial attitude while making, then eating their sandwiches and straightening the kitchen afterward. The bittersweet memory persisted. Nineteen years ago her daughter was here with her friends. They were girls then.

They were women now. But the same look of dread she'd seen so many times before now lay in their gazes when she said, "Let's take a walk down the beach."

Silence.

But she hadn't asked a question. She made a statement. "First, I need to take a pill."

Eunice stopped in the hallway outside the kitchen door and listened when she heard Ruby's wail. "She's going to make us skinny-dip and drown us one by one."

Annette ground out, "Ruby. Shut up."

Eunice retrieved her pill bottle from her tote bag. Lara was saying, "I can't. I can't do it."

Eunice pretended not to hear, took her pill with water, and the three friends followed her outside.

"I know this is difficult," Eunice said. They walked from the house, along the beach, and down toward the outcropping of rock. The fading evening sun reflected its golden glow on the ocean, which seemed such a living, breathing thing making its *slush, slush, slush* sounds. Why had that fiend chosen her daughter to swallow?

Or is that what happened?

That. . .drowning accident?

Dove had picked out her own clothes for years, so Eunice had been pleased when she asked, the day before she left for the Outer Banks, if Eunice would go with her to buy a bathing suit. She rather suspected Dove wanted to try and get a rise out of her by choosing one of those little string bikinis. Instead, Dove chose a more modest style than she'd owned in years. She'd tried it on and opened the dressing-room door. "Do you like it, Mama?" She'd turned and posed, looking into the three-way mirror to see herself at all angles.

"It's beautiful," Eunice said. "You look pretty, Dove. So pretty."

"Do I, Mama? Really?"

Eunice had laughed lightly, pleased that she and Dove were sharing one of those rare moments of camaraderie. So often they disagreed, but that was normal for a young girl learning independence.

Later, Eunice was to wonder. Was that really what Dove was doing that day? Did Eunice fail to see her daughter as she really was? Was Dove reaching out to her in a way she had not understood?

Reaching the rocks, Eunice put out her hand and looked at

the stark faces of the three friends who looked as if they'd lost their last one. They had. They, too, lost Dove, regardless of the circumstances. But Eunice had reached a point of no return, no matter how much the truth might hurt.

"Dove and I picked out her bathing suit the day before you girls came here," Eunice said. "Our last shopping trip together." Her determination for truth overrode the grief that threatened. "At the hospital, I was given a bag with a bathing suit in it. Then why?" She shook her head. "Why was my baby's bathing suit bottom washed up against these rocks?"

Lara felt it coming. She felt as green as that bathing suit bottom Eunice talked about. The ocean was swallowing the sun, then licking and slurping over the sand like a tongue flicking in and out. Each rising of the waves echoed with a hushed, hoarse kind of throaty laughter.

"I can't stand this," she wailed. Annette caught up with her as she ran for the house with her hand over her mouth. Her stomach churned.

She hated her reaction. Why couldn't she act like a mature woman, excuse that night as a fun time turned tragic? She rushed to the bedroom and found her bottle of purple pills. "I'll be okay," she said to Annette and locked the bathroom door behind her. She quickly washed the pill down with water, expecting that and her supper to defy her efforts.

"Yes," she said when Annette knocked and asked if she was okay. She leaned against the door and slid to the floor without a care about wet sand on her designer pants.

"I can't," Lara whispered.

twenty-six

"I can't."

That's what Lara had said that night on the beach when Annette dragged Dove in from the ocean and called them to help. Ruby had thought Lara was drowning and almost squashed her trying to get the water out.

"What are you trying to do?" Lara had screamed at Ruby.

"Save your life."

"That's not the way."

She and Ruby helped Annette lay Dove on her back. She was so limp. They stretched her out. Annette called her name. She didn't answer, just stared. Annette got on her knees and gave her resuscitation. She could hardly breathe herself. She slapped Dove's face back and forth, demanding she breathe. She stood. "Give her resuscitation," Annette ordered.

"I don't know how," Ruby said.

"I can't," Lara said.

"You have to," Annette said. "I have to call for help."

Seeing Ruby run off, Lara screamed, "Where are you going?"

"To get our clothes. We're naked."

She ran up to the house, behind Annette.

"Come back," Lara yelled. They disappeared into the house. She was left. . .alone. . .with that limp figure staring at her. She hopped around on the sand, like doing aerobics or a Bantu war dance with her arms holding her naked body. "I can't. I have to."

She heard a scream. It was her own.

Dove's eyes stared. Her mouth was open. She looked more alive when they first pulled her out of the water. But now. . .

Annette said she had to give it resuscitation.

Why did Annette make her do it? Annette had the training. *I do, too, but not as much as Annette. She's on the swim team. I've had lifesaving in PE, but that was funny, kissing on a rubber dummy.*

This was no rubber dummy.

Put my mouth on Dove's, that girl whose eyes are on me—blue eyes staring.

Lara dropped to her knees, took in a breath, closed her eyes, and lowered her head. Her mouth covered those cold, firm lips. Firm? Why weren't they soft? She could feel the teeth. The upper lip was slightly over the gums. Lara tried to push it down. It wouldn't go. She tried to close those eyes. The eyelids wouldn't go down.

Lara lowered her mouth to Dove's and forced her breath into it. She rose up and screamed. Her face lifted the dark cloudy sky. A plea for help from somewhere up there. But the moon hid its face behind a cloud.

She looked down long enough to put her hands on Dove's cold, damp, naked chest.

She pushed and cried and moaned and begged and pleaded. "Oh, please." She couldn't put her mouth on that thing again.

She's dead.

She can't be.

I'll die. So what?

She took a big gulp of air, put her mouth on Dove's again, and tried to force the air in. It wouldn't go.

Nothing moved except the shadows made by the moon playing hide-and-seek with the clouds. Eyes stared blankly, wildly.

It's a body. No breath.

I must make her live.

She straddled Dove, took a deep breath, violently blew into that open mouth. She stretched her mouth over it. Nothing happened except her own breath was leaving, and she felt like another one would not come. Her chest hurt.

She put her hands on Dove's chest again and pushed. "Wake up!" She cursed her, threatened her, slapped her. The slap bounced off. She grabbed her shoulders, cursing and demanding she wake up, get up, don't do this.

She won't breathe.

Annette had slapped her. Lara slapped her over and over and over and over. . .cursing, crying, screaming, begging.

"Lara!"

"Lara!"

She hears her name. *Is it. . .Dove?*

She looks at the cold, lifeless body. Only its hair is alive. She pulls the hair. It sticks in her fingers. She can't get loose. The thing has trapped her.

"Help."

She's being pulled away. The hair comes with her hands. The head comes with the hair. The body comes up with the head.

She loses her mind. Then Annette is slapping her. "Stop it! Stop it! We have to do something."

"Okay. Okay."

She breathes hard with every breath Annette tries to breathe into Dove. She pushes with every push Annette makes on Dove's chest. Annette should have done that in the first place. "Why did you make me stay here?"

Annette rose, breathless. "You didn't have your wits about you well enough to call for help. Neither could Ruby." Her shoulders drooped, and her voice softened. "You did all you could, Lara."

She shook her head. "I kissed a corpse." She turned and ran, throwing up as she went.

Annette yelled. "We have to dress her."

That stopped Lara. The acrid taste was forgotten. "Why?"

"The police will come. How will it look for her to be lying here naked?"

Lara realized Annette and Ruby were dressed. Anger flared up in her. "Like the two of us were out here naked."

Annette ordered, "We have to dress her."

Lara wailed. "I have to get dressed."

"Her first."

"Why?"

"Because." Annette took a deep breath. "She will harden."

Lara screamed. "I can't stand this." She looked at Ruby holding the green bathing suit top and looking like she was in the twilight zone, just waiting for someone to direct her.

Annette did. It took all three of them to put the top on the body. "Where's the bottom?"

"I don't know," Ruby said.

"Well, find it."

She ran to the ocean's edge but couldn't find it. "She threw it back. It must have gone out into the ocean."

Annette quickly took the bottom of her suit off, and they struggled to get it onto the body. It was loose, but at least she was covered. "Now we have to get dressed."

They all ran to the house.

Lara was covered in sand and vomit. "I have to brush my teeth and shower."

"You can't," Annette said. "How would it look if we get cleaned up and out there. . .out there. . . ?"

Lara nodded, found her bathing suit, and struggled into it. Annette found a pair of short-shorts and put them on along with her bathing suit top.

That's when they decided to hide the bottles. They shook, and their teeth chattered. "Maybe," Annette said, "we should drink coffee. In case. . .they can smell the alcohol."

"Okay." The three of them working together spilled coffee grounds all over, had no idea how many spoonfuls of coffee were in the filter or how much water made it to the pot, but they managed to plug it in. The pot began to perk.

They pulled cups from the cabinets without regard to any dust or bugs that might have accumulated. With a shaky hand, Annette poured hot liquid into the cups, spilling some, making stains.

"I need cream," Ruby said.

"No," Annette said. "Black coffee's supposed to sober people up. We don't want them to think. . .we've been drinking."

Lara sunk into a chair. "If we're not sober now, I doubt we ever will be." She'd meant it as an ironic statement, but it occurred to her that she would never be the same. She'd kissed a corpse. What. . .happened out there?

Sirens sounded in the distance. Lara began to shake, and the coffee dribbled from her mouth, down her chin, and onto her chest.

"We have to go out there," Annette said.

"No," Ruby said while Lara shook her head.

"It's not going to look right with us sitting here drinking coffee."

The coffee cups sloshed over when they all set them down. They ran from the house. The deafening sound of shrill sirens permeated that twilight zone with reality. Flashing, revolving globes lit up the night in neon colors and swirled over the still body dressed in a green bathing suit top and a black bottom that was too big.

Now Eunice was saying she had to go through it again.

Ruby went to the bathroom door and hissed, "Come out of there," while Annette and Eunice went into the kitchen.

"I'm coming," Lara said. "I'm. . .freshening."

Were things not so serious, Ruby could have laughed. Lara's statement sounded as silly as something she might say. Freshening!

But things were much too serious. When she walked into the kitchen, Eunice was watching Annette watching the pot make coffee. Ruby walked over to the pot. "Lara's okay. Must have been something she ate."

Eunice's gaze got stuck. Annette flashed Ruby a you've-just-won-the-idiot-of-the-year-award kind of glance.

Ruby grimaced and got cups. She closed the cabinet door.

"Saucers, too," Annette said.

Saucers. Well, yes. Otherwise they'd have coffee rings all over the floor and table before this night was over. Not wanting to chance walking four steps with hot cups of coffee in saucers, she set the empty cups. . .and saucers. . .on the edge of the table.

"Sugar and creamer," Annette said.

Ruby opened the sugar bag and set it in the middle of the table, put the container of powdered creamer beside it, patted them, then lifted her finger triumphantly. "Spoons," she said. "I'm not totally incompetent."

She had second thoughts when Eunice picked up the creamer, unscrewed the lid, struggled with the cardboard on top, tore it off, and screwed the lid back on.

Annette glanced at Ruby out of the corner of her eye, then took the pot over and poured the coffee.

Ruby slid the cups to the four places. She and Annette sat and watched the breeze stir the curtains.

Lara came in wearing fresh lipstick, sat in the waiting chair, murmured, "Sorry," and stared at her cup of black coffee like it was the green-eyed monster.

"Are you feeling better, dear?" Eunice asked.

"I took a pill," Lara said as if that were an answer.

Eunice put sugar in her coffee, then creamer. Ruby knew Eunice would take a sip, set her cup down, then ask her questions.

Nineteen years ago, Eunice's daughter had sat at that table. But it was not coffee they were drinking. The four of them had arrived late afternoon. They'd cleaned the place themselves since no one had stayed there since the place had been closed up in October. They'd made the beds, gone for supplies to stock the pantry. They'd driven down the streets with the top down on the convertible, waving to guys who would readily have accepted an invitation to a party. They confined it to flirting, however.

Evening came. They ate, put on their bathing suits, danced like church-going girls were told they shouldn't on the private beach while music blared from the car's radio, then returned to the house to eat and drink more. With night as their shroud, inhibitions fled, conversations became personal and turned to the topic of those days—the opposite sex.

"Have you guys. . .you know. . . ?" Dove asked.

"You mean. . ." Ruby wiggled her eyebrows. Lara and Annette giggled.

Dove pushed one side of her long blond hair away from her face. Her big blue eyes flashed. "Don't make fun of me. I mean it. I want to know."

"It's really no big deal to me. I have older brothers, and they're disgusting." Ruby sipped her drink. "Anyway, Charlie won't let me."

Dove's big blue eyes moved to Annette.

"Me?" Annette scoffed. "I'm president of the Christian student union. I can't do that." She grinned like she might or might not be telling the truth. "Every time I leave the house, my mom tells me to be sweet, and when I come home, she looks at me as if to ask if I have been."

Lara leaned forward, her dark eyes serious under her dark, arched brows. "I'm not spilling my guts about anything. But I'll tell you a secret. Jared and I are talking marriage."

Ruby squealed. Annette insisted upon knowing details.

Lara sipped her drink, set it down, and looked smug. "This is not an official announcement. He just mentioned marriage, and I have always said that a proposal must come with a dozen red roses, a background of soft music, champagne, and a big, white-gold diamond ring."

Lara turned to Dove, who was really going for that rum and Coke. "Have you?"

Dove set her glass down rather hard. "What? Miss Goody-Two-Shoes? The preacher's daughter? I wouldn't dare."

Ruby had the strong suspicion Miss Goody-Two-Shoes wasn't used to partying, either. Actually, none of them were. They'd tried a few things, but they didn't run with the fast crowd. This was just a. . .celebration. One of those few once-in-a-lifetimes. A taste of the forbidden.

Annette stood. "I think it's time we dared. . .something. What about a midnight swim?"

"It's not midnight."

"It will be when we finish. Just think. The moonlight on our glistening naked bodies."

"Naked?" Ruby said, while Dove sat with her mouth open. Lara chuckled.

Annette shrugged. "Why not? Our bodies get wet anyway. Why bother with bathing suits? This is a private beach. Let's be free."

Ruby huffed. "Easy for you to say. You have that swimmer's figure. I've got the chunky-cheerleader bod."

"Oh foot, Ruby," Lara said. "You parade it in front of the entire stadium. Anyway, I'm svelte." She posed as if being photographed. "I was asked to be a model once. My mom said it was beneath me." She shucked out of her suit and sent it sailing through the air. "Away with moms."

Annette ran to the door, looking over her shoulder. "Chicken!" Lara hurried toward her, and the two of them began cackling. They raced out the door.

Dove looked peaked. Ruby knew Lara had grown up around drinking socially, and it was no big deal to her. Annette didn't like it very much. Ruby had made her brothers share with her in years past, or she would have tattled. But she felt she didn't need it to be silly. "You're not used to this," she said and slid the glass away from her.

Dove smacked at Ruby's hand. "I can handle it." She reached for the glass and drank. "I'm not a prude."

"A prude?"

Dove giggled. "A. . .pr. . .rude. Got it? No, I'm not. I'm not a pr. . .rude." She giggled again. "Just. . .rude."

Ruby laughed. "We'll see." She took off her own suit and tossed it aside.

Dove looked sick. Was it the drinking? It wasn't as if they'd never had sleepovers in each others' homes, dressed after swimming, tried on each other's clothes, or showered openly in PE class for years. But going into the ocean naked and chance being seen was rather daring.

"Look, you don't have to do this. It's no big deal. We're just having fun. And kidding with you."

"Yeah. Fun. I do have to do it. It's the thing to do. You go on. I'll come."

Ruby wasn't sure, but looking over her shoulder, she saw that Dove was standing, her hands at her back as if unfastening her top. She kept looking back to make sure Dove was okay. By the time she reached the water's edge, Dove was walking toward them, tripping once. She dropped the top of her suit to the sand. Annette and Lara were out about chest deep, laughing, splashing, dodging waves. "Come on," Annette called. "This is so freeing."

Ruby walked in, still watching Dove wade unsteadily into the water. Fine, if she didn't want to take off the bottom of her suit. When she reached about waist-deep, she removed the bottom and threw it back on the beach.

"I want to be free," she said. A wave knocked her over. They all reached for her, but she came up unscathed and waded farther and put her hand on Lara's arm for balance. But who could be steady in the ocean?

When she thought Dove wasn't looking, Ruby made the motion of guzzling a drink, shook her head, crossed her eyes, and nodded toward Dove. Annette and Lara nodded as they understood and laughed. They could handle this. They'd watch out for each other. Anyway, the cold water should sober Dove up. Or maybe she was just self-conscious about being naked.

Now, nineteen years later, how could they tell Dove's mother about that night?

Then Eunice said it. "I want to know the truth."

The words were the same that she'd spoken at the funeral, but the sound was different. Back then, her voice had been a plea. Now, her voice was a command. Ruby knew the sounds. She'd spoken them often enough to her children. A whiney, singsong request of, "Clean your room," didn't mean the same as, "Clean! Your! Room!"

This was a "come clean" tone of voice.

Lara's hands moved to her lap, where Ruby felt sure her knuckles would be as white as her face.

Annette, with a steady hand, picked up the container of powdered creamer and shook some into her cup. The spoon *tink-tink-tinked* as she stirred. Was that some kind of centrifugal force that would keep the coffee in the cup like when one swings a bucket of water around fast—or would the coffee spill over?

Lara and Annette found their coffee cups as a focal point instead of Eunice's gaze, which fell on Ruby, who hadn't yet focused on her coffee but was waiting for Lara or Annette to respond. Annette always knew what to say.

But Ruby knew she was the only one of them who could get by with asking a question as if she were stupid. After all, she was an ex-cheerleader, and weren't they all supposed to be airheads? Almost as dense as a blond? She didn't think this was the occasion for a blond joke. She stammered, "Wh–what?"

"Everything. The top of that bathing suit the hospital gave me was Dove's. Not the bottom," Eunice said.

"It was mine," Annette said. "We were skinny-dipping."

"We dressed her," Ruby said. "But we couldn't find the bottom to her suit. We didn't want her lying there. . .like that."

"Thank you. . .for that." She looked from one to the other as if expecting some other explanation. Then she moved her hand in a sweeping motion. "This kitchen, for instance. I've had a lot of years to think. The policewoman said you all had been sitting at the kitchen table, snacking, talking, then decided on a late swim. Going for a swim right after eating could have caused Dove to have stomach cramps. Why was there no evidence of having eaten? The kitchen was spotless. Who cleaned it?"

Annette released her spoon but left it in the cup. That was unlike her. The coffee was well stirred. "We did."

Eunice's head lifted slightly. "You mean the four of you?"

"Three," Ruby said.

At Annette's quick glance, Ruby realized she should have kept her mouth shut.

"Before or after Dove drowned?"

They mustn't allow the silence to linger. That would make

them sound guilty of something.

"Before," Ruby said at the same time Annette said, "After."

Oh good, Ruby thought. *Now that I've lied and Annette wants to tell the truth after all those lectures about saying nothing, I won't be considered reliable.* She could just keep her mouth shut. . .like Lara. Except when she opened it to take in air.

"All right," Eunice said. "We have one before and one after. Lara, what do you say?"

Lara blew out a breath, and her head trembled from side to side. "I don't remember. I don't think I helped clean. I was. . . oblivious."

Eunice's shoulders rose with her breath. She exhaled. "Did she call out that she had cramps?"

They all stared at Eunice, then shook their heads.

"The police said you hit her."

Annette nodded. "I had to. That's the only chance I had of saving her."

"Why did you girls, one of you an expert swimmer, let my baby drown?" Her voice trembled. She asked again. "How did my baby die?"

Annette whispered, "Where do we start?"

Eunice said, "Start at the beginning."

"We had been drinking," Ruby said. "Quite a bit."

"We were so scared." Annette's voice trembled. "We didn't understand why we couldn't save her. We tried. We felt so awful about drinking. And being nude. We cleaned away the bottles and threw them into the trash out back. We weren't supposed to do those things."

"When did you clean up?"

"After we knew she was. . .not going to wake up," Ruby said. "Help was on the way. We wanted to hide. . .the bottles."

"The police found them," Annette said. "That made us seem

like. . .covering something up. And as if my hitting her had been because of a fight."

A hyperventilating sound came from Lara. "They left me. . . alone. . .with her." Her voice became a squeak. "I did the best I could."

The sun seemed to have dropped from the sky. The light of evening turned its back and withdrew through the windows, leaving behind ominous shadows throughout the kitchen.

Eunice pushed away from the table. "I see this is going to be difficult." She stood. "I'll get my Bible from my tote bag I left in the bedroom." She walked to the doorway, found the light switch, and they blinked as overhead light shone down upon the three as if they sat beneath an interrogator's bulb.

She left the kitchen.

"Oh Lord," Ruby said, praying for help. "She's going to make us swear on the Bible to tell the truth."

Eunice returned with the Bible and handed it to Ruby. "Turn to the back cover. Lift up the paper covering. Yes. It's glued down. Pull it up."

Why is she picking on me? Ruby thought. She began to cautiously lift a corner, fearful she was doing wrong.

"You can do better than that, girl. Do I have to do it myself?"

Ruby pulled, and as the dark maroon paper was torn away from the corner, she spied the corner of a white sheet of paper.

"Pull that out."

Ruby pulled the dark covering farther until she could pull out the white sheet of paper.

"Read it." Eunice sat down.

Ruby read it, then passed it to Lara, who passed it to Annette, who pushed it toward Eunice. The white paper, so long confined, cavorted in the center of the table. No one dared touch it.

A cool breeze drifted through the windows, chilled the air, and stirred the paper that represented a ghost of the past that had whispered, chided, threatened. Now it lived as if the beautiful, fine, golden-haired, brilliant blue-eyed girl were dancing, laughing, crying from her grave, vowing she would never be forgotten:

Mama,

Please don't hate me. It's so hard for me to tell you this, but I have to. Mama, I'm pregnant. I hate what I've done. I know the shame this can be to all of us, especially Daddy. Don't tell him. He always calls me his good girl. He can't say that now. I've failed you both. I'm so sorry. I love you both so very, very much. I don't want to hurt you. Please forgive me. I love you. Don't hate me.

Dove

Ruby got up and brought a roll of toilet tissue so they could wipe their eyes and blow their noses.

In the roar of silence, Eunice spoke. "Did you girls know?"

Annette sobbed. "I didn't know."

Lara shook her head. "No."

Ruby didn't say anything. Annette's and Lara's heads turned toward her. Eunice stared.

Ruby lifted her red-rimmed eyes to Eunice. "I suspected. Her actions that night were different. She seemed reluctant to take off her swimsuit. She'd never been shy about her body. It wasn't like we'd never seen each other without clothes. I think the reason schools call us the student body is because they lump us all in PE class and make us shower together."

The note blew toward Lara. She hugged her arms to herself. Annette closed the kitchen windows, then Ruby continued. "She waded out into the water before she took off the bottom and threw it toward the shore. I even started to say something about looking at that belly, but she stumbled, and we caught her. I shrugged that off as her having eaten and she'd really drunk a lot."

Ruby told about the conversation that night about boys. "The tone of it just wasn't right. But none of us was her usual self. When I was pregnant, I remembered how she looked lying on the beach. I told myself she was bloated with water. I had no reason to ever mention it. Had it been true, it was her situation that ended that night. Now I wonder if she had wanted us to know. If that's why she asked us about our behavior, as if she didn't know us."

Ruby reached out and touched the Bible. "I swear we never talked about that. I didn't know. . .anything."

Eunice searched their faces. "I thought she may have confided in you girls. That maybe she had tried having an abortion, but something went wrong. The medical examiner's report stated she was pregnant. I never told Henry."

Eunice tore off more of the tissue and wiped her face. She touched the note. "But she left this. I wondered if you girls knew her secret. Perhaps she left the note to prepare me, planning to confide in me later. Or—"

She took a ragged breath. "Had she intended never to come home again?"

They all sat pondering the questions.

What were the answers?

Annette got up and brought the coffeepot and began refilling the cups. This was a night that called for. . .at least. . .caffeine.

Then Lara's clear, distinct declaration shocked them all into deeper silence.

"I killed her."

The pot was tipped, the cup overflowed, and coffee ran out of the saucer and onto the table. Ruby yelled. Annette quickly returned the pot to the countertop and tore off paper towels. Ruby rolled out the tissue to help halt the flow.

Eunice hardly noticed the frantic efforts of the women trying to wipe up the stains left by the puddle of coffee. Her focus was on Lara. Eunice had waited nineteen years to hear the truth. Knowing herself as she did, she wasn't easily surprised by anything. But this, she never expected. Annette rinsed her hands and dried them. She returned to her chair. "No, Lara. That's not true." She stared at her friend. "You were on the beach when Dove was still alive."

"But it's my fault. I lied."

Relief replaced the pain in Lara's eyes as she began to tell her story. *Sometimes,* Eunice thought, *confession really is good for the soul. . .sometimes.*

"I didn't exactly lie, but I gave the impression that Jared had asked me to marry him. He hadn't. But I was jealous of the way he looked at Dove. He never cared about church until after he saw her; then he decided to go to some church activities. I could tell she liked him. He was my boyfriend. I couldn't bear to think she might take him away from me."

Eunice nodded. She had seen the interest in her daughter's eyes when Jared came to a church dinner they'd had for college students on Christmas break. Another time, one evening, Eunice and Henry turned off I-40 and onto I-240, heading to the cafeteria for dinner. When Henry made the turn, Eunice noticed a BMW like Jared's whiz by on I-40. The image of a blond woman behind the darkened windows made her think of Dove. But it couldn't be. Dove was spending the night with Ruby.

"Through the years," Eunice said, "I've wondered what my grandchild would have looked like. Do you think. . .the baby was Jared's?"

Jared's?

Lara had never thought. . .that. Jared had a roving eye and had a past reputation with the girls. She never thought there was, or could be, anything serious between Dove and Jared. Dove wasn't Jared's type. She was. . .the preacher's daughter. Now all sorts of speculations entered her mind. That night in the water had been so confusing.

Dove had swum out to Lara, then chided her to swim out farther. Lara had protested. Dove made the hen-cackling noise. Okay, she'd humor her. Dove was in a strange mood. She felt a twinge of guilt about that, too. Lara was used to drinking socially. She knew Dove wasn't. Something deep inside her wanted to see Dove topple from her pedestal. She was no better than anyone else.

They were both strong swimmers, so she took the dare. Then she felt Dove's hands on her. Was Dove in trouble? Lara got away. With all the sputtering, feeling the undertow, being too far out, hearing Annette and Ruby calling them to come back, she became afraid. Dove seemed to be pulling her out farther, saying things about her and Jared. Was she really going to marry him?

She was afraid of Dove's mood but unwilling to retract what

she'd said earlier because she did intend to marry Jared. . .someday. Dove began saying, "I hate you. I hate him. I hate. . .everything."

Lara had tried to save Dove when she realized she was in trouble. Dove was about to pull her under. She had to get away. She'd heard of the danger. She slapped her away. She'd heard that was the thing to do. She'd yelled at Dove to stop it.

"Stop it!" she yelled. "You'll drown us both." It seemed she was trying to push Lara under.

The sound that came from Dove was like a hysterical laugh. Lara thought she was scared to death. Or the drinking had made her lose all concept of anything. She was weak and scared and didn't know how to control Dove. Dove had her hands all over her head, her shoulders, and they rolled in the water. All Lara could do when surfacing was weakly yell, "Help."

"I hardly had enough breath to keep away from Dove's flailing arms, the waves, the tug of the undertow," Lara said. "I was swallowing too much water."

Annette reached them. She grabbed Dove from behind and had Dove's head in the crook of her arm. Dove had stopped struggling by then.

"I didn't know what was happening then," Lara said. "In my mind I needed to save myself. I needed to get away from her. I didn't know if she was so panicked she was trying to hold onto me, but instead she was pushing me under."

Lara looked straight at Eunice. "Now I think Dove was trying to kill me."

Eunice looked pained. Lara didn't hold back her thoughts, some of which had never come to her before. "I never remembered that night clearly. Such things weren't supposed to happen." She spread her hands. "I've been in shock for nineteen years." She spoke as if talking to herself. "Did Dove really want to drown me? Maybe the alcohol affected her brain. And her being pregnant would be the worst thing that could happen to a girl like that, then." Her voice softened. "Maybe for a moment, she did hate me. But Dove in her right mind would never want to harm anyone. Looking back. . ."

Lara shook her head. "So many times I've wondered why I wasn't the one who drowned. She was really. . .good." Lara put her hands over her face. "She was only eighteen."

Eunice moved Lara's hands away from her face. "Lara." Her voice was soft. "You, too, were only eighteen."

Annette felt the guilt of not having been more responsible. "I'm the one who suggested that midnight skinny-dip. Dove's mood change bothered me. I didn't want any conflict. We were there to have fun."

Eunice tore off some tissue and handed it to Annette. "Did she say anything else? Was she angry when she. . .went under?"

This dying woman who loved her child as Annette loved Tom, would love him no matter what he might do, wanted questions about her daughter answered before she died. Annette would try and forget herself for the moment and cater to Eunice's request. Why couldn't she, a championship swimmer, save Dove?

Hadn't she asked the same question herself?

Isn't that why she swam like a madwoman in college? But it did no good, so she stopped.

So much she'd wanted to forget. Too much she'd never forgotten. She told what she remembered.

At first she thought Lara and Dove were playing in the water. But they were out too far. Then the sound of their voices coming over the water didn't sound playful. They didn't come when she and Ruby called. Annette swam out. Dove seemed to be trying to push Lara under.

"I wasn't sure," Annette said. "All this was happening so

quickly, and we had the ocean to contend with. Like Lara said, I, too, thought maybe Dove had panicked and in trying to hold onto Lara was drowning her. When Dove came up, I hit her in the face. Dove went backwards and under. Lara emerged gasping for air. By that time, Ruby helped get Lara out."

Annette was thoughtful; then she looked at Eunice. "Dove was exhausted and stunned by my hitting her long enough for me to get her on her back and start swimming for shore. I was glad to hear her say for me to let her go, that she could swim. We were close enough to shore that I saw Ruby on Lara's back and wanted to hurry and help. I was exhausted and didn't think I could fight Dove again. I let her go."

Annette swallowed hard and took a few deep breaths before continuing. "We both were close enough to shore by then that we could soon have walked out. Dove said, 'Dear Jesus. Forgive me.' "

Sobs racked Annette's body. She rocked back and forth in the chair. Lara, Ruby, and Eunice were all sobbing. "That's where I made my mistake. I shouldn't have let her go. But I thought she was apologizing for whatever went on between her and Lara. I told her it was okay, that the midnight swim hadn't been the greatest idea.

"Dove didn't answer. I looked around and didn't see her. But Dove was not swimming with me. I began calling, swimming in circles as best I could. I felt something and grabbed. It was Dove. The waves were helping her get to shore. Her feet could touch the bottom. Ruby was standing, and Lara was on her knees. I called for help. They came running.

"I gave her resuscitation. That was supposed to make her breathe. It didn't. I knew Lara had taken a course in CPR. I left her there while I ran to call for help."

"I'm not sure what I did," Lara said. "It was awful. I couldn't believe it. That couldn't be Dove. And I was so confused by what had happened. I'd fought with her in the ocean. I'd had life-saving. Why couldn't I apply it? I couldn't hit her. If I had, like Annette did, maybe. . ."

"I told the police," Annette said, "that I hit her so I could save her. She was drowning. For quite a while they acted like I'd tried to hurt her. We didn't." Annette's voice was a high-pitched squeak. "We didn't want that to happen."

They all sat, silent except for the sobs they couldn't hold back. "I'm so sorry I couldn't save her." Annette's voice was strangled. "Please forgive me."

"And me," Ruby cried.

"And me-e-e-e," Lara pled brokenly.

Eunice got up from the table and left the kitchen, her every breath a sob. "We've talked enough tonight. Let's try and get some sleep. I need to take a pill." She left the room.

"I can't stand this anymore," Ruby said. "I hope she kills us now."

Annette sniffed. "I think she already has."

Lara took several gulps of air. "I died that night as surely as Dove did."

Fresh tears started.

Eunice came back in. She walked to the sink and took a pill, then returned to her seat at the table. "I want to ask you girls something else. Lara, you used to be so full of life, but when you returned from Europe, you were closed up like a rhododendron leaf in winter, and you've never opened up again. Ruby, you no longer sing like you did before. And Annette, you gave up swimming. Was that because of what happened here nineteen years ago?"

Ruby said, "Yes," while the other two nodded. "I couldn't stand up there, facing you, and sing a solo."

"You girls mustn't blame yourselves any more than I should

blame myself. I know what guilt can do to a person. It can destroy our effectiveness at being all the Lord wants us to be. We tell ourselves we aren't worthy. I've told myself I was a terrible mother. Dove should have been able to come to me with anything."

Ruby nodded vigorously. "We tell our children that, Eunice. And our mothers told us. How many of us really confide in the one who cares the most?"

Eunice smiled wanly. "I know. But when they don't, we feel like failures. So I want you girls to know I didn't bring you here to condemn you. I wanted to know the truth as much as possible and let you know that if you needed forgiveness for anything, I am offering it."

The surprise on their faces revealed they thought she had wanted to condemn them. She must set them straight. "If you hadn't done all you could to save Dove, I would forgive you. But I believe you did. She would not have died that night unless she wanted to. I think she killed herself."

Their downcast eyes indicated they believed the same.

"Now, I'm asking you to forgive me for the various phases of grief I went through. They were many, including condemnation, anger, resentment. But the Lord took that from me years ago. I want to tell you this. I have not been a perfect woman. Oh, we all say we're sinners and laugh like we stole a paper clip or didn't tithe until we had enough money. But I sinned big-time." She smiled. "But I'm forgiven, which means I'm clean as a whistle."

"Oh, Eunice," Annette said. "Your life is a beautiful example of a Christian woman."

"If so, that's because of the Lord Jesus using my life, which I want Him to do. And I want you girls to know I hold no resentment toward you whatsoever."

"We've felt so guilty," Annette said.

Eunice nodded. "I know about guilt. We can be so slow to

forgive ourselves. It doesn't seem right for us to pick up the pieces of our sins and go on as if they never happened. We think we don't deserve our blessings. Then we listen to preachers like Henry, who remind us how good and great God is. How Jesus suffered so our sins could be forgiven. But sometimes we insist upon our own suffering, as if that will absolve us. We even wonder at times if we are Christians."

"I don't think I am," Lara said blandly.

Lara wasn't quite sure why she said such a thing. Maybe because of the hours of each woman confessing, searching her soul. What would one more truth hurt?

Curiosity lay in Ruby's and Annette's eyes. Lara looked at Eunice. Her eyes held something Lara hadn't been cognizant of for nineteen years. Her expression was full of love and kindness. Hadn't she heard her?

Lara felt an explanation would be in order. "I don't have that relationship you talk about, that closeness and talking to God. Oh, I've prayed. But I've never. . ." She felt embarrassed. "Never asked Him into my heart. That seemed so silly and childish."

She felt like the air had gone from the room. They all sat like statues. Maybe she shouldn't have changed the subject. She lifted her hands helplessly. "I've wanted to believe it. I mean, what else is there? I've read books about it. Like the apostle Paul says, if the salvation story isn't real, we're all miserable." Her short laugh was ironic. "I've been there."

They smiled at her as if they knew what she meant. Now that she'd gone this far, she might as well continue. "So I've done what I thought was right. I go to church. I give part of my earnings. I help the poor. I've gone with Ruby and Annette to visit the sick and take food and cards."

"You're right, Lara," Eunice said after a long moment. "It is childish to ask Jesus into your heart."

Lara laughed shortly. She nodded as Eunice said, "Jesus says we have to come to Him like a little child, trusting, asking, admitting we're weak and helpless."

"I've been afraid of having to admit that maybe I didn't do everything I could to save Dove. Maybe I hadn't really wanted to. Why couldn't I? Why. . . ?"

"Lara, Lara," Eunice said, getting her attention. "You've already told what happened. Of course you're to blame for anything you did wrong. But my daughter was responsible for her actions, too. Before and during that night. Whatever you have done or didn't do is not the issue now. Because of sin within the human heart, we need to ask God's forgiveness, invite Jesus in. Accept that forgiveness, and start life anew."

Lara had never. . .humbled herself in such a way. But somehow she knew this was a life-and-death issue, as much as the events of nineteen years ago had been. Like she'd seen little children do in pictures on the walls of the church, she folded her hands, bowed her head, closed her eyes, and said, "Jesus. Forgive me. Come into my heart. Amen." She raised her head, opened her eyes to their smiles, then quickly closed her eyes again. "Oh, and thank You."

She took a deep breath. Why didn't they talk? Why didn't she see a blinding light or hear something other than the same old ocean? She lifted a hand helplessly.

"Don't worry," Eunice said. "It'll come."

"What?" Lara asked tentatively.

Eunice smiled. "The assurance that you belong to Him. Your salvation is secure. Oh, you won't be perfect, but you don't have to live with guilt or fear. That's been conquered, and it will continue to be conquered daily if you just turn it over to the Lord."

"I've known that all my life," Annette said. "And yet I have let guilt eat away at me."

Ruby snorted. "And I've tried to eat the guilt away."

"I understand," Eunice said. "Even though we're forgiven, we suffer the consequences of our actions. And it usually takes a lot of living and failing before we learn to turn everything over to the Lord. I want to thank you girls for coming here with me, letting me burden you."

"No," Annette said. "You have unburdened us."

Ruby and Lara agreed.

She stood. "I can't stay awake any longer. That pill is getting to me. And Lara, you are now like a newborn baby in the kingdom of God. And babies need sleep." She yawned, then blinked. Her eyes had difficulty staying open. "Don't you girls have something that can help you sleep?"

Ruby's and Annette's gazes questioned Lara.

She nodded.

They awoke to a new day of sunshine streaming through the open windows. Eunice was the last to come into the kitchen. "I smell coffee."

They all went out onto the porch with their cups. Annette and Ruby sat on the steps. Lara and Eunice sat in the rocking chairs. "The ocean doesn't look so ominous this morning," Eunice said. "We should at least wade in it. The ocean is to be respected, but it's not the enemy."

Soon, the four of them in shorts and tank tops frolicked at the edge of the water, delighting in the playful tickle of water and sand beneath their feet.

After a while, Eunice reached into her pocket. "There's something I need to do." She took the white note and tore it into pieces, walked farther into the water, and tossed them into the ocean. She watched the pieces of paper go with the flow of the tide, in and out until they disappeared. "That's what God does with our sins."

She turned and walked back to the edge. "I don't want Henry to know what I've told you girls here. That note lay hidden in my Bible as a big question mark for nineteen years."

"But it was like an answer for us," Lara said. Annette and Ruby agreed.

"Yes," Eunice said. "Opening up that hiding place was an answer for me. Bringing it here."

"Imagine that," Ruby said and grinned. "Finding answers to life in the Bible. Who would have thought it?"

They laughed at the irony of that statement and the foolishness of humans so often neglecting to live up to what they know and are taught.

"Hmmm," Lara said. "I think I'll read that book."

Eunice wanted to stay another day, determined that they all concentrate on the positive. They rode around the Outer Banks, visiting places of interest, enjoying the sunshine, and eating at a unique seaside restaurant.

Eunice complimented them. "Your adversities have made you strong young women."

"Really?" Ruby beamed. "I thought they made me fat."

Late into the evening, they walked and talked and cried some more. They remembered Dove, the beautiful, sweet girl they had known and loved. "Remember those things," Eunice said. "Let go of that tragic night. Remember the good."

She could say from experience, with confidence, "If we turn everything over to the Lord, good really does come from the worst of things."

They spent another night, walked on the beach in the early morning sun, enjoyed a final cup of coffee while sitting on the porch, then left for home.

During that drive, like four friends, they had no lack of conversation.

"That turned out to be like a well-earned vacation," Ruby said. "I haven't had one in years."

That got a rise from Eunice. "He gets a couple of vacations from church, Ruby."

"Right, but it doesn't always coincide with the radio station. Anyway, we can't afford to go anywhere. We take the girls up to Craggy Gardens for a picnic. Take them to a lookout on the parkway and say, "You can see five states from here. Now how many other families take a vacation in five states all in one day?"

Annette told about her honeymoon to the Grand Canyon years ago and more recent trips she and Tom had taken to visit her parents in Florida.

Lara talked about the various sights she'd seen in Europe, making it sound much more exciting than it was because she'd been so unhappy at the time. Before that, she'd gone to Hawaii and the Caribbean with her family.

"The most wonderful trip I've had was to Israel. That was quite a few years ago," Eunice said. "After my bout with cancer. The church thought that would be good for me and Henry. It was." She turned her head toward the backseat. "Did you girls hear me and Henry talk about it? We had a special evening at church for that."

They remembered, but none of them had gone to that event. Carley was only a couple weeks old then, and Ruby had stayed home with her. Annette didn't remember what she had going on. Lara recalled there was no way she would go without Ruby and Annette.

Through the years, they'd heard Eunice and Henry mention places they'd seen.

Eunice told them of sites that had brought the Bible to life in a way her studying could not have done. She could not think that anyone, a Christian in particular, could go to the Holy Land without feeling closer to God.

"What was your favorite experience there?" Annette asked.

"Oh, overlooking Jerusalem while riding on a camel," she said.

They laughed with her. Then she told of life-changing experiences like riding in a boat on the Sea of Galilee, floating in the Dead Sea, walking along the edge of the Mediterranean Sea, standing on the Golan Heights looking at Syria and Lebanon, going to Bethlehem, sitting on the temple steps.

Ruby said, as if such a trip were a possibility, "We've been friends for years, but do you think we could stand each other, in the same room, day after day?"

"Well, you can take what you will from this story." Eunice forced a serious look on her face and looked from one to the other. "I heard about this man who took his wife and mother-in-law to the Holy Land. The mother-in-law had a heart attack and died. The funeral home director said they could ship her back to the United States for fifteen hundred dollars. But they could bury her in Israel for two fifty. They talked it over. The wife was willing to bury her mother in Israel. But the man insisted she be shipped back to the United States.

" 'Why?' the man was questioned."

Eunice lowered her head and peeked at them as she finished. " 'Because,' the man said, 'I heard that over two thousand years ago, a man was buried here, and He came back to life.' "

Eunice reveled in their laughter. How good it was to see these three women relaxed and enjoying life, with the look of contentment in their eyes.

Lara was amazed that Eunice could talk about death and joke about it. More amazing was that she could listen and not feel like throwing up. She said something she never thought she would even want to say. "Go with us to Israel, Eunice. You could teach me so much."

"No," Eunice said. "You three need to go together. It is the Lord who teaches. And you will discover there's something special about walking over the same stones on which Jesus walked, seeing where He lived and died and rose from the dead."

Eunice laid her hand on Lara's arm. Lara did not shrink but welcomed the touch. The warmth lingered after the touch was gone.

Lara looked in the rearview mirror at Ruby and Annette. Their gazes met. What was happening here? They were talking as if taking a trip to Israel were a reality.

Were their lives. . .at last. . .on an even keel?

Could they accept and find what Eunice had deep within herself?

Abiding peace?

Henry came bounding across the porch and out to the driveway before Lara could stop the car. They were ready to pile out after that long drive with only one short stop for lunch.

"I'll take the suitcase in," Ruby said.

Eunice didn't say anything. She was already in Henry's arms, being held as if she'd been gone for three weeks instead of three days.

She moved back from his embrace. He had tears in his eyes. He'd missed her.

Without turning her loose, he spoke to the others. Then he asked Eunice playfully, "Did you get those girls straightened out?"

The friends laughed as if that were a joke. Eunice hadn't told him that was what she had planned to do. She'd only said she needed to go back to where it happened, and Henry had nodded. He'd told her he didn't need to. He had the scrapbooks, the memories—that was what he wanted to remember.

She could have told him now that she had gotten herself straightened out. Instead she looked up at him and smiled. "I think so."

"Good," he said.

"It feels good to be home," she said, looking up at him.

They told the friends good-bye and walked into the house with their arms around each other, joined physically at the hips, joined emotionally in the heart, joined eternally with their souls.

He gently caressed the side of her waist and looked tenderly into her eyes. "I have a pot of coffee waiting and a few tidbits of—" His speech halted for a moment. "Get that gleam out of your eye. It's not gossip; it's. . .sharing."

"Good," she said and laughed. "I can hardly wait for that coffee."

"Curt came over and brought some hostas and helped me plant them out back where I wanted a border. We had supper together."

"What did you cook?" Eunice asked.

Henry gave her a look. "Pizza."

She gave him a look, so he added, "Supreme."

"How's he doing?"

Henry nodded as he spoke. "Better. He's thinks something will come of Shelby's taking that girl in on a trial basis. Brian's optimistic, too. He came to the office and talked about the positive changes in Shelby. That young girl is with them now. Although Shelby said it was a trial basis until you got back, he was hoping it would be more." His eyebrows rose. "He said he couldn't understand how anyone wouldn't want a little newborn baby. Of course he was talking about Shelby."

"Now, Henry. A person shouldn't adopt if they can't love the child."

"Of course Shelby would love the child. She's a loving person. I've seen her grow up. I've seen her with her sister's children. You can't fake things like that all the time."

"No, Henry. I agree she's a wonderful girl. But people don't always feel the way we think they should. Some aren't made to be good mothers."

"Hogwash!" He became adamant. "How can anyone look at a child and not love it? It's perfect, beautiful, God's creation."

She sighed. "Henry. Do you like spiders?"

He cringed. "That's not the same as babies."

"They're God's creation, too, and quite beautifully made. You, yourself, have commented on the beautiful webs they weave." She smiled. "Remember showing me that one with dew on it, sparkling in the sunlight. Ah, a masterpiece, like stained glass in a church window."

He shivered. "If the spider would stay out of the web, I'd like it better. But there's no use talking to you, woman. You twist things."

"No, you just give up when I'm right."

"Right?" he snorted.

He looked at her for a long time. Then he got out of his chair and took a step toward her. He held out his arms. She rose and fell into them, against his chest. He enfolded her. He was her strength, her love, her life.

"I love you, Henry."

"And I love you, my dear, more than anything. What will I do. . . ?" he asked, as if there were a spider in his web.

She shook her head against his chest. "You'll do," she whispered. "Don't worry. You'll do. You can do all things. . . ."

His chin moved against the top of her head. He said, "Yeah." She dared not look up to see if his eyes reflected the hoarseness of his voice. "That's what I preach. All things. . .ah. . .Eunie."

"Henry, stop it."

He did. But his breath came in little gasps, and his chin moved on her hair. His arms around her tightened.

"Henry, stop it. I'm here, Henry. I'm here."

Annette's gaze had lingered on Eunice and Henry until Lara turned the car onto the road and left the touching scene behind. For a moment, she'd felt that tug of loneliness. Her thoughts moved to Curt. How blessed to have a mate with whom you are completely one. She'd had the excitement and passion of a young woman in marriage. She was middle-aged now and sometimes longed for a relationship with a mature man. She thought she could have had that with Curt.

She had no time for regret or remorse, however. The past three days had given her a sense of inner freedom she had not felt since she was a girl, naked in the ocean, proclaiming that free feeling. That had been a pseudo-freedom. There was none apart from the freedom that Jesus gave to one who let Him into his or her heart.

Eunice had put things in perspective for her. She would not spend time with regrets but with counting her blessings. A burden had lifted from her shoulders. She had let go of the past; she had a business, friends, and a wonderful son she was eager to see.

She saw the full bloom of spring all around the big Victorian house. The warm afternoon sun welcomed her as she took her suitcase from the car and bade her friends good-bye.

As Annette struggled through the doorway with her suitcase, she heard Sudie, who worked in the gift shop, announce, "Your mom's here."

"Mom." Tom bounded through the room. They hugged. He lifted her bag to take it upstairs. "I'll be down in a minute, and you can tell me all about your trip."

A few minutes later, she sat with her son at a table, he with a soda and she with a cup of steamy, aromatic cappuccino. She didn't tell him about the past but about the places they saw, where and what they ate, the beauty of the beach and the ocean, the camaraderie the four experienced, the differences between flatlands and mountains, the jokes and laughter, the mention of a trip to Israel.

"And how did things go here?" she asked after they had exhausted her subject, in which he displayed what seemed to be genuine interest.

"Great," he said. "No problems." He mentioned that coffee and teatime had just ended and he'd finished cleaning up the restaurant. Her heart overflowed with joy. Her boy was growing up. Showing responsibility. Maybe she should reconsider Curt—

Her thoughts stopped. Her eyes widened, and her mouth dropped open. She couldn't believe what she was seeing as her gaze focused on the birdcage.

twenty-nine

Tom?"

Annette heard his intake of breath. "Ma'am?"

"What happened to the birdcage?" Her gaze reverted to him.

His eyes widened. "It fell over. I tried to straighten it out. I guess I didn't do too good a job."

"It fell?"

"Yes, ma'am."

She shook her head. "That birdcage is attached to a sturdy base. It didn't just fall over."

"Well, Mom. I had a few of my friends over and one of the. . .people. . .knocked it over."

"People?"

"Well, yeah. A friend."

Annette took a deep breath. "You mean a girl, Tom?"

He shrugged and nodded.

"Do we have to have this discussion?"

He shook his head vigorously, his eyes wide. "No, ma'am. I'll go to my room."

"No, Tom. That's not what I mean. Did you forget about having friends here when I'm not home?"

He growled. "I guess so."

"Then we do have to have the discussion again."

He shook his head. "No. I know the rules, Mom. But I didn't think it would matter if I had a few guys over."

"And the guys turned into girls, huh?"

"Well, I sort of said you wouldn't be here, so some of them invited some girls."

"How many?"

"Well. Six at first."

"At first?"

He nodded. "Then I was the oddball, so I invited a girl. She wasn't sure I was telling the truth about others being here so she brought some girlfriends. When they found out they were outnumbered, they invited a few others over. I mean, they think this is a great place. The food and all."

"You had a party."

He nodded. "Yes, ma'am."

"Dancing?"

He sniffed up a lot of air. "Some."

"The kind I think is atrocious."

"Well, we're from different generations."

Annette nodded. "So when did that happen?" She pointed to the birdcage. "Was someone dancing with it?"

She thought she was being facetious, but his beet-red face said that was true.

"She. . .tripped."

Annette tapped her fingers on the table. She didn't ask; she told him. "She was drunk." A worse thought struck her. "Or on drugs."

He was quick to answer. "No, Mom. No drugs. I wouldn't allow that. It scares me as much as it does you."

Annette felt herself trembling. "But you let them drink."

"I didn't let them. They brought it." He threw up his hands. "They sneaked it into the drinks away from me for a while, but after I knew it, I thought, why not try it myself?"

"You've never tried it before?"

His silence was an answer.

She looked at the birdcage, then back at him. "Was she hurt?"

He grinned. "She didn't seem to feel it."

Annette didn't grin back, so his face sobered.

"Was Marcella here?"

"A little while."

"Did she drink?"

He shrugged.

"Tom. Drinking can cause problems with a pregnancy. It could affect the baby."

He looked concerned. "I don't know what she did."

"You should, Tom. She was in our home."

She held out her hand. "Your car keys, please."

She didn't relent at his cajoling, explaining, apologizing. "How do I get to school?"

"I'll take you."

"That's punishing yourself," he said.

"Maybe I should be punished," she said. "I guess I haven't raised you right. I thought you knew better. I never expected to come home to this. I'm disappointed in you, Tom. Disappointed."

He jumped up so quickly she thought the tottering chair would overturn. "No, Mom. It's not your fault. Everybody knows you're perfect. They all say it. Well, I'm not."

He'd been angry with her before but never because he thought she was. . .perfect.

She kept her hand on the table, palm up.

He went to the key rack, returned, and tossed the keys on the table. Her fingers closed into her empty palm.

He seemed to have moved away from her overnight. She was getting things straightened out at the beach. Then she came home to this.

Tom apologized the next morning with what seemed to be true

repentance. Over the weekend, he stayed home and studied for final exams. He was exempt from two. A couple of his friends came to apologize for the birdcage. She thought Tom might have put them up to it, but at least they did it.

She determined to keep him grounded long enough so that he understood consequences followed disobedience, no matter how inconvenient it was for her to take him to school and pick him up. He again became a model son.

On Monday morning, when Marcella came into work, Annette told her the rules and that drinking could harm her baby. Marcella cried.

"Did you lie to the people you're staying with?"

She nodded. "I told them Tom was having a party, but I didn't say you wouldn't be here." Her sorrowful eyes looked at Annette. "Am I fired?"

"I blame Tom for this. But I don't want to hear anything like this again."

"I won't. I promise. I'm sorry."

Annette believed she was. "I forgive you."

Hearing the tinkle of the bell, Annette turned. Curt came in and asked someone to hold the door for him. Annette did while he struggled with a long object with the top covered with paper. He grinned like a cat that returned the canary.

Ignoring customers, he gestured for her to tear off the paper, as if it were not obviously a birdcage. She did. "Oh, how beautiful." It resembled the other Victorian one, perhaps slightly more ornate. She stood back while he took it to the empty corner.

His smile vanished when he turned. "You have misgivings?"

"Not about the birdcage itself. But how did you know? Does everybody know?"

"Not everybody," Curt said. "Just the church and half the town."

Annette shook her head and grinned along with him when he said, "Just kidding. Very few know." He motioned toward a table. "Let's sit down."

Marcella came immediately. "Could I get you something?" she asked sweetly. She and Curt smiled at each other. After one glance at Annette, however, she looked like she might cry again.

They both ordered coffee.

"Tom called me when things got rough over here and the guys didn't want to leave," Curt said. "I came over, decided who should drive whom home, ordered them out, and threatened them with bodily harm and worse. I said I'd tell their parents if I heard anything about this being laughed at or talked about." His face was serious. "Tom and I had a long talk, Annette. He's a good boy."

She nodded. "I'm sorry you got caught up in this."

"I'm glad he felt he could call me."

Annette nodded. "So am I." Her steady gaze met his. "You're making yourself indispensable."

"Have I overstepped the bounds? After we. . .you. . . decided—"

Marcella came with their coffee and set cups in front of them.

Had he overstepped the bounds? Looking into his deep blue eyes that spoke of his affection, she could almost forget the more recent issues that had been dominant in her mind—Eunice. . . Dove. . .Tom. . .

Her gaze moved to the birdcage. Under the circumstances, had he gone too far with such a gift?

The old birdcage had been empty. There was no dove, because there was no Dove. Perhaps she could put a dove in there. A reminder of a lovely girl who died. She could think of her now without that big hole in her heart, that fear, that guilt, that stain. She was free. She was forgiven. Yes, she would like a dove in that cage. In the Bible, the dove was a symbol of the Holy Spirit.

"What it needs," Annette said, "is to be draped with silk flowers and a dove put inside. And I want the cage door left open. When anyone asks, I will say it represents the Holy Spirit, who cannot be caged but is ready to alight upon anyone who is willing to accept Him."

"What a beautiful thought," he said. His eyes met hers. She looked away quickly but not before she saw the light in his. What had he seen in hers? Had she averted them quickly enough? Then he said, "We can sit like this and talk occasionally. Let me bring you flowers like before. At least, be friends."

Annette studied her cup of coffee. Maybe, someday, she would tell him that it wasn't the birdcage or flowers that won her over. It was his little-boyish charm when he, so normally confident, was nervous, wanting to give her a present, but afraid he'd done something wrong.

When she was in the first grade, a neighbor boy she liked very much had given her a nickel. She took it home and showed her mother. Her mother made her return it, saying she mustn't take money from anyone. She returned it, and the boy looked as if she'd stuck a pin in his balloon, broken his favorite toy, punched him in the stomach. He didn't cry, but his face and eyes would have looked better if he had. She never forgot that look. Annette figured she had destroyed him forever. The next week, however, he gave the nickel to Patty, who went around showing it to everyone for the rest of the year. Annette lost her first boyfriend over that nickel.

Laying her hand on Curt's, Annette smiled.

"Thank you," she said.

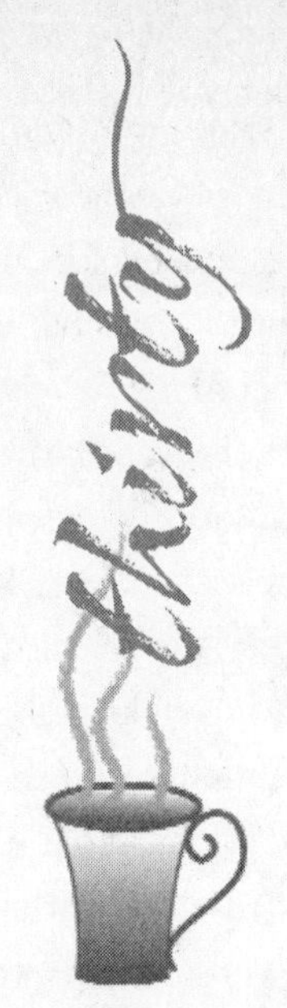

Shelby had been mortified that Marcella didn't know not to drink while pregnant. The morning after her dad explained about the party, Shelby and Brian went to the Masons' and asked if they could go ahead and take Marcella to their house instead of waiting until the school year ended.

The Masons seemed eager to get on with their plans of moving. Marcella looked dejected. Shelby helped her pack. On the way to her house, Marcella apologized. She had been pleased when Tom asked if she wanted to stay and he'd invited a few people over. "We didn't plan to do anything wrong."

Shelby heard her sob and turned to look at her in the backseat. She was crying. Marcella looked up at Shelby. "I guess that's the story of my life."

Brian spoke kindly. "Marcella, most people don't intend to do wrong or hurt anyone else. That's why we have to be taught what's right and how to let the leadership of the Lord guide us." He paused. "We'd like to help you with your decisions if you'll cooperate."

Shelby cast a glance toward Brian, who looked straight ahead through the windshield. She hadn't agreed to a long-term arrangement. She'd told Eunice she would try this. That evening, she didn't attempt to talk to Marcella about anything other than the layout of the house and her room.

Brian would take Marcella to school. She would ride the bus to Annette's Kitchen after school. Shelby would pick her up from work; then she'd do her homework. She did laugh when Brian went into his antics about the use of the kitchen table.

"I'm growing out of my clothes," she said.

Shelby looked her over. Her heart lurched at the most beautiful shape a woman could have—pregnant. She squelched the threatening sadness. *Think of others, not yourself.* "I'll bet you could wear some of my clothes."

"My parents will get anything I need. I just have to let them know."

"In the meantime," Shelby said, "let's try mine and see if you like them."

Marcella did like some of her shirts that could hang loose over her jeans. When Brian walked by the doorway, she said loudly, "I can try Brian's shirts next. Bet I could wear his."

The two pretended to argue about that. Brian had a way of making young people relate to him. Marcella was a pretty neat girl herself.

The next day, Saturday, Shelby's dad invited the family for a cookout since Shelby and Brian's deck was hardly big enough for more than a small grill and a couple chairs. Francine brought her brood. On the way back, Marcella asked if Shelby and Brian were going to have children.

Over the pain of it, Shelby told her she couldn't.

After a long silence, Marcella asked, "Do you want to know how I got pregnant?"

Shelby had asked Marcella to wait until they got home for an explanation, then Brian decided he had an errand to run. They sat at the countertop that separated the kitchen from the dining area, sipping iced tea. Marcella explained that she had no excuse. She'd thought her parents favored her older sister, who was smart and talented. Marcella was the one always getting into trouble.

"Nothing big," she said. "But talking in classrooms, not having all my homework done, making poor grades, hating piano lessons and not practicing." She shook her head. "They kept comparing me to my sister, and I just couldn't measure up. I thought they didn't care. Then Nick, an older man—" She said that in an exaggerated way. "Two years older. He paid me some attention. Said I was awesome. We were in love. Who needed parents when you had Nick?"

She shook her head as if scolding herself. "I soon found out. As soon as I thought I was pregnant. It was Nick here one day, vanished the next. He didn't know me. He acted like I was some kind of ogre out to ruin his life. I know this sounds awful, but I thought about abortion."

They were silent. Shelby figured Marcella expected a lecture. There was no need. Shelby just said it sounded awful. Also, the leaders of this program at church used Scripture and taught these young girls in this situation about right and wrong.

After a moment, Marcella said, "So I told my parents."

Shelby anticipated the worst. That wasn't what Marcella said. "They were wonderful. Even my sister." She got teary. "Said they would help any way I wanted. I could stay there. I could keep the baby or give it up for adoption. I could go to a home for unmarried girls. I could go to relatives. I could go to a place like you have here where church members help. They'd heard of this church. Another girl from my hometown came here awhile back."

"Your family sounds like wonderful people."

Marcella nodded. "They are. They call every day and will come to see me when I want them to. But I just didn't want to stay there where everybody knew me. Here, everybody's been so nice. They don't act like I'm some insect."

Suddenly Marcella yelled, “Oh!”

Shelby jumped. “What’s wrong?”

Marcella grabbed Shelby’s hand and put it on her belly. “What is that?”

Shelby laughed. “It’s kicking.”

Her lips trembled. “Did I hurt it?”

Shelby laughed, delighted. “It’s supposed to do that. That means it’s healthy and strong.”

After a couple days, Eunice invited Shelby, Brian, and Marcella to her house for a fried chicken dinner. Afterward, the three women cleaned up the kitchen while Brian and Pastor Hogan went out on the front porch. “This is what women do,” Shelby said with mock sarcasm. “The cooking, the cleaning.”

Later, they all settled in the living room and looked at scrapbooks Eunice brought out. Their daughter had been beautiful, with fair skin, blond hair, and blue eyes that seemed to jump from the photographs.

They all laughed as Pastor Hogan and Eunice told stories about their daughter. Love was in their words and on their faces as they reminisced about a girl called Dove, who died.

Then Eunice showed scrapbooks of their foster children. Love abode there, too.

“I’m learning something,” Marcella said.

Shelby was glad. She had a strong suspicion Eunice was trying to impress upon her that motherhood was not just giving birth to a child.

Marcella smiled. “You’re showing me how important a family can be and how loving, aren’t you?” She took a deep breath. “Even if I gave my baby up for adoption, I could make people happy like you and Pastor Hogan were with foster children. Or maybe my baby could go to a couple who would love it.” She looked down at the picture of a little boy. "I'm sorry I ever considered. . .abortion."

"Pray," Eunice said. "The Lord will lead you to do the right thing."

Shelby, Brian, and Marcella prayed together when they had devotions before going to bed.

Marcella said, "I don't know how to be a mother. I need to learn things. Talk to people like you and Mrs. Hogan."

Shelby began to realize that she didn't know how to be a mother, either. She'd heard women say they had to learn as they went along. She began to teach Marcella what she knew about cooking, cleaning, organization, shopping, budgeting.

She laughed about it after a few days. "You know what, Marcella? I've never been so organized in my life. I'm teaching myself instead of you."

"Right," Marcella said. "I'll never learn to wash dishes, so you have to do that."

"Practice makes perfect," Shelby said.

When Marcella brought home her report card, she'd made all As except one B. "You're a bright girl," Shelby said.

Marcella huffed and made a face at Brian. "I could have made all As if he didn't hog that table."

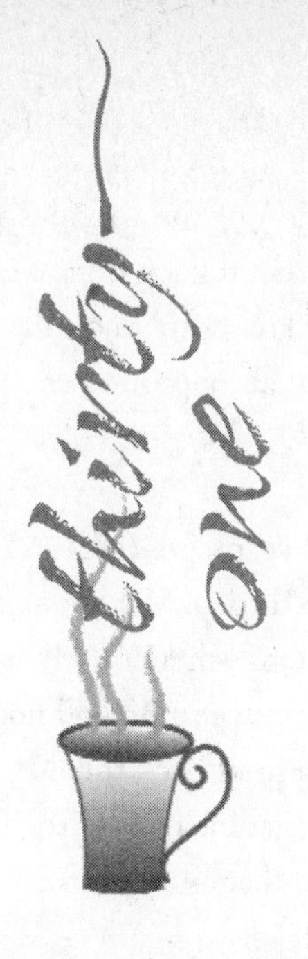

I'm sorry, but he can't be disturbed for the rest of the afternoon."

"Tell him Mrs. Gerard is here to see him."

The receptionist peered over her bifocals with a look of "you're not who you say you are, and you're not going in even if I have to arm wrestle with you."

"The ex–Mrs. Gerard."

"Oh. Yes." She stood. "Please, come right this way. I'll take you to his suite. Mr. Gerard is expecting you." She led Lara to an elevator.

Hmmm, Lara thought. He left the afternoon free. . .for her? Well, she had called to say she was flying all the way from North Carolina to London just to see him.

"Lara." He rose from a high-backed leather chair, walked around the huge desk, and strode across the executive suite with his arms extended. "You look fantastic."

A week ago, she would have said, "It's the clothes." But she felt rather good lately and decided to respond, "Thank you, Jared. You look terrific, as always." She took his hands.

He laughed lightly. She would have said that regardless, but he really did. Age served him well, complete with the expected silver sprinkled through his dark hair at his temples and the deep creases at his mouth.

"Here, have a seat. Can I get you something. . .to drink?"

She sat on a couch. "Ice water?"

"Sure." He walked to another section of the spacious room and went behind the elegantly curved bar, took ice from a refrigerator, and poured two glasses of water. He set them on the table in front of her and seated himself in a chair opposite her. "What brings you here? Business? Pleasure?"

"Us."

She knew he could say what he had years ago. *It's over. There's nothing more to say.* If he did, at least she'd tried. She took a sip of the water and returned the glass to the table, then looked at him.

He returned the look with a pleasant expression and nodded.

"I want to explain why I was such a mess back then."

He shook his head. "I knew, Lara, that incident at the beach changed you. You can't lose a friend like that and stay the same."

"It was worse than you can imagine."

"I doubt it," he said seriously. "For several years I've thought about talking to you. Then I'd think I might be stirring up something better left alone."

She nodded. "I thought so, too, for nineteen years. But it wasn't. I want to set the record straight. Confess what I did. I knew you were attracted to her. I saw the gleam in your eyes. And in hers. I gave her the impression you and I were to be married."

She told him about that night, Dove's being so distraught. "All these years, Jared, I thought it was my fault she was so upset that she wanted to kill me or to kill herself."

He put his hands on his knees. "You didn't kill her, Lara. I did." Distress filled his eyes and his voice. "And my baby."

"Oh, Jared. I didn't come to make you confess anything. I wanted to explain why I was such a lousy wife."

"I know why. Because I was a lousy husband."

No wonder, she thought. He had lived with a worse sense of guilt than she. If they had talked, maybe things would have been different. But they hadn't. They'd tried to ignore it, but it didn't go away. "So you knew about the baby."

He nodded. "When she told me, she had that great expectant look in her eyes. She thought I would marry her. First, I told her to have an abortion. That almost killed her. Then I told her I would support the child. I would play a part in the child's life. I watched her die right there before my eyes."

He got up and stood behind his chair, propping his arms on the back. "But I couldn't marry her. She didn't have money, background. . .and of all things, she was a preacher's daughter." He shook his head as if that were ridiculous. "What could I do? Give up my parents' dreams for me and be put out in the street? Become homeless? Live in a box? And the idea of having a baby was even more ridiculous."

"Well, Jared, why—"

"Lara." He interrupted. "You know why. She was gorgeous. And a challenge. But she made an impression on me. Dove saw something in me that no one else did. She saw. . .a soul. She tried to convert it. There was a genuine sweetness about her. Maybe it really was the personal relationship with Jesus she talked about. She made me think about it seriously."

His laugh had an ironic sound. "Not seriously enough. I made her think about the physical side of things. I knew she was inexperienced and loved me." He looked down at his hands. "I took advantage."

"You loved her, Jared?"

He looked toward the ceiling, then back. "After she died, I loved her. I loved the ideal of her, what she was and who she was before I destroyed her. Before she died, I loved her less than I loved my freedom, what my friends would say, what my parents would do. I loved me more than I loved my unborn baby. A path was laid out for me by my ancestors. Nothing would stand in my way."

Lara was fascinated by this man she didn't know. He wasn't boasting; instead he stated a truth that condemned himself with every word. How could he say that so openly? Maybe. . .because she was just the ex-wife, the failure. She smiled inwardly. That was the past. She was no longer a failure.

"We were both young and immature, Jared. Instead of letting you know what I was going through, I turned to alcohol."

"And I turned to women. After a while, I thought I was killing you, too. Divorce seemed better." He scoffed. "After several years of so-called success. . ." He motioned with his hand, indicating the opulent suite in which they sat. "Along came Gladys."

"Gladys?"

He grinned. "Gladys was a saucy, sassy secretary that I didn't like from the get-go. But she was the secretary to the CEO. Really smart, knew her stuff, organized, spoke her mind." He laughed. "She seemed to think I was the sorriest kind of human being she'd ever come across. I didn't care at first. I tried to charm her just to get the better of her. You know, make her care, then toss her aside. I was a master at that."

His face clouded, and a faraway look came into his eyes. He looked out the window without focusing on anything in particular. She almost didn't hear his words. "She reminded me of Dove."

Lara opened her mouth to protest that the Dove she had known was never saucy or sassy. But his mood stopped her. She waited.

He faced her and continued. "Oh, not in looks. And Gladys wasn't innocent like Dove. But her faith reminded me of Dove. I didn't want to see that at first. When I admitted that, it was my undoing. I realized I wanted to do the same to her that I had done to Dove. Undo her faith. Show her it didn't save her. It didn't keep her from being a human being like the rest of us. Her morality was a sham."

He shook his head. "But I couldn't. Gladys was different. She'd had a rough life, was raised with four brothers that she talked about being mean as snakes. She wasn't taken in by me. She asserted her faith, and if I or anyone else didn't agree or like it, she had the attitude that we had our chance and if we didn't take it, we could just go to hell in a handbasket."

Lara laughed. "She said that?"

He nodded.

"Well, who won?"

Jared gave her that sly look. "I did."

Lara felt something close in her throat.

He grinned. "You see, I didn't care for that handbasket deal and began to investigate her faith. Even went to church and started reading the Bible so I could argue with her. Oh, I'd heard the basic arguments and had said them. All religions are alike. Sure, I believed there's one God and He's the God of all. But that Jesus-in-your-heart stuff, no. Well, it started to get to me. It seemed like it could be real."

Jared returned and sat in his chair. "But getting back to Dove. I told her two days before her death I wouldn't marry her. I didn't want a baby. I would see that she was taken care of. I'd support the baby. Or she could get rid of it. I'd pay for an abortion. She went ballistic."

Tears gathered in his eyes. "She began to hit me. Of course, all I had to do was grab her arms and hold her away. She kicked and screamed until she finally calmed down and collapsed to the floor. It was sickening. I'd never seen anything like that. It showed her weakness, and I told her so. I told her to get up and act like an adult. I hadn't forced her into anything. She should have had sense enough to use birth control if she didn't want a baby."

He sneered, and Lara knew it was at himself.

"The overriding thing that entered my mind was that she was

trying to trick me into marriage." He lifted his hands. "After all, what a prize I considered myself." He shook his head. "Her death hit me hard. I did everything I could to erase it from my mind. Even got married. And you know. . ." He shook his head and looked disgusted with himself. "You know what a prize I am. The booby one."

"Now, Jared—"

He lifted a hand to silence her and blinked at the moisture in his eyes. He smiled. "So finally I gave up to the Lord Jesus, and I married Gladys. We have three children. Life is good. . .basically."

"What do your parents think about you and a secretary?"

He shrugged as if it didn't matter. "They mellowed through the years. Maybe we all grew up some. When a problem arose, the family behaved like Gladys was from outer space, which I tend to agree she might be." He laughed, and Lara knew he loved the woman.

She was sorry. She was glad.

He continued. "Gladys was more sensitive than she ever let on. That hardness was real but also a front. When she seemed not to notice a snub from my family, I'd say, 'Gladys, you have any more of those handbaskets available?' She'd look at me. I'd send her an 'I love you' look. My mom would say, 'What are you talking about?' and I'd say, 'Oh, it's a private joke, Mom.' "

Lara laughed with him. He was not the Jared she'd known.

"I think eventually Mom got the idea that when she was sarcastic or snobbish, it brought up that private handbasket joke. She even began to take pride in her daughter-in-law who was an executive secretary, as if that were a novelty."

Lara looked into his eyes for a long time. "I think I like you, Jared."

"Yeah. Sometimes I do, too. Because. . ." His eyes clouded. "I'm a saved sinner." He shook his head. "Who would have thought several years ago I'd ever say such a thing? I dislike my past. Gladys has helped me overcome the guilt. Well, only Jesus can do that, but having a wife like her makes a difference. He sent her to me. Why He loved me, I don't know."

He finally stopped talking. "How have you been, Lara. I mean, really?"

"Closed up. Going through the motions. Until recently. Jesus freed me, and I'm learning to let go."

He nodded. He understood. Something in them communicated without words.

After a long moment, he said, "I did love you, Lara."

"You don't have to say that."

"I know. I loved Dove. I loved you. I just didn't know it. I love you now for who you are, who you were, what you went through, are going through."

"But you're 'in love' with Gladys."

His long eyelashes swept down over his eyes as he nodded.

She smiled faintly.

He looked up. "Did you love me, Lara?"

She thought about it. Love was not so easily defined. "Not like I wanted to. Jesus said we're to love others as we love ourselves. I didn't love me."

He nodded.

"Jared. You're a Christian and a married man. But I get the strong impression you're flirting with me."

"Well, you're still a very attractive woman."

"Well, mister. You and your Gladys can go. . ."

He held up his hands. "The handbasket thing?"

Lara laughed. "No, I was going to say you and Gladys can go and have a wonderful life together as far as I'm concerned."

His gaze swept over her. "I like you."

"Yeah. And I like you, too."

He stood and motioned with his index finger.

She went to him. His arms enfolded her, and they both sobbed, then broke apart.

"I love you, Lara."

"I love you, Jared."

They smiled. He swiped at his eyes. Jared Gerard with tears on his face. She loved this Jared. He was not the Jared she had married. She was not the Lara he had married. It was as if they had just met.

She searched her purse and pulled out a tissue to wipe her cheeks with.

"Do you want to come and meet my family?"

"Thank you, but no, Jared. I want to get home. . .soon." She walked to the door.

"Have a good life," he said.

She glanced over her shoulder. "You, too. Good-bye, Jared."

He nodded, blinking at the fresh moisture in his eyes.

She left. This was good. She and Jared now loved each other. They were friends in Christ. They would likely never see each other again. She glided along the hallway, down the elevator, wings on her feet.

She was free.

That's what Eunice had emphasized. Let go, let Jesus. Maybe she could begin to live.

The image of a handbasket faded as she caught a glimpse of heaven. She lifted her face to it. The clouds parted, and they were rimmed with gold. A ray of sun streaked through and she smiled.

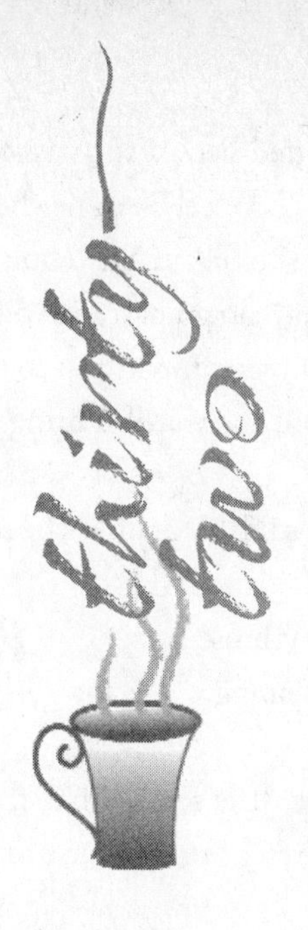

Annette was so proud of Tom. She and her friends sat together, watching him walk across the stage to get his diploma. He had accomplished much during his high school years. That was confirmed by letters of acceptance from several universities. Annette rewarded him with the return of his keys and a gift certificate for a new electric guitar he'd been wanting.

When Ruby and Lara came for lunch on Saturday, Tom brought up their tray. Lara gave him a sculpture she got in Europe of a figure playing a guitar. Ruby gave him a card. He read it and laughed.

"What is it?" Lara and Annette asked.

Ruby put her finger to her lips and shook her head. "A secret for now."

He nodded and thanked them. Ruby wouldn't say what it was, just looked smug. But Tom had seemed pleased. Probably was a joke. Tom said he'd bring dessert soon and went back downstairs.

Annette was thrilled at the change in Lara. Annette and Ruby had given their hearts to the Lord years ago but hadn't turned all their guilt and grief over to Him. Lara was now like someone who'd been released from prison, and spiritually she had been.

While they ate, she told them about Jared and how she no longer had any regrets there. She'd stayed in Europe to visit art museums that she'd seen years ago while in an alcoholic stupor. She could see them now in a new way, and it whetted her artistic passion. "I might try and paint again." She laughed. "I do feel like a newborn."

Ruby snorted. "Ah ha! That's why she did it. She's going to count this as her birthday so she won't have to go past thirty-nine. She's starting over. Foul! Foul!" Then Ruby grinned. "But to show how kind I am at heart, I have a present for you. I'll bring it to you later."

"And I have a pie for you," Annette said. "A double-chocolate cheesecake."

"You guys don't need to give me anything."

"Believe me," Ruby said with meaning, "I want to." She wouldn't say what it was.

"Tell you what I want," Lara said. "Let's take that trip to Israel. It will be my spiritual birthday present to me. Or. . .maybe it's God's."

"I don't have that kind of money," Ruby said.

Lara's eyes lit up. "I'll pay for it."

Ruby huffed. "I'm not a charity case."

"We're friends," Lara said.

"Are we? Or just stuck together because we got stuck in the past?"

"Speak for yourself, Ruby," Annette said. "I can't imagine going someplace like that without you two. But I can't with things like they are here."

"What's wrong?" Lara asked.

"I told you about that party Tom had while we were at the beach."

"But that was a one-time thing," Ruby said. "That happens with teens."

"I know," Annette said. "But I was gone only three days. How could I even consider taking a trip to Israel and leaving Tom here alone? It's out of the question."

Before they could answer, Tom appeared with their dessert.

If he thought it strange they became suddenly silent, he didn't show it, just set their desserts down like a young gentleman.

After Lara and Ruby left, Annette went downstairs and asked where Tom was.

Marcella was cleaning off a table. "He said he had something to do."

Annette wondered what he had to do that he hadn't told her about.

At 11:30 p.m., she was still wondering.

After midnight, she heard a car coming up the drive. The tires screeched as if the car were stopping and starting. Tom must have had car trouble. A door slammed. She walked toward the door. The porch light shone on Tom, fumbling with his key while trying to unlock the door. He dropped it. She opened the door. He almost fell inside, missed the key, and laughed.

Annette got the key and closed the door. From the looks and smell of him, it wasn't the car that had trouble. He'd been drinking.

"What in the world do you think you're doing?"

He stumbled away from her. "Whatever I want to do."

She grabbed his rumpled shirt. "Come into the kitchen. We have to talk."

He jerked away. His words were slurred, and he pointed an unsteady finger in her face. "You don't tell me anything. I'm not telling you." He rocked forward. "Anything."

"What are you talking about?"

He leered at her, and his finger pointed in another direction. "Go to the kitchen. We gotta talk."

Annette thought he probably needed to sleep this off before they could have a serious talk. However, he stumbled to the kitchen and plopped into a chair. With his forearms balanced on the table, he nodded while she made cups of instant coffee for them.

She expected what happened. He picked up the cup, took a gulp, and with an unsteady hand set the cup down onto the stain he'd just made by the coffee spilling out. She did not know what to say to this stranger residing in her son's body.

He ran his finger around the top of the cup. He stuck his finger in it, then licked it. He played with the stain on the tablecloth. She didn't know if he was thinking or sleeping with his eyes open. "Go to bed, Tom. We'll talk in the morning."

He shook his head, then picked up the cup and downed the rest of the coffee. Finally he leaned back. "Now," he said. Then he began as if what he had to say had been dammed up inside him for a long time. As he talked, she didn't care about half sentences or slurred words. Her son was hurting.

"I went to get you some flowers," he said. "I talked to Curt. I told him you wanted to go to Israel, but you couldn't because of me. I asked him if he would stay here or if I could stay with him. And you know what?"

She was afraid she did.

"He said he would like that, if you approved. Then I asked him when you two were going to get married. He said you dumped him."

Annette was shocked. "He said that?"

Tom shrugged. "I don't know. That's what it means." He huffed. "Called it off. . .whatever. The night of the party, Curt and I really got along. He was like a dad. You didn't tell me. You asked me how I felt about your marrying him. I was pleased, so I was trying to treat him like I thought I should act toward a dad. Then I find out you dumped him." He leaned toward her. "You're not getting any flowers."

"Tom, I'm sorry. I just have had other things on my mind." What good would it do to say she had been dealing with the past, with breaking up with Curt?

He nodded. "That's okay. I'm not important. I can get along okay. Won't be long 'til I'm eighteen." He chuckled. "Already gave myself a party."

Annette refused to sit and listen to anymore of that drivel. She stood. "Go to bed, Tom."

He stood. "Okay. But I'm going to call Grandma and Grandpa. Tell them I'm coming to Florida."

Annette headed for the stairs. He followed, then got ahead of her, looking down at her as he held onto the railing and ascended the stairs. "You're perfect. And I'm not. I'm not staying here anymore. You don't trust me."

She'd never seen such a hurt-little-boy look on a young man asserting his independence. "Good night, Tom." She followed to make sure he got to his bedroom. At his doorway, he made a motion of swatting her away, then with his arms and legs straight out, he fell face down onto his bed.

Soon, a raspy noise sounded from his throat.

Annette was still sitting in the dark, in her oversized chair in the living room, when she heard Tom's footsteps on the hardwood floor in the hallway. Then the steps were muffled across her carpet. He stopped somewhere behind her and stood silent. Annette stared at purple mountain peaks towering into the blackened sky.

From behind her he said tentatively, "Mom?"

She breathed out a shaky breath. "Yes."

"I'm sorry."

She made a single nod. "Yes."

"Would. . ." He cleared his throat and began again. "Would you like some. . .coffee? Or tea?"

Her intake of breath was ragged. She managed to nod. "Coffee, please."

A time to tear and a time to mend.

Which would it be?

A faint streak of pink appeared beyond a mountain. The night didn't want to give way. But light is more powerful than darkness. Light invades darkness. Darkness does not invade light.

A time to keep and a time to throw away.

Tom resented her perfection. Would he hate her imperfection? Was it not better to be resented by your son than hated by him, disrespected by him? This was just a phase in his teenage years; that was all. Everyone went through it. It was painful.

He's been a good boy. I should just let it go. He'll apologize. He already did. I forgave him before he apologized. He's my life. My flesh. My blood. My boy. My son. My heart. My reason for living.

He switched on the hall light, and the windowpanes were darkened. Her view was no longer visible. Just "through a glass darkly." The apostle Paul wrote that. *Ah, he understood life. So much we see as if looking through a dark glass. The view is obscured. Too often I've seen too much too clearly. If I tell him. . .*

He's a child.

Yes, so was I. But. . .old enough. Oh, God. What to do? I've prayed that way even when I wasn't praying. My whole life has been a prayer of what to do. I was wise before I was nineteen. I knew where I was going and what I was going to do and how to make decisions. Since then, I've known nothing. . .I know nothing. . . .

Tom brought a tray and set it on the table beside her. He brought over an armchair and sat on the other side of the table. The skin beneath his eyes was puffy, but he'd at least combed his hair. He was waiting for whatever tongue-lashing she might have for him.

"Tom," she began, "you've been a good boy. I've been proud of you. You say I'm perfect and you're not. You have been exceptional, except for last night and the night of the party. That is, as far as I know."

"Mom, I've tried to be all you want me to be. And live up to the hero image of a dad I don't remember. But I've made mistakes." He sighed. "I haven't done any of the biggies, you know?"

She glanced at him with a lift of her tired eyebrows.

He snorted. "I'm even. . .one of the few. . ."

"Virgins?"

He laughed an embarrassed laugh. "Well, I prefer to say one of the few who abstains. When I signed that pledge card, I meant it. That's not easy, Mom. I admit my thoughts condemn me. My thoughts aren't always the purest."

Annette was shaking her head. "Tom, I've always said you could tell me anything. No matter what. But you don't have to confess to me that you're a human being with weaknesses and temptations. I know that comes with the territory."

"What I'm trying to say, Mom, is I'm not perfect, but I try."

"I know how that is. Maybe I should have let you know that I'm not perfect. I've wanted you to think I am. I've wanted. . .to be."

He scooted to the edge of his chair, facing her. "You are, Mom. I guess I just get to feeling so inadequate. I know I'm a Christian. I know I shouldn't have had that party. I shouldn't have been drinking. I got so tired of being good. I just wanted to be part of a crowd for a change. Is it so wrong to. . .just let go. . . sometimes?"

She had been the same age as her son when she felt that way. "Tom, I want to tell you a story. A story of four young girls who started out to have fun and a perfectly innocent rendezvous with experimentation and of what it led to. You may despise me when I finish. You will not think me perfect. It's a chance. . .I have to take."

"Mom." He grabbed her hands. "You don't have to tell me anything. I love you. I could never hate you. I'm sorry for the things I said."

She shook her head. "I do need to tell you. And I don't know if I'm telling you this to help you. . .or to help me."

"Mom." His voice was a plea.

She told him the story, except the unnecessary details. The death was enough, a result of an evening that started innocently. . . and led to the darkest night of one's soul.

"Oh my Lord." She heard his breath. "That wasn't profanity, Mom. That was a prayer."

"I know. It's been my prayer for twenty years."

"I'll never drink again, Mom. I swear."

She shook her head. "That's not what this is about, Tom. To drink or not is between your conscience and God. What I'm saying is what I've said almost every time you've left this house."

He made a sound. "Be careful."

"Yes."

"Oh, Mom. I'm sorry."

"You've already apologized. I already forgave you before you asked."

"I know that. I knew it before I came in here. Mom, I'm sorry you've had to go through this."

A time to love and a time to hate.

A faint streak of light shone beyond the windowpane. "Turn out the hall light, Tom, and let's watch the sun rise."

He switched off the light and returned to the chair. She looked at her son as he stared out the window. Her son was becoming a man. He could never have that little boy fascination, adoration, for his mother again. She was a human being who made mistakes, who sinned, who suffered, who had reasons for being who she was and who she wasn't. He knew her secret. Where would it lead?

A time to search and a time to lose.

He would have to search his own heart and life. It would take time to understand. Or accept. Or learn about his mother, to view her in a different way.

A time to mend.

The sky blazed in glorious color. Her son's face in the window turned from gray to pink to gold and began to fade so quickly.

Tom must now discover who he was. . .apart from his mother.

The beauty faded. The sky hung light gray over aged purple mountain peaks. A shade of green began to be visible.

A time to be born and a time to die.

This night they had died to each other in a child-parent relationship. What would be born of this?

A time to embrace and a time to turn away.

Her son stood. He looked tall, haggard, tired, sorrowful, different, older, somewhat mature. Dark stubble outlined his young face.

"Mom."

Annette looked up. She rose from the chair. Her son took her in his arms. He embraced her, held her tight while she sobbed against his shirt that he'd slept in. When had he become so tall?

Overnight, her little boy had become a man. His mother had become to him a person.

thirty three

Ruby sat straight up in bed, and her arms flew out to her sides.

"What the. . . ?" Charlie rolled over and fell out of bed. He got up and switched on the light. "What's going on?"

Ruby stared. "You got out of bed."

"You hit me," he said.

She cleared her throat. "I did?"

He rubbed his face. "I'm sure I have a fist print to prove it. What's going on?"

"I was asleep."

He snorted. "Well, good. I sure hate to think what would have happened if you'd meant to hit me." He looked at the clock and mumbled. "Two o'clock in the morning."

Ruby sat up in bed, staring into the darkness. She'd dreamed the Rapture had come and she'd been left behind. But later she'd learned that wasn't so. Everybody in America had gone to Israel, and she was the only one left at home to cook, clean, and shop. . .and she didn't have anybody around to complain to. What a nightmare.

For the rest of the night, she tossed and turned. Charlie groaned a lot.

Just as she dozed off into a restful sleep, the alarm sounded. She and Charlie groaned.

The day went from bad to worse. By the time she returned from lunch with Annette and Lara, Ruby was like a teapot ready to whistle.

To top it off, Jill came in wearing a swimsuit that looked like the top was almost off. "Where did you get that thing?" Ruby blared.

"Peggy outgrew it, so she gave it to me."

"Well, you've outgrown it, too. You wear something else or keep a T-shirt over it."

"Maa–umm."

"You got it, babe. I'm the mom."

"I'm going to be late."

Ruby shrugged. "So? That's the story of my life. Won't hurt you. Just make a grand entrance." She pointed her finger. "Wearing your T-shirt."

Jill's huff could have blown down the little pig's brick house. Oh well, deep breathing was good for the lungs. With that thought, Ruby figured her daughter's lungs were the best in the country. She muttered at the tablecloth. "Look at you. Coffee and Coke stains all over. I just put you on there this morning. Okay, so I'm just a maid. A doormat. Work, work, work so somebody can have another pair of shoes, or a DVD, or a lipstick, or something. I'm a slave."

She jerked the tablecloth off. A saucer that had been covered by an upturned corner of the cloth clattered to the floor. It broke into three pieces. *Well good! One less to wash.* Habit turned her to the right, where she would open the door to the basement and throw the cloth down the laundry chute whose official name was The Stairs.

Second thought turned her to the left, where she flung the cloth onto the floor atop the three-pieced saucer. "There! Take that! You crummy old cloth. All you're good for is to run up the water and electric bill." She looked around for something else to throw.

It walked in.

"What's wrong, honey?"

"Don't honey me!"

Charlie shoved the tablecloth out of the middle of the floor with his foot. He didn't even care that she'd thrown it. Sure. She'd pick it up later and wash it. So what if the dishes were broken? There were others. After she broke all those, she could just go work her bootie off and buy some more.

Charlie plopped into a kitchen chair. She hoped he wouldn't show that dimple, because if he did, she might melt and forget she was mad at the world.

The girls whispered at the doorway, apparently having seen the whole episode, making under-the-breath comments like they didn't know her. Well, they didn't.

"You want to know what's wrong? Okay. I'll tell you. I never get to go anywhere."

Charlie stared. "You just got back from two hours at Annette's."

"Two hours! You go to those religious conferences—at the beach no less! The girls go to camps and clubs and meetings and practices and parties and—" She stopped for a breath. "Two hours, you say. Well, my friends are going to Israel. That's going to take at least two weeks, not two hours. What am I going to do?" She pointed at the floor. "Break dishes and do the hokey-pokey on tablecloths."

"Good grief, Mom," Kristin said from the doorway. "You just went to the beach."

Jill poked Kristin's arm. "Shut up."

To Ruby's surprise, she did. And Ruby decided not to say, "Sweet Christian girls don't say 'good grief' or 'shut up.' They say 'hush.'" That would get her into that do-as-I-say, not-as-I-do bit.

"Come sit down and listen for a change," Ruby said.

"Maa–umm." That whine again. "The party's at two o'clock."

"Yes, and if you don't go, your life might be changed forever, right?"

"Right."

Ruby's swimstroke drew the girls into the kitchen. "Let me tell you about a life-changing party."

"Ruby." The tone of Charlie's voice meant, do you really want to do this? That one word brought them into the kitchen looking like they were about to enjoy a horror movie.

She ignored Charlie. She had innocent daughters, sixteen, thirteen, and eight, who needed to know about more than birds and bees. They needed the facts of life.

"I was in college," she began. "I knew it all. We were drinking. Having fun. Went for a swim in the ocean. One girl died. She drowned."

"An accident, Mom," Jill said.

"Yes and no," Ruby said. "None of us wanted that to happen. We were young girls who didn't understand the danger." She told them that the trip to the beach had been a revisiting of the guilt that had plagued her for almost twenty years. "I want you to know that my warnings to you are not just words. They're based on experiences I've had. When you do wrong, God will forgive. But you still have to pay the consequence. I'm just now beginning to let go of the guilt I've felt for almost twenty years.

She felt drained. The girls lowered their gazes when she looked at each one. Should she have told them this? "So, I think this isn't really about Israel. It's about wanting to raise you right and not really being sure how to do it. I want to protect you. But it comes out as yelling and complaining."

She looked at Charlie. "I used to sing."

"Mom," Jill said, "you still sing."

"No. I just blend with others in the choir."

They stared. Carley came over to her with tears in her eyes and hugged Ruby. Ruby patted her shoulders. "I'll be okay."

"I love you, Mom."

"I love you, too, baby."

Carley didn't say, "Don't call me baby," but instead smiled up at Ruby.

Jill said, "Mom. I'm sorry."

"Me, too," echoed Kristin.

"Girls," Charlie said. "Go clean your rooms. Don't come out until it's done. Anything left thrown around or on the floor will be thrown in the trash, and it won't be replaced until you get a job and replace it. Understood?"

"Yes, sir."

Ruby lifted her red-faced, red-eyed, swollen fat face to her husband. She stared at him. He had spoken calmly, firmly, and they had answered respectfully.

She stared.

Charlie glanced at her and back at the girls. "Just a minute. Things are going to be tight around here for a while. Your mom's going to Israel. Now," he said, "you're dismissed. Go clean your rooms."

Ruby sat like a petrified tree while Charlie cleaned up the mess on the floor. He poured her a cup of coffee. In a few minutes, the girls appeared in the doorway.

"Your rooms—" He stopped when he saw what was in Carley's hands. She brought in her piggy bank and set it in front of Ruby. Jill laid down twenty dollars. Where did she get that? Ruby didn't ask. Kristin laid down two ones and some change. Charlie reached in his pocket and brought out forty-six cents.

Ruby was crying for a different reason now. She didn't want to go to Israel or anywhere, just stay with her wonderful family.

"Okay," she said. "This is a start. At this rate, I can go to Israel in about. . .let's see. . .seventy-three years."

They laughed and blinked away their tears.

"This is so sweet, girls. But I can't." She pushed at the money.

Charlie's hand came down on hers firmly. "Yes, you can. You've taken care of us all these years. Let us do something for you."

She nodded. "Oh, I love all of you so much. You're everything to me. More than any trip."

"Mom," Jill said, "you can take the money that's in my college fund."

Ruby gawked. "You don't have a college fund."

"Everybody has a college fund."

"Yeah, right," Ruby said. "Like everybody has a new sports car, the most expensive tennis shoes, a curfew of three o'clock in the morning, no rules. We know all about it. Been there, done that. But you have something others don't have, and that's ingenuity."

"Ohhh." Jill grinned and nodded. "You mean live at home for another eight years and go to the cruddy local college. I can get a student loan and work study. Better yet, I can be like Grandpa and walk to college barefoot, backwards, uphill in a blizzard."

"See? Didn't I say you have ingenuity?"

"There's another thing," Charlie said. "I have this small bank account that's for emergencies, retirement. . .or trips to Israel."

The girls jumped up and down with glee, hugged Ruby, and said they loved her. Her peripheral vision saw white teeth. That meant Charlie was smiling. She dared not look.

Why was he so eager to get rid of her for two weeks?

After Jill left, wearing her T-shirt over her swimsuit, Charlie suggested Ruby make some lemonade and they go out into the backyard and lounge. Lounge? She rarely lounged, but it sounded good.

Surrounded by mountainsides becoming lushly green, hedges of yellowbuds at their fence, the dog barking and running wild because the cat was chasing him, the kittens meowing, Carley and

Kristin yelling over the sounds of their CDs of two different kinds of music, Ruby relaxed into the chair.

"What happened in there?" she said.

Charlie set his glass down. "You stopped being in control and telling us what to do. You admitted you did something wrong. You shared with us. You're normally on top of things. Doing for us. Working, cleaning, feeding, and we just don't measure up. This afternoon, you gave us a chance to see a hurting human being whom we love. We can understand that, Ruby, because we all have our hurts and concerns."

Ruby's hands tightened around her glass. "What are your concerns, Charlie?" She'd never asked that before.

"I'm concerned about the distance between us. I thought when we were dating the fireworks would always be there. I thought I must have put them out. You never lit up again after Dove's death. I thought it was our marriage. Maybe I wasn't what you thought I should be. We used to sing together. You got caught up with the children. It's a good life, but somewhere along the line, I sort of lost you."

"I've always been here."

"Yes, and we have a good marriage. You've made this a comfortable place. It smells good, like food."

"I had my fill. You like me fat, Charlie?"

"You're not fat. But with each extra ounce you've put on, it's just that much more of you to love. I didn't realize until today that you're afraid, like most of us."

"I'm letting it go."

His head turned toward her. "Ruby. I still have that spark for you. Do you. . .for me?

She took a deep breath and looked away. "I could. . .if. . ."

"If?"

"Get rid of Maybelle."

For a minute she thought he'd swallowed his lemon. "What?"

"You favor her. She sings all the important solos. A pageant comes up, I think, 'Uh-oh. Here comes ol' Maybelle again.' "

"Old?"

"Not in age. That's part of the problem. *Ol'* is a derogatory term."

"Mmm, using big words now."

"I do know a few. And that was a kind one. I could have said something worse."

He leaned forward, swung his legs over, and sat on the edge of the lounge chair. "What do you mean, get rid of her? Murder? Or just do like the wicked stepmother did with Snow White and have her taken out in the woods to get lost and have to look for seven little men?"

Ruby stared at him, her nostrils flared and her chin lifted. "Seven, seventeen! I don't care how many, just so she quits looking at one cute, dimpled, curly-headed choir director."

Charlie's laughter echoed across the mountainsides.

She balled up her fist. "What's so confounded funny?"

"You're jealous."

"Yeah. I'm jealous. And I'm mad. And I've had enough. You want her, just pack up and go."

"Oh, you couldn't pry me out of here with a crowbar, sugar. I knew it was in there somewhere. At times it surfaced like a pilot light coming on, and I would wait for the flame, but you'd turn it off. I thought it was the awful thing that happened before we married. I would help you get over it. Later, I thought you were sorry you married me. You wouldn't sing with me anymore."

He was right. She had driven him away.

"I tried to make you notice me," he said. "I saw the way you sort of twisted your face and curled your lip when something displeased you. You did that about Maybelle, so I kept showing her attention, put her up front just to see your displeasure. I wanted you to care what I did. Well, praise the Lord, it's here."

She couldn't believe it. "You do that. . .to make me jealous?"

"Sure. I knew how much you and I used to enjoy singing together. I understood why you couldn't after your friend died. But I thought it was just an excuse when the children came and you said you didn't have time to practice. I started using Arlene for solos and duets."

"Arlene?

He chuckled. "That's the reaction I got then. You didn't care. Arlene was an older woman, so it didn't bother you. So I decided that I'd use a young, pretty girl to sing solos and duets. I thought you might get jealous, but you never did. How would it look if I suddenly stopped having her sing?" He grinned. "You are jealous."

"I. . .guess I might be."

"Then you sing with me." He jumped up and reached for her hand. "You're the only woman for me, Ruby. Nobody else is like you. One in a billion. You're beautiful, and fun, and. . .he wiggled his eyebrows and pulled her off the chair. He claimed her with his arms and his lips. Above the din of life, Ruby's heart sang.

Summer came, and so did Hospice.

She and Henry could have managed for a while longer, Eunice knew. But she didn't want to burden him any more than necessary. She could talk about every little ache or pain, need for additional medication, her increased fatigue, waning appetite, and what symptoms to expect next.

Church members and friends kept them inundated with food. When anyone saw a dish that needed to be washed or a chore to be done, they did it. She couldn't imagine having done that much for anyone, but they said she had and were honored to be able to help her and Henry in any way.

That was one blessing of knowing ahead of time that she was dying. She was discovering how many caring, wonderful friends she had. After she died, they would take care of Henry, she knew, and it comforted her.

She didn't go to every church meeting anymore. Increased medication limited her attention span. She could still do almost anything she'd done before, just more slowly, and her desire to do things decreased.

She was at church on Sunday morning when Ruby and Charlie sang a duet and dedicated it to her.

Annette's Tom had formed a band. They came often to play and sing for her. Tom brought his kitten to play with its kitty-sister, both animals gifts from Ruby.

Henry named Eunice's kitten Eve. "Like the first woman," he said. "And in honor of the first lady of my life."

Eve followed Henry, sometimes scratching out his plants. Henry laughed and scolded the kitten. Then he'd pick Eve up and hold her close to his face. Eunice watched, smiling. The kitten would be something for him to hold. . .to talk to.

That evening when they sat in the swing on the front porch she told him. "Henry, I am healed," she said. "Not of cancer, but of all that might cause me any dread of meeting my Creator. You know, dying is a healing, too. And I'm going to be reunited with our daughter."

She felt his hand move over hers, which she had rested between them on the swing.

"Henry, you must be glad about that. Don't let any bitterness or regret stain your life. Don't let it be a noose around your neck, ready to hang you. Don't let it be like a dirty ol' ring around your collar. Rejoice in what we had. Remember, you told me things like that when I couldn't stand the loss of our daughter. You brought me through it."

He squeezed her hand. "We did it together. I wasn't strong, Eunice. I acted like it, hoping it would come true."

"It did."

"Yes," he said. "I think I became a better pastor, a weak, incapable man who had to lean on the Lord wholly, fully, which is what I needed. I was a smart young man, higher IQ than most around me. I was going to change the world. I had to learn." He put his arm around her. "He gave me you. My great blessing. He blessed us with a daughter for eighteen years. No, I can't complain."

She nodded. "He gave us other needy children. Some have become such fine people."

"Yes, we've had a good life. I love you, Eunice."

"What are you going to do without me, Henry?"

He looked off toward the lush green mountain peaks. "I'm going to walk into that pulpit, say the right things, encourage the congregation, tell them the truth of how I can't even stand, I can't even walk without the Lord holding my hand. And that He's held it for seventy-five years and never let go. I'm going to be encouraging. I'm going to be admired. I'm going to act like a good Christian witness. And it will all be true, Eunice."

The smile on her lips vanished when he choked out, "Then I'm going to come home and be the loneliest man alive."

She leaned against him.

After a long moment he said, "Someday, I will retire and become a gardener. Maybe I'll write about things I've learned. You see, I can get mad at God. I can question Him. I can tell Him things aren't fair. Just like anybody else. But He's blessed me, led me, walked with me, guided me all my life, and I can't deny that. I can't not believe in Him, and for that I'm so grateful. That's the greatest blessing. Some don't grow up to know He exists. They don't know, Eunice. How blessed we are to have known all our lives. To grow up believing, learning Scripture, knowing right from wrong, knowing the truth."

"The truth shall make you free. . . ," she said. "Are you free, Henry?"

"Yes, love. I'm free."

She nodded. She wouldn't tell him about the note that Dove left. That was Dove's private business. She had sinned. She had suffered. She had paid. She was set free.

Years ago, Eunice had asked his forgiveness for anything and all things she'd ever done against him. Instead of asking what she'd done, he'd said, "I forgive you. Please forgive me."

"For what, Henry?"

"Anything and everything. Even a person's thoughts condemn them, you know. The Bible says when we sin, it is against God. If we get His forgiveness, who is anyone else to condemn us? When He sets us free, we are free indeed."

Now, Eunice closed her eyes. "I'm free."

His arm tightened around her.

On Sunday, Pastor Hogan preached about adoption. Shelby knew he did it just for her. He didn't talk about people who adopt children, but the point was unmistakable. She was not a blood relative of Jesus. His blood wasn't flowing through her veins. He loved her anyway. But He shed that blood for her so she could be adopted into His family. She was a child of God. . .through adoption.

She'd heard sermons like that, but they'd never had an impact on her before.

What if Jesus had said His blood wasn't flowing through her veins, and she would have to spend eternity separated from Him?

The thought was devastating.

But God loved her.

He adopted her!

She was a child of the King, with an eternal inheritance.

He never said, "You're not one of my chosen race, my chosen people." No, He said, "Believe that precious blood shed by My only Son was for you, and become one of My children. I will adopt you and love you forever."

She began to see that adoption was a special condition, a choice made freely out of love. The whole idea took on a different perspective. A husband and wife having children was natural. Choosing to take a child not of your own blood was a special choice.

"Act," Eunice had said, "and the feeling will come."

Shelby had acted by taking Marcella in, and the girl had become like one of her and Brian's family. As Shelby watched the tummy over that baby grow, she began to love them both. She could love that baby. She felt it kick. She saw the ultrasound. A little girl was in there.

A perfect, beautiful little girl who needed parents.

She wanted to tell Eunice.

She called, and on Monday evening, she took supper to Eunice and Henry. She and Marcella ate with them while Marcella's kitten played with its sister. After supper, Henry went outside to check on the kittens while the women straightened the kitchen. When they finished, Marcella reached into her shirt pocket.

"I have something to show you, Mrs. Hogan." She pulled out the ultrasound picture. "Isn't she beautiful?"

Shelby felt she knew how an expectant mother felt. She was as proud of that picture as Marcella. Eunice took the picture and sat down in a kitchen chair. Marcella and Shelby stood over her. "Oh, yes, she's beautiful," Eunice said. "Look at those tiny little fingers and toes. Keep this. We didn't get pictures like this when I was carrying Dove."

"I love that name," Marcella said. "Would it be okay if I named my little girl Dove?"

While Marcella glowed, Shelby pulled out a chair to sit in. Eunice said, "That would be lovely, Marcella. My daughter would be pleased that you named this baby after her. I am pleased."

Marcella took the picture and kept glancing from it to Eunice while she talked about how she appreciated the church people, especially Eunice, Shelby, and Brian.

"I've learned so much." She looked at Eunice. "You loved your daughter so much." Her glance went to Shelby. "And Shelby talks about what a great mom her mother was. I know how much she'd like to have a baby. She's made me realize how special a mom is. I know she's not old enough, but she's been like a mother to me."

Eunice could almost see the joy bells that had been ringing in Shelby's mind. It was in her eyes, in her smile, in the soft pink glow on her face as if she were the expectant mother.

The young girl sat down. "When I thought I might have hurt this baby because I drank some alcohol, I was so scared. I didn't want anything bad to happen to my baby. I don't know how I ever thought of getting rid of her as if she were a piece of garbage."

Eunice sensed what was coming. Judging from Shelby's pale face, she did, too.

"That's why," Marcella announced after taking a deep breath, "I'm going to be the best mother any baby ever had. I'm going to keep my baby."

"The church will be here to help you, Marcella. Don't forget that." She patted the girl's arm. "Now, why don't you take that picture out and show Henry? And check on those kittens."

Eunice knew by the look on Shelby's face that she felt as if she'd jumped off the high dive and landed with a belly flop.

"That's not what I expected," Shelby said. "I've said so many things about not being able to replace anyone else in your heart. And I was so against adopting a child. I've changed, Eunice. I don't feel that way now. I have empty places in my heart I want filled. And I thought. . ."

"Shelby," Eunice said. "Think of what you just said. The Lord knows what is in our hearts even if we don't. He has lessons to teach us. He knows if this child would be a replacement for your mother and for your barrenness."

Shelby nodded.

Eunice shook her head. "The baby God has in your future will not be a replacement. When you learn that, your love will be deeper and stronger, and your child will not be a replacement for anyone or anything. Your child will have its own room in your heart."

Okay," Ruby said when they met on Saturday for lunch. "Lara, I'm going on a diet to lose ten pounds before fall. I'm not a pig, and I'm not going to eat like one anymore. I don't think pigs are held in high esteem in Israel anyway. So in a few weeks, I'm coming to Lancaster's to say, 'Dress me!' "

A big smile came on Lara's face. "With pleasure." Lara and Annette applauded. "I've tried to get you there for years."

"Do you cut hair and give manicures?"

Lara laughed. "No, but I can recommend my hairdresser."

"You know," Annette said, "every time I mention we're going to Israel, I'm told we might get blown apart over there."

"Ha!" Ruby shrugged. "I've been blown apart right here for years. At least I'll be blown apart into Paradise."

"Paradise?" Lara looked at Annette. "Do we believe in Paradise?"

Annette shrugged.

"Jesus did," Ruby said. "He told the thief on the cross he'd be with Him that day in Paradise. That's good enough for me."

Tom came up with their tray and set their plates in front of them. "I'll have no dessert, thank you," Ruby said smugly. "By the way, Tom, how's your kitten?"

"Normal." He laughed. "His favorite plaything is the corner of my bedspread. He scratched the furniture, tore up a window screen trying to get out, sleeps in my socks, and causes Mom to scream threats at me when he even looks like he wants to go into her place of business."

"You want to keep mine when we go to Israel?" Lara asked. "I think she'd like to spend time with her brother."

"Sure." He grinned at Annette. "I could use the company. It's going to be so lonely here without my mom." He sniffed, pretending to cry.

"I said this before, and I'll say it again," Annette warned. "I'd better not find one cat hair downstairs where we serve food."

He leaned over, his mouth open, his forefinger against his thumb. "Is that a people hair?"

They all looked. Annette gasped.

He straightened. "Just kidding."

"Looks like you two are back on an even keel," Ruby said.

Annette nodded. "I've decided to trust my son. I can't make his decisions for him. But Curt will be staying here with him. They're both looking forward to that."

Ruby turned to Lara. "Is your kitty tearing up your condo?"

"Not at all. I got her a ball of yarn. She plays with it. I didn't think I could have an animal around me. Before. . .I couldn't bear the thought of even touching one. But that sweet little Val just curls up in my lap while I'm reading and looks at me like I'm the greatest person in the world."

"How many other persons does Val see?" Ruby asked.

Lara just sighed and attacked her food as if she liked that, too.

Annette asked why she named her Val.

"That's short for Valentine. You know, like a heart. And when I cuddle her, I can feel that little heart beating, and she's a constant purr. When I wake up at night, I hear that little purr, and it's comforting."

"Well," Ruby said, "there are more where that one came from."

"One's enough, thank you. Oh, let me show you what I've done." Lara dug into her bag and brought out several cards. On each one was a painting of one or two snow-white kittens, with big blue eyes. One was playing with red yarn. Two sat in a basket, looking curiously straight ahead. Another peeked out from behind a chair.

"You did these," Ruby said. "They're adorable."

Annette agreed. "These would make wonderful greeting cards. Or these could be illustrations for children's books."

Lara nodded. "I'd love to make something like these into books. I mean, that little kitten is a delight. She's always doing something different and surprising. I have the pictures but not the words."

"Oh, I can help there," Ruby said. "I'm never at a loss for words. I'll do that part."

"Agreed," Lara said. "And one other thing. If anything comes from this, I'd like them to be called Dove cards or Dove books." She seemed hesitant. "You know, like representing the Holy Spirit."

"Perfect," Annette said. They smiled and nodded when she added, "Eunice was right. When we turn things over to God, so much good can come from the worst of things."

Later in the week, Curt stopped in at the restaurant during coffee and tea hour. He lingered afterward, so Annette got a cup of coffee and sat with him.

"I wanted you to know," he said, "that Henry's sermon Sunday caused me to examine my attitudes and responsibilities. His thoughts on adoption made me realize anew how we're to view each other. We're all sisters and brothers in God's kingdom. I just want you to know that my offering to stay here with Tom while you're in Israel is something I want to do because it's right. Not just to get closer to you." He added quickly, "Although I'd love to do that. I would even like to tour Israel with you."

She shook her head. "This is something my friends and I need to do. I would like to tell you about that, Curt. I want you to know the real me."

He leaned back against his chair. "Everybody I know shares the same opinion. You're about as perfect as a human being can get."

"There's the catch," she said. "The human part." She exhaled briefly. "I have a story to tell you that might change your mind."

"Good. I've been afraid of your perfection, your goodness." He leaned forward, his brow wrinkling. "Does this mean I'll have to confess all my indiscretions?"

"That's your choice. I want to do this because it's made me what I am, colored my life, or perhaps I should say it's stained my life. You may have heard that Eunice and Henry had a daughter who drowned when she was a teenager."

"I've heard that," he said.

"I was there."

She told him about it and how it had affected her life, as well as Ruby's and Lara's. "I don't think we have to tell everything that happened in our past to those we care about, unless the events are life-altering and affect the relationship. That was life-altering for the three of us. People who knew accepted it as a tragic accident and forgot about it over the years. We hung onto it. We didn't think we deserved to be free of it. That's why we want to go together and walk where Jesus walked, learn to let Him live in and through us."

"I'm glad you told me," Curt said. "It helps me understand Shelby better. And myself." A look of enlightenment crossed his face. "And you. That was part of your reticence about us marrying?"

"Everything I've done has been tainted by that tragedy. I've told Tom, and it helps him understand me better. I wanted this kind of honesty between you and me."

He settled back while the waitress came over and refilled their cups. After she moved away, he said, "I guess I have to confess, too."

"Not confess about what we've done or not done, Curt. Just share what we've learned from our successes and failures."

He nodded. "I guess, well, I have a few skeletons, too."

"Really?" she asked.

He looked across at her. Something in his deep blue eyes wouldn't let her look away. He picked up his cup. He took a sip. "Hot," he said. He quickly lowered the steaming coffee and licked his lips. His hand trembled lightly, and the coffee sloshed over.

He looked at the brown liquid staining the white cloth. He lifted his gaze to meet hers. "Sorry."

"It's all right." She smiled. "Happens all the time."

She did not look away from the man who she knew and didn't know. . .but wanted to know. She reached for his hand.

He caressed hers tenderly. "I love you," he said.

Annette didn't know how her life would be changed by going to the Holy Land. But she knew it would. That would be a spiritual journey. But she would not forget and would return to consider the personal, how he held her hand, gazed into her eyes, and said, "Come back to me."

Thirty Six

"There's a special light in your eyes, Eunice. What is it?"

"Oh, many things, Henry. Sometimes I can't seem to think clearly. The medication, you know. But going through my mind were some lines from Walt Whitman's poem that I taught for so many years. I may not remember it, but I'll try." She began:

> *"O past! O happy life! O songs of joy!*
> *In the air, in the woods, over fields.*
> *Loved! Loved! Loved! Loved! Loved!*
> *But my mate no more, no more with me!*
> *We two together no more."*

"Oh, Eunice. . ."

"No, Henry. The joy, the love, the happy life. That's the part to remember."

"Yes."

"I see heaven, Henry. I don't want to leave you, but it's my time. I want to go, and I don't want to go."

He couldn't speak. He got on his knees next to her recliner and put his arm across her and held onto her shoulder. His wife, his life. "I love you, Eunice."

"Henry. Look at me."

He did, and she could only shake her head slightly at his face that he felt was crumbling.

Her voice was weak. "Henry. Go. . .escape to your study. . . your sermons. The last thing I want you to hear from me is me saying I love you. I love you, Henry."

Henry got up, touched her shoulder, kept his hand there a moment, memorizing the feel of the cloth, the flesh, the bones, the life. . .he knew all that. She'd become a habit. . .a ritual.

No. He'd stopped that. . .long ago.

What would he do. . . ?

He obeyed her and escaped to his study.

Escape?

He'd thought it was a refuge. God's Spirit spoke to him. He felt God's presence. He could lose himself in preparing a message for the people.

It was not so much what they needed but what he needed or was learning himself.

God says this.

Learn this, Henry.

Then tell the people.

A refuge.

A strength in time of weakness.

A comfort in time of distress.

An answer in time of doubt.

An assurance in time of little faith.

An escape?

Yes!

An escape from trivial human pursuits into dependence upon God.

Footsteps falter. God carries you.

You're empty. God fills.

You hurt. God heals. Healing sometimes came through death.

Death is healing.

Eunice would be healed.

I have been healed.

Yes. God is an escape. A crutch.

And oh, how we humans need that crutch.

Thank You, God.

She didn't want Henry to remember seeing her die but to remember her alive, saying she loved him. In death, no matter how many stood with you, you stood alone before your Creator. What was it like? This death?

Her Bible lay on her lap. The one with the back inside flap torn away. She touched it. She had wanted the truth. Her daughter's friends had needed to face the truth. The truth lay in that book. Truth about creation, who and what we are, God and eternity.

She didn't know all the answers.

But she had the truth.

Jesus said, "I am the way, the truth, the life."

Her daughter's friends were going where Jesus walked.

She felt a smile. *I'm going where Jesus walks.*

Something from the Psalms came to mind. "Your goodness and unfailing love will pursue me all the days of my life, and I will live in the house of the Lord forever. My cup overflows. . .with blessings."

She pictured it. The cup overflowing, leaving proof of God's presence that could not be contained.

She heard music, saw incredible light, a door closing and another opening. She smiled. Her eyelids fluttered; so did her heartbeat, her anticipation. She saw the image of someone as if floating, running toward her, one arm outstretched, the other holding the hand of. . .a child.

She heard her breath go out. Nothing came in. But that was

all right. She remembered something. The important thing in life is not how many breaths we take, but the moments that take our breath away.

She felt light, lifted, as if God had sent His love, on the wings of a. . .

Dove!

YVONNE LEHMAN lives in the panoramic mountains of western North Carolina where she directs the Blue Ridge Mountains Christian Writers Conference. Her writing has won her numerous awards including The Dwight L. Moody Award for Excellence in Christian Literature, Romantic Times Inspirational Award (first in nation), National Reader's Choice Award, and Booksellers Best Award. Her books include adult mainstream, inspirational romance, historical, the young adult White Dove series, and the biblical *In Shady Groves* (reprinted as *Gomer* in Guideposts' "Women of the Bible" series). Recent titles include *Carolina, South Carolina, His Hands*, and *Strings of the Heart*. Her women's fiction title, *Coffee Rings*, is her fortieth book.

DISCUSSION THOUGHTS ON *Coffee Rings*

The story you've just read lends itself to themes that are pondered by Christians and those outside the faith alike. How do we answer questions for ourselves and others?

The entire Bible offers the answers to how we are to live. Yet the most learned theologians admit they do not know all the answers to everything. Therefore, the purpose in providing Scripture verses is to stimulate discussion, not necessarily to give a complete answer.

My hope is that these verses will lead you to study the Word and allow God to speak to your heart. I encourage you to think about the verses listed below, but it's also important that you take a few minutes to examine where in the Bible these words occur. What are the subjects covered by the book of the Bible in which they appear? Be particularly careful to examine their immediate context. You can often tell this simply by looking for paragraph breaks, subheads, footnotes, or other study aids that may be included with the text of your Bible.

Studying the Bible is ultimately a conversation between you and God. Be sure that it's a long enough conversation for you to get out of it everything God wants you to hear. We are admonished to "work hard so God can approve you. Be a good worker, one who does not need to be ashamed and who correctly explains the word of truth" (2 Timothy 2:15).

Questions to Consider and Scripture to Ponder

Chapter One

Eunice Hogan has just been told she has six months to live. She thinks, *What am I supposed to do?* What would you do?

Her husband says, "We believe in miracles, you know." What is a miracle? Do miracles still happen? Has God performed a miracle for you?

"Does God give you the Holy Spirit and work miracles among you because you obey the law of Moses? Of course not! It is because you believe the message you heard about Christ" (Galatians 3:5).

Chapters Two and Three

Annette agrees to marry Curt only if his grown children approve. Should these two mature adults make decisions based on what their grown children think? Suppose the parents disapprove of the mate choice of their grown children. Is one instance right and the other wrong?

Chapter Seven

Annette loves Curt, yet she felt relieved when they broke up because she wondered if she would have to tell him about her past if they were to be married. Must one reveal one's past to the person one plans to marry? If a mistake or event in the past affects one's present state of mind, should it be revealed to a prospective mate?

Shelby experienced ridicule from her family when she disagreed with her dad's decision to remarry after her mother had been dead for only six months. She grieved after her mother died. Her dad grieved over losing his wife during the four years of regressive illness. Was Shelby right in objecting to the serious relationship her dad wanted?

Is there a time limit on grief? Who decides a time limit?

Why is communication so difficult between family members, friends, or other Christians?

"We can gather our thoughts, but the LORD gives the right answer" (Proverbs 16:1).

CHAPTER NINE

The church has a program to help young girls. Does your church speak out against abortion? Does it offer an alternative?

Henry Hogan has told the church that Eunice is dying from cancer. How does your church respond to such news? What can you do to show concern?

"Faith that doesn't show itself by good deeds is no faith at all—it is dead and useless" (James 2:17).

" 'I assure you, when you did it to one of the least of these my brothers and sisters, you were doing it to me!' " (Matthew 25:40).

Chapter Ten

Eunice has kept the coroner's report secret from her husband for nineteen years. Is that right?

Do you tell your family, husband, friends everything? Why or why not?

Chapter Eleven

Lara says she's lived with her life-affecting event for nineteen years and asks what she can do. She answers herself by saying she will "do what millions do. . .live with the consequences." Do you know people who let the past affect their present?

Do you live triumphantly despite "the consequences"?

" 'Everyone who believes in him is freed from all guilt and declared right with God' " (Acts 13:39).

"I can do everything with the help of Christ who gives me the strength I need" (Philippians 4:13).

Chapter Thirteen

Curt is trying to make peace with his daughter Shelby. He knows "when you fight with someone, it's hard making up." When you have a fight or disagreement with someone, do you admit being wrong? Do you say you're sorry?

What was your last fight about? Is there a possibility you could be wrong?

" 'If you forgive those who sin against you, your heavenly Father will forgive you. But if you refuse to forgive others, your Father will not forgive your sins' " (Matthew 6:14–15).

" 'Forgive us our sins, just as we have forgiven those who have sinned against us' " (Matthew 6:12).

Shelby says, "I'm not a real woman," when she finds out she can't bear children. What is a real woman?

"Be honest in your estimate of yourselves" (Romans 12:3).

Chapter Fourteen

Henry Hogan bowed his head, but he didn't pray for health or that the food would nourish their bodies and their bodies would be used for God's glory. Are our prayers before meals something like that?

How often do we thank God for blessing that food, nourishing our bodies, and using us for His glory?

Do you appreciate good health? Do you tell God that?
What have you taken for granted lately? Do you talk more about your problems than your blessings?

"How we praise God, the Father of our Lord Jesus Christ, who has blessed us with every spiritual blessing in the heavenly realms because we belong to Christ" (Ephesians 1:3).

Chapter Fifteen

Eunice might be able to prolong her life by taking chemotherapy and radiation. She questions what kind of life that would be. After making her decision, "a peaceful feeling settled over her as she communicated with her Lord." Have you felt God's peace?

If not, have you "let go and let God"?

"Let the peace that comes from Christ rule in your hearts" (Colossians 3:15).

Eunice reads, "Dying is a form of healing if we have accepted Jesus in our heart and lives." Do you agree?

From what are we healed upon dying?

" 'Death is swallowed up in victory. O death, where is your victory? O death, where is your sting?' " (1 Corinthians 15:54–55).

What is "quality" of life? A prolonged one? Is there purpose in prolonging your life if the results are only longer illness?

Have you talked about funeral plans with your loved ones? Should you do that before illness occurs?

Chapter Sixteen

Annette recognized Shelby's hurt and said it was dangerous. How can you recognize when someone is hurting?

Should you consider that an angry, negative person might need your love more than a lovely person with a problem?

" 'If you love only those who love you, what good is that?' " (Matthew 5:46).

Chapter Eighteen

After Shelby's mom died, Shelby cried that she was sorry she hadn't told her how much she loved her. On a regular basis, do you tell your loved ones that you love them?

" 'I command you to love each other' " (John 15:17).

Chapter Nineteen

Eunice knows God has forgiven her. Should she confess to her husband? Would that hurt or help their relationship?

Should you reveal something that eases your conscience but hurts another?

"Remember that the temptations that come into your life are no different from what others experience. And God is faithful. He will keep the temptation from becoming so strong that you can't stand up against it. When you are tempted, he will show you a way out so that you will not give in to it" (1 Corinthians 10:13).

Chapter Twenty

Eunice yielded to temptation and committed adultery with the choir director. Eunice was sorry and sought God's forgiveness. Should she have remained in the choir? Is it hypocritical to behave like you're morally upright after you've had an affair?

How should Christians behave when they sin?

Are they worthy to lead in church?

" 'Let those who have never sinned throw the first stones. . . . Go and sin no more' " (John 8:7, 11).

"The more we know God's law, the clearer it becomes that we aren't obeying it" (Romans 3:20).

"If we confess our sins to him, he is faithful and just to forgive us and to cleanse us from every wrong. If we claim we have not sinned, we are calling God a liar and showing that his word has no place in our hearts" (1 John 1:9–10).

"In the same way, their wives must be respected and must not speak evil of others. They must exercise self-control and be faithful in everything they do" (1 Timothy 3:11).

"An elder must be well thought of for his good life. He must be faithful to his wife, and his children must be believers who are not wild or rebellious. An elder must live a blameless life because he is God's minister" (Titus 1: 6–7).

Eunice kept thinking, *It never happened,* as if wishing her sin away. Are there things in your life you wish never happened? How do you handle them?

Henry says their expected baby is their miracle child. Can the results of one person's sin become another person's blessing?

" 'Everyone who believes in him is freed from all guilt and declared right with God' " (Acts 13:39).

Chapter Twenty-Two

Ruby questioned, "Would we be friends if it wasn't for. . . ?" What is a friend?

Does the Bible define friendship?

"Here is how to measure it—the greatest love is shown when people lay down their lives for their friends. You are my friends if you obey me" (John 15:13–14).

"There are 'friends' who destroy each other, but a real friend sticks closer than a brother" (Proverbs 18:24).

Annette, Lara, and Ruby feel God is punishing them by making them relive the past. Do you look at unwanted situations as punishment from God?

Can you find blessing in those unpleasant times?

" 'He gives his sunlight to both the evil and the good, and he sends rain on the just and the unjust, too' " (Matthew 5:45).

"Jesus said, 'Come to me, all of you who are weary and carry heavy burdens, and I will give you rest. Take my yoke upon you. Let me teach you, because I am humble and gentle, and you will find rest for your souls. For my yoke fits perfectly, and the burden I give you is light' " (Matthew 11:28–30).

Chapters Twenty-Three Through Twenty-Six

Lara, Annette, and Ruby face the past. Do you need to revisit the past in order to settle things finally? Did the characters?

Dove, a Christian young woman, left a note that could be taken as a suicide note. Her actions the night of her drowning suggest suicide. Do Christians commit suicide?

Can persons who kill themselves go to heaven?

In the note, Dove asked Eunice not to tell Henry she was pregnant. Eunice kept that secret from her husband, along with other secrets. Was Eunice wrong in not telling her husband? Would she have been wrong to tell him since her daughter asked her not to? Is withholding the truth the same as lying?

Is there ever a time when lying is permitted for a Christian?

"If you claim to be religious but don't control your tongue, you are just fooling yourself, and your religion is worthless" (James 1:26).

"Those who love to talk will experience the consequences, for the tongue can kill or nourish life" (Proverbs 18:21).

"The Lord hates. . .a lying tongue" (Proverbs 6:16–17).

Chapter Twenty-Seven

Lara says she is not a Christian. Yet she attended church, gave money, visited the sick, donated food, and wasn't living in sin. Eunice said, "We even wonder at times if we are Christians."

Are you positive you are a Christian? How can you be?

Are you able to tell other people how they can be sure they will go to heaven when they die?

"If you confess with your mouth that Jesus is Lord and believe in your heart that God raised him from the dead, you will be saved" (Romans 10:9).

Chapter Twenty-Eight

"Imagine that," Ruby said and grinned. "Finding answers to life in the Bible. Who would have thought it?"

Do you find the answers you need in the Bible? Why or why not?

"Jesus told him, 'I am the way, the truth, and the life. No one can come to the Father except through me' " (John 14:6).

"Dearest friends, you were always so careful to follow my instructions when I was with you. And now that I am away you must be even more careful to put into action God's saving work in your lives, obeying God with deep reverence and fear. For God is working in you, giving you the desire to obey him and the power to do what pleases him" (Philippians 2:12–13).

Chapter Twenty-Nine

Annette comes from the beach, feeling peaceful, then discovers her son, Tom, was involved in a drinking party. He becomes belligerent because she didn't confide in him about her breaking off the relationship with Curt.

How much should parents tell their children? Do you tell them about your wrong choices when they are young or wait until they start making their own mistakes?

Chapter Thirty

Eunice constantly admonishes, "Pray." Do you pray without ceasing?

Since Jesus prayed for us, should we do any less than pray for each other?

" 'I am praying not only for these disciples but also for all who will ever believe in me because of their testimony' " (John 17:20).

"Pray without ceasing" (1 Thessalonians 5:17 KJV).

"Don't worry about anything; instead, pray about everything.

Tell God what you need, and thank him for all he has done. If you do this, you will experience God's peace, which is far more wonderful than the human mind can understand. His peace will guard your hearts and minds as you live in Christ Jesus" (Philippians 4:6–7).

"Listen to my voice in the morning, LORD. Each morning I bring my requests to you and wait expectantly" (Psalm 5:3).

Chapter Thirty-Three

Annette, when talking to Curt, said she didn't think one had to admit forgiven sins to other people unless those actions affected one's present state of mind. Do you agree? Disagree?

How much and what are we required to share about our sins?

"We are each responsible for our own conduct" (Galatians 6:5).

"Whatever you do or say, let it be as a representative of the Lord Jesus, all the while giving thanks through him to God the Father" (Colossians 3:17).

Chapter Thirty-Four

Eunice has said, "Act and the feeling will come," implying love is action. How do you show that love is action?

Once more he asked him, "Simon son of John, do you love me?" Peter was grieved that Jesus asked the question a third time. He said, "Lord, you know everything. You know I love you." Jesus said, "Then feed my sheep" (John 21:17).

Eunice said to Henry, "I'm free." What did she mean?

Can we feel "free"?

Are you sad, depressed, defeated? Why?

"Those who wait on the LORD will find new strength. They will fly high on wings like eagles. They will run and not grow weary. They will walk and not faint" (Isaiah 40:31).

"So if the Son sets you free, you will indeed be free" (John 8:36).

Henry Hogan is not naive, but he never blames Eunice for any indiscretion. Is it realistic that one can be that strong spiritually? Do you consider his silence as cowardice or denial? Is he practicing what he preaches about love and forgiveness?

Do you blame and criticize instead of loving and forgiving?

"The greatest of these is love" (1 Corinthians 13:13).

"As we know Jesus better, his divine power gives us everything we need for living a godly life. He has called us to receive his own glory and goodness!" (2 Peter 1:3).

" 'No eye has seen, no ear has heard, and no mind has imagined what God has prepared for those who love him' " (1 Corinthians 2:9).

" 'For God so loved the world that he gave his only Son, so that everyone who believes in him will not perish but have eternal life' " (John 3:16).